WATCH
HOW
WE
WALK

A NOVEL

Jennifer LoveGrove

ECW PRESS / MISFIT

Published by ECW Press
2120 Queen Street East, Suite 200,
Toronto, Ontario, Canada M4E 1E2
416-694-3348 / info@ecwpress.com

This is a work of fiction. Names, characters, places, and incidents either are the product of the author's imagination or are used fictitiously, and any resemblance to actual persons, living or dead, business establishments, events, or locales is entirely coincidental.

LIBRARY AND ARCHIVES CANADA
CATALOGUING IN PUBLICATION

LoveGrove, Jennifer, author
Watch how we walk : a novel /
Jennifer LoveGrove.

ISBN 978-1-77041-127-2 (pbk.)
ALSO ISSUED AS: 978-1-77090-468-2 (PDF);
978-1-77090-469-9 (EPUB)

I. Title.

PS8573.O8754W37 2013
C813'.6   C2013-902486-7

Editor for the press: Michael Holmes /
a misFit book
Cover design and photography: David A. Gee
Author photo: Sharon Harris
Type: Troy Cunningham

The publication of *Watch How We Walk* has been generously supported by the Canada Council for the Arts which last year invested $157 million to bring the arts to Canadians throughout the country, and by the Ontario Arts Council (OAC), an agency of the Government of Ontario, which last year funded 1,681 individual artists and 1,125 organizations in 216 communities across Ontario for a total of $52.8 million. We also acknowledge the financial support of the Government of Canada through the Canada Book Fund for our publishing activities, and the contribution of the Government of Ontario through the Ontario Book Publishing Tax Credit and the Ontario Media Development Corporation.

Ontario
Ontario Media Development
Corporation

ONTARIO ARTS COUNCIL
CONSEIL DES ARTS DE L'ONTARIO
50 YEARS OF ONTARIO GOVERNMENT SUPPORT OF THE ARTS
50 ANS DE SOUTIEN DU GOUVERNEMENT DE L'ONTARIO AUX ARTS

Canada Council
for the Arts

Conseil des Arts
du Canada

Canada

1

▼

THE FIRST LINE WAS SMALL, timid, and red. I was scared, but it was the only way through. I breathed deeply and drew the line longer, pushed harder, and it bloomed.

It hurt. I clenched my teeth, then smiled.

I etched another line, perpendicular to the first. It burned, clear and pure, both pain and pleasure, sheer release. Red beaded and dripped down my arm, but I didn't look away. Compared to everything else that had happened, it was nothing.

I clenched my fist tight, then opened it. Something surged through my veins — a warm rush, a high, and then, exquisite release.

I stretched out my arm and admired my newfound craft. A perfect red letter L.

It seemed only natural to discuss it with her, and just as normal when she responded.

What do you think? Pretty, isn't it?

Little poppies, little hell flames.

Do you like it?

No. You're a freak. Better do what I say. Or I'll tell.

Footsteps padded above me and stopped at the door. Someone was listening. I shoved my tools in the drawer and switched off the lamp. I sat still and silent, trying not to move or even breathe, willing myself invisible.

WHEN I WAS A LITTLE GIRL and people asked me what I wanted to be when I grew up, I said what everybody else said: a Full-Time Pioneer. That's what we were all supposed to be — obedient brothers and sisters who spent all their time going from house to house, knocking on doors, spreading the Armageddon virus. The people would smile and nod in approval, at me, then at my parents, then back at me, their joyous, too-bright heads bobbing in a sea of Pharisees.

At the meetings — Tuesday nights, Thursday nights, and Sunday mornings — I would sit down, cross my legs, smooth my skirt, and open the latest issue of *The Watchtower*. We'd all read it together and answer questions about it, sing some songs, and pray. I thought it would be like this until Jehovah took over and killed everybody else off, and gave us — the loyal sheep, on the right hand of God — eternal life in Paradise on Earth.

If I hadn't finally figured out things were not what they seemed, I might still be there, sitting in the Kingdom Hall, waiting.

AS A TEENAGER, I DEVELOPED something like claustrophobia, but it happened mostly when I was alone. Thoughts would rush my brain and keep coming and coming, one after another, thoughts of Uncle Tyler, of Lenora, and it would overwhelm me and I couldn't breathe. It was the house, I told myself, the same old creaking house, and I needed to escape. I still lived at home then, with my parents making all the decisions, in the same town where the elders seemed to be perpetually peering over our shoulders. Every day, the walls inched toward each other, closing me in.

It began with the house, but then I became claustrophobic within my own skin. Hunger, exhaustion, cold, pain, even pleasure — all of them had abandoned me. I felt nothing. A chrysalis of numbness had grown thick around me. If I spoke, my voice sounded distant, and when I listened to others — at school or at the Hall — it was as though I was under water. If my parents forced me to eat, I picked at the pasta or grilled cheese on my plate but I tasted nothing. That was just as well; I had also developed a paralyzing fear of throwing up. I would go to great lengths to avoid germs, gagging, and even the vaguest mention of vomit. Sometimes I would dream that I was about to throw up, and I would jolt awake just in time, shivering and panicked. Then I would recede back into numb immobility. I was a prisoner in my own body, trapped no matter where I was or what I was doing. I started to wonder if I even existed anymore.

One fall day at school I sat and alternately stared at the teacher or down at my books while I pinched the insides of my arms. Purple bruises blossomed. By 3:00, I had four of them on each arm, evenly spaced apart.

I started to feel more alert then, and by the time I got home, I had come up with a way to get outside of the haze of myself, to escape the thick fog around me, and find her, my sister, and bring her back home.

2

▼

THE TOWN THEY LIVE IN has two stoplights, some stores and banks and a library, an arena, one high school, lots of farms, at least a dozen pagan churches, and one Kingdom Hall. There are about seventy-five brothers and sisters in their congregation, and the worldly people know who they are. Every weekend, Emily's family and most of the other Witnesses go out in service, from house to house talking about the Bible. Emily knows it's wrong, but most of the time, she dreads it. Her stomach aches with nervousness and her hands are tiny, hard fists in her yellow mittens.

Her father pulls the car into a driveway in the country and turns off the engine. A rusting pickup truck, its windshield smashed, sits up on blocks near the garage. The porch sags as though falling from the house, the walls' white paint is peeling, and one of the windows is boarded up. Though the sidewalk isn't shovelled, footprints from the front door imply that people do live there. The sky clouds over, shadows fade, and it's darker than it should be on a Sunday afternoon.

— Are you ready, Emily?

— I think I have frostbite. In my feet. Maybe I should stay in the car this time. Emily hunches into her parka, a stubborn blue iceberg in the back seat.

— Lying is a sin. He opens the car door.

— Out you get.

The name on the mailbox is "Bales" and Emily shivers, her whole body, her thoughts — everything shakes but her toes, which really are numb. Tammy Bales is one grade above Emily, but three years older and much bigger. She should almost be in high school by now. Tammy throws rocks at her during recess and calls her a JoHo. *Do not take the Lord's name in vain.* Sometimes, on the worst days, Tammy calls her a JoHo Shitness, over and over, right up close. "JoHo freak," she yells in front of all the other kids. They laugh, everyone laughs at Emily, the loser who doesn't even get birthday presents, and the teachers shake their heads. *Turn the other cheek.* But Emily turns red instead. Once she tried to be as tough as her sister, so she stammered, "Sh-shut up!"

— What did you say? Tammy Bales grabbed the collar of her shirt and twisted, pulled Emily to her red face, bumpy with acne.

— Nothing. Emily could only mutter, and Tammy shoved her, disgusted. Emily landed face down in the sawdust in the jumping pits, choking.

It's Emily's turn to speak at the door. Her parents say she's ready, they rehearsed for two hours the night before.

Good afternoon. My father and I are just making some calls in your neighbourhood, coming by to talk to you about the state of this world and about hope for the future . . . Emily wears her navy blue polyester dress with a mouse embroidered just above the hem. The style is too young for her, it's childlike, and her tights are too small. They're itchy and the crotch has slid halfway to her knees, and she must take small ridiculous steps. Emily wonders if she is allowed to say *crotch*.

— What did you say? Her father grabs her arm, hard, and roughly turns her to him.

— What did you just say?

— Nothing. I coughed. I'm cold. I think I'm getting a cold. I didn't say anything!

Her father says nothing, looks at her for what feels like a full five minutes. They walk up the driveway toward the farmhouse, the snow crunching like broken glass under their boots.

— Straighten up. We're almost to the door. Do you remember what you're going to say? Do you have the magazines ready?

She nods, as her stilted footsteps tromp double-time with his to keep up. *Please God, Jehovah, don't let Tammy Bales answer the door. Please give me the strength to do this right on my first try. Please let Dad not be mad. In Jesus' name, Amen.* Emily knows that she has to say *in Jesus' name, Amen* after a prayer or God won't hear; it's like a stamp. A letter won't get beyond a mailbox without a stamp, and Jehovah won't get your prayer if it's not sent *in Jesus' name, Amen.*

Emily and her father creak three steps up to the door,

where the doorbell glows orange, and she knows it will be hot to the touch.

She presses it and jumps back, landing on her dad's foot.

— Calm down, Emily. You'll do just fine.

There are thumps like footsteps, or maybe a dog, and some rustling, but no one comes to the door.

— I guess they're not home. Emily turns to leave. Her dad grabs her shoulders and swivels her back toward the door. He knocks vigorously and it echoes as he peers through the screen door window.

— You know the rule. We knock three times before we move on to the next house.

There is another thud from inside, and Emily's bowels rumble and she needs to go the bathroom. Soon. She winces, and no one answers.

She closes her eyes and presses the doorbell one last time. They wait, but there is only silence now, and then the clang of the loose eavestrough on the side of the house as the wind blows.

They drive on, and at the next house, an old woman answers the door and listens, nodding, to Emily's entire speech. She smiles, takes the magazines, says nothing, and closes the door.

3

▼

THEIR THREE-BEDROOM HOUSE is on the outskirts of town, and there's a linen closet at the top of the stairs, near the bedrooms. Emily knows her mother hides the gifts there, but they're already wrapped, so she can't tell what they are. Every day she fights the urge to peel back the wrapping paper and peek. Sometimes she even mutters, "Get behind me, Satan!" but then feels like she's done something wrong, because you shouldn't *make a mockery of God.*

— Don't you want to open yours now? Maybe just a little look? I won't tell Mom.

— Be patient, Ems.

Lenora smiles calmly and returns to underlining her *Watchtower* magazine in preparation for the meeting.

Lenora has a tiny bit of yellow highlighter on her right cheek. It looks like egg yolk, or the smear of a dandelion. Emily doesn't tell her.

She closes Lenora's bedroom door behind her, and the house is quiet except for the clatter of her mom making dinner. Cutlery rattles, the water blasts then stills, the oven door clangs shut.

Emily can't wait any longer.

She tiptoes to the closet, opens the door, crawls inside, and pulls the door shut behind her. It is dark and musty, but Emily isn't afraid. She digs a flashlight out of her skirt pocket and switches it on with a click, sharp and too loud, like when her dad cracks the knuckles on his good hand. She hopes no one heard. After a pause, she lifts up each blanket one at a time and sets them aside in sequence, making sure she doesn't get the sheets and bedspreads and pillowcases out of order; her mom will notice.

She worms her hand beneath a rough wool blanket spattered with pink roses and slides out a silver rectangle. Her name is on it. Without making any noise in case her sister hears and tells on her, Emily peels back a corner of the shiny paper, careful not to tear it. She tilts her head and shines the light beneath the paper to see if she can tell what it is, but can't see anything but more paper. Her mom must have known she would look and double-wrapped it. More than anything, Emily hopes it's the huge encyclopaedic *Circus World* that she saw in the giant bookstore at the mall in the city. It's heavy enough. What else could it be? She smiles and bounces up and down a little bit on the pile of blankets; a miniature celebration dance. But she loses her balance and starts to slide. She grabs at something, anything to stop herself, but reaches only blankets and keeps sliding. She braces her hand against the closet's wall to keep from crashing, but it's too late.

She thuds against the door, but it doesn't open. She holds her breath, leaning there, hoping that no one has heard her, hoping that she hasn't ripped the wrapping paper.

— What's going on up there?

Emily says nothing. She hears her mom move chairs and lay plates on the table.

— Hurry up and get downstairs. Dinner's ready.

Emily doesn't move. She tugs at the paper a little more and tries to look, but the reflection of her own shadowy, scrunched up face — top teeth gritted over bottom lip — glares back, and guilt burns through her like an electric jolt. She is cheating. Surprise Day is still a week away.

After Lenora thunders down the stairs, Emily puts the blankets back, flicks the flashlight light off, and climbs from the closet.

— HOW WAS SCHOOL TODAY, girls? Their mother pauses between bites of her pork chop and potatoes, which she has cut up into tiny, even pieces. Emily pauses before she answers, unsure if it's one of her dad's no-talking-at-the-table nights or not. Those happen, along with no-talking-in-the-car, a couple of times a week after he's had a bad day. This time, he says nothing, and she and Lenora answer in unison.

— Okay. They look at each other and laugh.

— Do you have any homework? Their father doesn't look up from his food when he talks.

He holds the fork in his right hand, between his middle and index fingers and thumb, spearing food and putting it in his mouth rhythmically, without speaking. The last two fingers on that hand are missing. He has a pair of round, pink stubs left and that's all. Sometimes people stare, but Emily's used to it. It's been that way since before she was born, but when he was her age, he still had all his fingers.

Emily sometimes wonders how much it hurt when the car accident tore off his fingers. Nothing that compares has ever happened to her. What hurt more, the bone being crushed or the skin burning off? Or did he pass out during the accident before he felt any of that? Who else was there? How badly were they hurt? Other people talk about car accidents they've been in, but although this tragedy is decades old, they're not allowed to ask about it.

— I'm already finished my homework.

Lenora got straight As during her first year in high school.

— What about you, Emily?

— I don't have any today.

— Good. You can both get started on the *Watchtower* article for Sunday's meeting. You can help your sister with the bigger words, Lenora.

— I'm already done that too. I'm working on the next one.

— Good girl. Emily, ask your sister if you need any help with this week's. If she doesn't know, ask your mother, and if she can't help you, then you can ask me.

— All right.

Emily had already tried to read "Exposing the Devil's Subtle Designs," which was all about immorality in music and worldly people and how to *fight against independent thought*, but her mind kept wandering. Isn't all thought independent? How can you think someone else's thoughts? She doesn't always understand everything in

the magazines or at the meetings, but she gets the important points, like the Ten Commandments and the Last
Days, Armageddon and the Resurrection. She can even
list all the books of the Old Testament, in order, by heart.
Lenora promised to help her with the New Testament.

— I have a question though.

— Don't talk with your mouth full, Emily. Her mother
frowns and readjusts the napkin in her lap.

— Sorry.

No one says anything for a while. Emily runs her toes
along her chair, counting the round bumps in the leg. Six.

— What is it, Emily?

Her father, now finished, sets his fork down and looks
at her.

— Well . . . She falters. She has gone over this in her
head a hundred times, and still her face goes red. How
will she ever give a talk at the Kingdom Hall in front of
everyone someday if she can't even ask her dad a question
at home?

— Go on.

Emily breathes in deeply and pushes it out. The edges
of Lenora's napkin flutter across the table.

— I want to be on Library Staff. At school. It's not after
class, it's only—

— You know better than that, Emily. You're not allowed
to participate in extracurricular activities.

Extracurricular activities are what worldly kids do. It
means stuff at school that is not mandatory, and kids from
the Hall aren't supposed to be part of that, because it will
make them miss some of the meetings or have *bad association*. But Emily knows that some of them join teams and
clubs anyway.

— But it's only at recess or at lunch. It's not after

school, so I wouldn't miss any meetings. I'd be putting books away by myself instead of being outside with worldly kids.

— Your sister doesn't do extracurricular activities at the high school; it would be unfair.

— I don't mind. Why not let her spend her time in the library instead of with worldly kids? I know what kinds of immoral things kids talk about at recess, not to mention the swearing—

Ever since Lenora got baptized last year, their parents have treated her more like a grown-up. Emily tries not to be jealous, but it's hard.

— I don't think it would hurt, Jim. Could be worse things than volunteering in the school library. Her mother takes a long sip from her glass and as she swallows, her father looks over at her and narrows his eyes.

— Easy, Vivian. Moderation.

He waits and no one says anything. Emily's mother empties her glass and sets it down, hard. Emily bites the insides of her cheeks.

— I'll talk to the elders and see if they think it would be appropriate.

Emily grins and high-fives Lenora. If she doesn't get *Circus World* for Surprise Day, maybe she can convince Mr. MacKay, the librarian, to order it.

— Thanks, Dad! Can you ask them tonight? Can you call Brother Wilde right now?

— Patience, Emily. In due time.

SURPRISE DAY ISN'T A REAL holiday. Their mom invented it so that Emily and Lenora don't feel left out when all the other kids at school get lots of new toys and clothes for Christmas. Of course no one has ever actually admitted that aloud; they wouldn't be allowed to celebrate it if they did. Just like no one has to tell Emily not to mention Surprise Day in front of other brothers or sisters from the Hall.

Emily sits on the thick brown carpet in front of the coffee table, while Lenora lounges on the floor, leaning against her favourite armchair. Her arms stick to the brown vinyl and make a peeling noise when she moves. Their parents perch on either end of the itchy orange floral sofa. Across from the couch, the television is dark. Next to the closet, a gun rack hangs on the wall. Their mom complained so much about seeing their dad's hunting rifles there, he put them just out of sight, in the front corner of the living room closet, and now they hang their coats and hats and scarves on the gun rack. He hardly ever goes out hunting anyway.

Each of them holds a gift on their lap. Emily likes the heaviness of her thick silver package, and she keeps lifting it up and setting it back down. She does this twelve times before her father tells her to sit still. She can hardly wait to tear the paper off and start reading.

For their father, Emily and Lenora helped their mom pick out some new ties to wear to the meetings; he'd been wearing the same three over and over. That was easy, but they'd argued over what to get their mom. They agreed on a necklace, but Emily wanted to get one with a pendant of the comedy and tragedy theatre masks, since her mom used to be an actress. Lenora thought that was a bad idea.

— You know Dad always gets mad when Mom mentions her past, before she was in the Truth. Then they'll fight and it'll ruin Surprise Day. You don't want that to happen, do you?

Emily shrugged.

— I guess not. Her mom has a box at the back of her closet full of photographs and programs from plays she was in. It's behind her old boots. Emily doesn't let on that she knows it's there. She loves to look through it when Lenora is babysitting her and on the phone for hours. Her mom wore all sorts of different costumes, from puffy Shakespearean dresses to silver princess gowns and even a black witch outfit. Emily tries not to look at that one, since witchcraft is Satanic, but she loves all the other pictures. Some are even from the newspaper, with her name in bold letters under a picture of her in Elizabethan costume: *Juliet, played by Vivian Golden*. There are even some from when she and Uncle Tyler were kids, like the one where they're holding hands in homemade robot costumes.

Their dad never talks about her acting days and whenever their mom or someone else does, he always says something like *that was then and this is now* or *that was a long time ago* and that's the end of that conversation. Lenora is right; they shouldn't risk making their parents fight. They settled on a plain silver locket instead.

Emily doesn't know what Lenora's gift is. Her mom wouldn't tell her. It's wrapped in red and green wrapping paper that's covered with fat, stripy candy canes. Her father runs his hands through his short salt and peppery hair.

— That's not very neutral gift wrap, Vivian.

Everyone is quiet and Emily can hear the crickets outside. Seven chirps before her mother speaks. She shrugs her thin shoulders.

— It was on sale.

— That's not the point. It's inappropriate.

— There's no Santa Claus or Christmas trees on it, it's not that bad.

— It's not what we discussed.

— Fine. Her brown hair bounces as she stands, and falls across her face when she reaches for Lenora's present.

— Hey! Can't I just open it and throw away the paper? Come on!

Her mom snatches the box, stomps upstairs, and slams the bedroom door.

Ten minutes pass and no one speaks. Emily doesn't know what to do; she can't open her gift when Lenora has nothing. They wait and wait, and avoid looking at one another, and then their mom returns to the living room and they all exhale at once.

— Here. She thrusts the same box, sloppily wrapped in plain red paper, at Lenora.

— Gee, thanks.

Their father says a long prayer about thankfulness and obedience and forgiveness. Emily thinks he's going slowly on purpose, to make her wait even longer, but then feels guilty for criticizing her dad's prayer. She'll ask Jehovah God to forgive her later, when she says her bedtime prayer. Together they murmur "Amen" and it's finally time to open presents.

— Youngest first! Youngest first!

— Okay, okay. Her mom smiles a little and Emily is relieved.

— You go first, and then Lenora.

Emily rips the paper off as fast as she can and throws it behind her. It's her book! It's *Circus World*, five hundred glossy pages of elephants, trapeze artists, jugglers, tigers, and her favourite, the tightrope walkers.

— Thank you thank you thank you! Emily hugs the book to her chest and grins.

Lenora opens hers neatly, not shredding the paper like Emily at all, then folds it up and gives it back to their mother to reuse.

— All right! Lenora cheers when she finds her very own Walkman in the box. She pulls the headphones over her dark blond hair, switches on the radio, and closes her cat-like green eyes.

— I'm going to open mine later.

Their mother sets her gift aside and looks straight ahead, jutting her pointed chin toward the window. Their father sighs.

— I guess that means it's my turn.

He smiles at Emily and Lenora, but it's a fake smile. It doesn't look like he's paying attention to what he's doing, and he sneaks glances at their mom when he thinks Emily isn't looking. Their mom isn't interested in opening her gift at all; it sits beside her untouched as she stares out the window and swishes the rest of her coffee around the bottom of her mug. Their father holds each tie up and admires it in turn, but Emily knows he's still angry about the worldly wrapping paper. She's glad they didn't get their mother the theatre necklace after all.

4

▼

SNOW FALLS IN THICK SWIRLS, and Emily tilts her head up, smiling — winter is her favourite season, even though it contains Christmas. The cold and snow simultaneously calm and thrill her; her whole being overflows with a buzzing peace that no one but her can understand.

She's walking home from school by herself, amid the shouts and the snow angels of her worldly classmates, though Lenora is supposed to meet her at 3:30 every day. Their parents set up this arrangement at the beginning of the school year, when the bus routes changed. The Morrows' house is on the edge of town, and used to be the first stop on the after-school route, but as the town grew, Emily's family and their neighbours were no longer considered rural. The walk takes about half an hour, and Emily enjoys doing it alone, it makes her feel more grown-up. A couple of weeks ago, Emily made it all the way home without Lenora, even though she walked as slow as she could. Lenora got in big trouble when she showed up half an hour later.

— She's just a little kid, what were you thinking? She could have been kidnapped or run over!

Lenora claimed she'd told them she needed to stay late after school to use the library, but their mother didn't believe her.

— I'm not that little.

Emily knows how to walk on the side of the road and move over for transport trucks, she isn't stupid enough to get hit. As for the kidnappers and the child molesters, she would fight them off, she would wail as loud as possible and run away, she would scream like they teach the women at the Kingdom Hall. Jehovah would protect her, she would pray out loud, she would shriek, and also grab a stick and poke out their eyes. They wouldn't be able to see her and that's how she would escape.

Screaming, however, is most important. The elders won't believe you if you don't scream, because if no one hears you, there won't be any witnesses, and you need a witness to prove to a Judicial Committee what really happened. Some sisters have said they were attacked, but there was no evidence that they fought anyone off, so everybody knows it was just an excuse to commit immorality. They have since been disfellowshipped, and no one in the congregation is allowed to speak to them.

Lenora was grounded for two weeks for not walking Emily home from school, and after dinner that night, she cut out the last page of one of Emily's Trixie Belden mystery books and chopped it into a thousand pieces.

— I told you to always wait for me! Snarling, scissors held above her head, Lenora shredded nouns and verbs and adjectives and they floated to the floor like terrible confetti.

TODAY SHE DOESN'T MIND the walk home alone, and she catches snowflakes on her tongue, kicking at the powder already accumulating on the ground. Her mom would tell her not to eat the snow, that it's filthy and polluted, but Emily thinks this way is acceptable: she catches the flakes in mid-air, they cannot be dirty if they haven't even touched the ground yet. The snow falls straight from heaven into her mouth.

Emily is also happy because they don't have to go to the Kingdom Hall tonight, even though she knows it's wrong to feel that way. It's just that she gets bored sometimes, and the meetings are so long. She's glad that she won't have to wear a dress or sit silently for two hours, because it's Monday, and the meetings are on Tuesdays, Thursdays, and Sundays, which is also the day they go out in door-to-door service. Sometimes they go on Saturdays too.

Cars move past more slowly than usual, and Emily hopes that Lenora will be able to see her through the snow. A few more drive by but no one stops, and she is halfway home. Emily looks down to check her watch, and something hits her in the face — an explosion, she stumbles, she can't see — cold, sharp clumps of ice slide down her cheek and neck. It stings more than a slap across her face.

— What's the matter, didn't Jesus save you? You gonna cry, you little Jesus freak?

Tammy Bales laughs shrilly in front of her. Even with one eye closed, Emily sees her pick up another handful of snow.

— Shouldn't you be out knocking on people's doors, you loser?

Emily says nothing, and silently prays, *Please Jehovah, make Tammy stop persecuting me, please don't let her hit me again, in Jesus' name, Amen.*

— What's the matter, freak, you scared? Tammy laughs again and raises her arm. Instinctively, Emily ducks.

— You're pathetic, you and your whole family. We almost set the dogs on you yesterday, you and your nerd father, all dressed up carrying your Bibles around.

Tammy shoves her, and Emily trips over her own feet and falls onto the side of the road. A car sounds its horn, swerves, and keeps going.

— That's right, we were home yesterday, but we didn't answer the door. We hid behind the curtains, my mom and my sister and me, laughing laughing laughing at you!

Emily gets up and tries to walk past her, tries to ignore her, but Tammy blocks her way. She concentrates and bites her cheeks — she will not cry in front of Tammy — and they stand in the snow at the side of the road, facing each other. Tammy isn't even wearing a hat or gloves.

— Say something, you freak!

— No! Emily tries to shout, but Tammy is faster and bigger, and pushes her down again. Emily lands in the ditch, and then Tammy is on top of her, knees pinning her arms down in the slush as she piles fistfuls of ice and snow in her face. It feels like thousands of needles stab her cheeks. Emily cannot scream, there is too much snow in her mouth, and this snow is not from heaven, it is filthy. Emily gags and gags and she can't get up.

— Hey! A car door slams but Tammy doesn't stop.

— Get off my sister, you slut! Lenora screams at

Tammy and pulls her off, while someone else hauls Emily up by her wrists.

— You okay, kid?

Emily doesn't recognize her. She wears a black and white striped hat, big boots up to her knees, a short plaid skirt, and a black wool coat. Her black eyeliner is thick around her eyes and her lips are black too.

Emily starts to cry, and spits out the dirty snow, and the strange girl wipes Emily's face with a tissue. A tall boy with a shaved head and black leather jacket leans against the blue sedan. A half-smile sits crooked on his face and his arms are folded across his wide chest. He pulls a cigarette from a blue and white package and lights it, still watching Emily. She has definitely never seen either of them before.

Lenora, bigger than Tammy and even louder, chases her a few paces down the road. They stop, and Lenora's hands are on her hips and she's looking down, shouting right into Tammy's face.

— Pick on someone your own size, you loser! Just because you failed almost every grade doesn't mean you can beat up little kids!

— Fuck off! Tammy's face is scrunched up and she takes an unsteady step backwards. She looks back toward Emily and Lenora's friends.

— No, fuck you, loser! Lenora's blonde hair blows and whips around her head like she's in a tornado and her feet are wide apart and her cheeks blaze. She spits, and it lands very close to Tammy's feet.

— Now get lost. It'll be worse next time.

— Whatever. As if I care. Tammy shoves her hands deep into her pockets and starts walking down the other side of the road. Emily watches her fade into the snow and disappear.

— Let's get out of here. Get in the car, Emily.

Emily stays where she is. She doesn't know the girl driving the rusting car, or the silent boy who stares at them, and they'll get in trouble if they get a ride from worldly kids. Snow pelts her face and stings her eyes and her wet coat and boots are too heavy for her to move in.

— Lenora . . . She tries to whisper.

— We're not allowed—

— Hurry up! It's freezing! Lenora opens the door to the back seat and pushes Emily in.

— Just drop us off before the bend in the road by my place, okay, Marla?

Emily doesn't argue. Lenora knows what's right and wrong, so this must be okay. Maybe there are different kinds of worldly people, the kind to avoid — persecutors, like Tammy Bales — and the kind who aren't so bad, who even help you. Maybe Lenora even Witnesses to them, maybe she gives them copies of *The Watchtower* and *Awake!* and pretty soon they're going to start coming with them to the meetings. Before high school, her sister often convinced kids from primary school to come to the Hall with them, until they started asking their parents if they could stand out in the hallway with Lenora during the national anthem at school too, and then their parents made them stop.

Emily tries to picture Lenora's friends sitting attentively on Sunday morning, but then sees the boy in his leather jacket slumped and scowling, legs sticking out in the aisle, an unlit cigarette tucked behind his ear. The sisters would cluck and frown at Marla's thick black eyeliner and lipstick and short skirt. Still, imagining them at the

Hall makes Emily feel better as they drive through the slush, closer and closer to home.

Then Lenora turns to the boy and touches his shoulder.

— Give me a drag, will you?

He turns around, winks, and hands Lenora a cigarette. Emily goes rigid next to her. She's never seen Lenora smoke before. Cigarettes and drugs are against their religion. Lenora puts it into her mouth and sucks on it, as her eyes crinkle and she coughs a little.

— Shut up. Lenora responds as though reading her mind.

— Don't look at me like that. And stop crying. Good thing I came along when I did, seeing as you can't take care of yourself. She dabs Emily's face with her damp scarf and it scratches her cheeks like sandpaper. The cigarette smoke fills the car and hurts Emily's nostrils and she sniffles. Until then, she didn't even realize she was still crying.

She says nothing about the smoking. What would have happened if Lenora hadn't been there? Maybe Tammy would have beaten her up so badly that she'd still be lying in the ditch, unconscious, as the snow fell and covered her. She could have frozen to death and no one would find her until the spring, a sodden lump on the side of the road. It would be her own fault for not being able to stand up to Tammy. No one picks on Lenora; she's strong and isn't afraid of anyone. Emily doesn't know why Jehovah God didn't make her more like her sister.

The girl driving the car turns the music up so loud they can't hear each other. The three teenagers pass the cigarette around until they pull over. There are smears of black lipstick on the end of it. Emily feels as though she's been dropped into an unfamiliar universe, one happening at the same time as the regular world, but just off by enough to be completely wrong. She decides she'll have to find out more about her sister's secret life. Just like Trixie Belden, she'll have to be a detective and start following Lenora. Maybe she'll even figure out some way to make the two universes back into one.

— Thanks for the ride. As they get out, the boy rolls down his window and Lenora leans in toward him, and they murmur to each other, smiling. Then she waves her arm toward Emily.

— Sorry about all this. She grabs her sister's school bag and carries it the rest of the way home for her.

— You're not going to mention this to Mom or Dad when we get inside, are you?

Emily is not a tattletale. Sometimes she forgets that she's not supposed to mention certain things and talks too much, but she doesn't believe in ratting on her sister. Lenora always has a good reason for everything, even if it seems wrong at first. One day, soon, she will be able to fend for herself, but for now, she owes Lenora, and Lenora knows it. They will keep certain things from their parents, and Emily will not be a threat. They will protect each other.

Emily shakes her head, no longer crying, and pictures Tammy's back, her jacket flailing in the wind as she slumped away. Maybe Tammy will never make fun of her again. Maybe she will finally be left alone.

Emily wonders if Jehovah made Lenora show up like that, just in time.

5

▼

THE BASEMENT WAS COLD and dark. I sat hunched and cramped in a small arc of yellow light from a desk lamp. Outside, the wind wailed and shoved the snow into drifts against the house. It had snowed for two days; school was cancelled and there weren't enough ploughs to keep all the roads clear. I had brought the coffee maker down with me, and the air smelled acrid and sharp. I had no need to venture upstairs. My stomach contracted and twisted in on itself but I ignored it. Hunger helped keep me awake. I hadn't slept for a couple of nights. The snow blocked the light from the windows and I was losing track of the days.

I yawned in spite of myself. The clock read 3:02 a.m. I still had a lot of studying to do for geography and history and English literature. Exams were two days away.

I had to stay awake. I pushed back my chair and stood up, stretched, shook my limbs. The room tilted and began to lurch and spin. Darkness crept into the edges of my vision. I grabbed the side of the desk and rested my hands on my knees. Better. I breathed and decided I could have some of the carrot sticks I'd brought down earlier.

Their crunch was unnaturally loud and I cringed. Swallowing solids felt foreign and awkward but I forced it all down with another gulp of lukewarm coffee. Eating had begun to disgust me, but I couldn't risk passing out. I had to stay awake. It was my only way out.

I forced myself to focus and keep alert the best way I knew how.

I turned off the lamp and sat back down to let the bulb cool. There were shapes in the dark, masses I no longer recognized as sofa, chair, desk, boxes. They looked to be very slowly moving, in silent unison, toward me. Circling. Black shapes blocking all the exits. I tried not to move. My arms and neck prickled.

Is that you?

Concentrate! There isn't much time.

I opened the drawer next to me and without needing to see, removed a small cardboard box. It held a red light bulb and I set it on the desk before me. I unscrewed the still-warm bulb from the lamp and replaced it with the red one. I switched the lamp back on and the room glowed hotly.

Next I took all the contents from the same drawer and set the stack of paper and envelopes and notebooks on the floor. I lifted a board from the drawer, revealing the false bottom that I'd created, just like the one Lenora had built in her dresser a decade before. I gently took out another box and set it on the desk. In it was a sampling of my favourite implements: box cutters, penknife, razor blade.

I smiled. I soaked a tissue in rubbing alcohol and wiped down each of them. This would energize me, this would keep me awake. I just had to choose which. My hands shook from all the coffee. The thin, braided bracelet bounced lightly around my wrist. I ran my fingertips over it as I often did when I felt overwhelmed, and I began to focus.

I pushed up my sleeves. The lattice on my arms was intricate. I always took care to be symmetrical, but it was difficult. A row of Ls on my skin: perfectly spaced as though marching in a determined little row, ready to escape from my fingertips and leap into oblivion.

I had another dream about you.

Oh yeah? What was I wearing? How did I look? Hot?

Stop it. It wasn't like that.

You sure about that?

It was winter and you were wearing that black leather biker jacket. You were walking in front of me, and I kept trying to catch up, but the faster I ran through the wet snow, the farther away from me you got.

Serves you right.

I shouted your name but you didn't hear me. You just kept walking.

Oh, I heard you, all right. I just had better things to do.

Then you disappeared.

After the dream, anger like a blast from a furnace. I hated my parents for letting her go. I hated them for their lies and their silences. I'd bitten the insides of my cheeks and dug my nails into my palms until they bled. That hadn't been enough.

I miss you.

I'd etched and etched that night until I could stop crying, until I no longer felt the burn of all our blame.

After that, there wasn't much space left on the tops of my forearms, so I had to move to the more delicate insides of my arms. That night, the hate wasn't just for my parents or the elders; it was also for myself. Everything that had happened was, in some way or another, my fault.

This time, I chose the box cutters. I scratched a series of straight lines, each two inches long and a half inch apart. One line for everything I did wrong, and one for everything I didn't do at all. The first couple burned and stung, but I got used it, and didn't mess any of them up by flinching. They were perfect.

My hands stopped shaking, and I went back to studying until daylight, and then I went to school.

6

▼

ON WEDNESDAY NIGHT, EMILY'S DAD starts Family Study late. He's been over at Brother Wilde's, discussing some problem, and when he returns, he says they'll do an article from one of last year's *Awake!* issues, called "What is Spiritism?" Usually they study whatever *Watchtower* or *Awake!* article is scheduled for the next meeting.

— Why aren't we doing this Thursday's *Watchtower* article? Why are we reading an old one?

Emily's mom doesn't wait for him to answer.

— Jim, it's late. The kids have to get up for school tomorrow. She crosses her arms in front of her chest and doesn't sit down at the dining room table.

— It won't kill us to skip one Family Study so the girls can get enough sleep for once.

Emily's dad ignores her mother, and flips through the old magazines until he finds the article he's looking for. Then he rubs his eyes and looks up as though he's waking up from a long nap and has forgotten where he is.

— Where's your sister? We can start as soon as she gets to the table.

Emily's mom sighs, not a real one, but a loud, fake exhalation.

— I'll go get her. Emily runs out of the kitchen and down the hallway to the bathroom. It's locked, and before she can even call Lenora's name, the shower blasts on and muffles any sound on either side of the door. Emily yells and knocks anyway, but there is no response. It's her turn now to sigh, but hers is real, a breath full of disappointment and fatigue, and she rests her forehead against the wooden door frame. At her feet, snaking beneath the door and into the bathroom, is the telephone cord.

She doubles her knocks, pounds both fists now, and still nothing, so she cups her ear to the door. Nothing beyond the steady pulse of the water is audible, and because it's a lie, it seems even louder.

When she comes back to the kitchen, she sits down at the table, defeated, and doesn't look at her parents.

— Is your sister still in the shower?

Emily shrugs.

— She didn't answer.

Her mom shakes her head and sits down across from Emily, her arms still crossed. *Folded*, thinks Emily, just to be safe, *her arms are folded.*

— We can't start until we're all here. Did you tell her we're waiting for her?

— I don't think she could hear me. Emily bites her lip, debating whether or not to tell them about the phone cord. She still owes Lenora one for rescuing her from Tammy Bales. Then again, aren't they even because she didn't mention the cigarette?

— This is ridiculous. It's way too late. Her mom takes a long sip from her cup and glares across the table.

— I'll get her moving.

Her dad strides out of the kitchen and toward the bathroom. Emily's stomach clenches — will she get in trouble for not telling them about the phone? What will happen to Lenora when she's caught skipping Family Study and on the phone instead? And who is she talking to? She follows him out and watches from the doorway.

First he bangs on the door and tells her to shut off the water and get to the kitchen immediately. When that doesn't work, he tries the door handle again and again, as though it might somehow unlock at any moment. The shower still blasts and they hear nothing else. Emily can't remember a time when Lenora ever refused to come to Family Study or to the Hall. This must be was her mom meant about "teenagers" and "hormones."

— What the . . . ? Her dad finally notices the phone cord.

He grabs the slack outside the door and yanks it as hard as he can. Something crashes in the bathroom, then there's a yelp like a kicked dog, and the water goes off.

They all head back to the kitchen in silence, with Lenora trailing behind them, rubbing her forearm. There's a black bandanna tied around her head. She doesn't look at any them.

Emily sneaks a glance at the clock and it's already after 10:00. They've never started a study later than 8:15, and it's always been finished by 9:00.

— We will not be studying a recent article tonight. Her dad leans his head on his hands, and Emily wonders if he is tired too. He's not even yelling at Lenora or grounding her or asking who she was talking to in secret, locked in the bathroom. It's as though he doesn't know what to do, and so just begins the Family Study as planned.

— Let's pray. He bows his head and, on cue, they all do.

— Oh Jehovah God, we pray in your glory tonight that You might keep us free from Satan's wiles . . .

Emily tries hard to pay attention, but her mind keeps wandering to Lenora. She doesn't even have to ask, she knows she was talking to a worldly person, probably Marla; why else would she try so hard to hide it?

— Something very serious happened to Brother Wilde and his cousin Richard. Emily's dad begins, then stops. The magazine in his hands shakes. Her mom sighs.

— Jim, are you sure this can't wait? Everyone is tired, including you.

— Why do you drink from a mug with a lid, like a baby cup? Lenora doesn't even look up as she asks, as though she doesn't care about the answer.

Their mom glares across the table.

— Because. It keeps my coffee warm.

Lenora snorts, then coughs. Their dad exhales and squares his shoulders.

— I understand that this is a school night, but learning about Satan's evil ways is more important than getting up early for school.

Emily's dad explains that Brother Wilde's cousin, from a nearby congregation, recently moved into an old house and has since had strange experiences. Emily doesn't know why Lenora cares about their mom's cup; this is far more interesting.

— Strange how? Emily's pen is poised above her

Kingdom Hall notebook. She's excited to be up this late; it's almost like a party.

— Unexplained disturbances. The walls shake in the middle of the night, doors slam, and dishes rattle and sometimes smash on their own.

— Perhaps his children are unruly and lack discipline. Maybe there's a draft. Emily's mom looks at her, grins, and rolls her eyes.

— Brother Richard lives alone. He's investigated all possible explanations. There were no animals trapped in the walls, the shelving was all secured properly, and there aren't any earthquakes around here.

— So the house is haunted? Emily's eyes are wide and she leans forward.

— *Haunted* is a worldly term. There are no such things as ghosts.

— Demons, then, I meant demons. Is it demons?

Across the table from her father, Lenora snorts again. Emily's face reddens.

Emily's mom flips through the *Awake!* magazine that her father hasn't opened yet. Emily wonders if they are actually going to read it or not, and if her dad will ask questions from it, or if he's just going to tell them this story about Brother Wilde's cousin. They've never had a Family Study like this before. Usually they take turns reading the paragraphs aloud; then her father, the head of the household, asks a question, and Emily, Lenora, or their mom answers. They do that for each paragraph until the article is finished. It's like a rehearsal for Thursday night's meeting, where they'll do the same but as a congregation.

— Well, Brother Richard didn't know what was causing the problem with the house. He searched the place for weeks. Then one afternoon, cleaning out the basement, he finally discovered the issue.

He pauses again, looking at Emily, who is not fidgeting or daydreaming at all, she is paying attention, and then he looks at her mom. She reads something in the magazine, but Emily can't see which article.

— Vivian! Pay attention! Try to set the proper example.

— I'm listening. She doesn't look up.

— The basement. Something evil in the basement.

— But what was it? What did he find?

— Don't raise your voice, Emily. Jehovah God values self-control.

— Sorry. She nearly whispers, hoping that he'll finish the story.

— What did he find?

— He discovered that there was an old Ouija board left in the cellar, hidden under some loose boards in a corner.

Her dad tells them that Brother Richard decided to get rid of the Ouija board immediately. Without telling anyone, he took it out to a forest in the country and buried it deep in the ground. But the house shook again a few days later. This was months ago, in July when it was very hot and humid, but his basement was always cold. He didn't want to go down there but he knew that he had to.

— Sure enough, the Ouija board was back. Just sitting there at the bottom of the basement stairs. Waiting for him. As though Satan was making a mockery of God.

Richard didn't know what to do after that, he didn't know that he had to burn it, so he moved into his trailer in the yard and told everyone he was renovating the house. When it got too cold to stay out there, he moved back in but the noises and the shaking continued. He didn't want to tell anyone in his congregation because he was afraid they would think that the Ouija board was his, and then he might get disfellowshipped. After he could endure no more, he called his cousin, Brother Wilde, to help him and Brother Wilde told Emily's dad the whole story.

— Satan is very powerful. We must constantly be on guard against him. That this happened today, to someone near us, illustrates Satan's earthly strength and sovereignty.

— Jim, I really don't think this is the kind of stuff you should be telling our youngest child before bed. You'll give her nightmares!

— Simmer down! This is the end of the story. There was no demon activity in the house when they first arrived, but Richard said that was not unusual, it didn't happen every day, and when it did, it was mostly in the middle of the night.

— They put the Ouija board in a plastic grocery bag, along with some newspapers and matches. Brother Richard had already packed his axe and some dry wood in the trunk of his Buick. They prayed constantly.

— So they were going to burn the demons?

— Well Emily, they were going to burn the Ouija board, in order to eliminate the demon activity. If the object no longer existed, then the demons would have to move on, they would have to go elsewhere.

— Were they scared, Dad? Were you scared when they told you?

— It is right to fear Satan. But we must trust in God's protection — and have faith. Next they locked everything in the trunk and drove to the partially frozen lake outside of town. They hacked the Ouija board into hundreds of pieces.

Her dad rubs his moustache with his good hand, then continues.

— They built a small bonfire on the beach and burned all the bits and splinters and waited until—

— What did it look like? Emily can't help but interrupt.

— What did what look like?

— The Ouija board. What did it look like while it was burning? Could they see the demons? What did they look like?

— See, Jim? You see? You're getting her all worked up. She's not going to sleep at all tonight.

— But I want to know! Did they have horns? Knives for teeth? Could you see their faces?

— Emily, you know that demons are invisible to humans. The Ouija board probably just looked like a burning piece of wood, no different from anything else.

Her dad sighed and shook his head.

— They headed back to Brother Richard's car, unlocked the doors, and were about to get in. Then Richard started to shake and yell, 'No no no' over and over again. I swear to the one true God Jehovah, that sitting right there on the passenger seat, intact, waiting for Brother Wilde, was that Ouija board.

Cold creeps up Emily's neck like a spider and her skin tingles. Even her mom looks up and frowns. Lenora has said nothing the entire time they've been seated at the table. Emily is pretty sure she hasn't heard a word of the story.

— What happened? What did they do?

— Nothing. For now, Brother Richard is staying at Brother Wilde's until they ask the district overseer what to do next.

EMILY'S MOM TUCKS HER IN bed, and they pray together, and then she asks Emily if she is scared.

— No. Jehovah protects people who are good and free from sin.

— That's right. You have absolutely nothing to worry about, and besides, we're just down the hall. She kisses Emily good night on her forehead.

A short time later Emily hears her parents shout at each other, but can't make out what they are saying. She tries to fall asleep but the image of the demonized Ouija board is stuck in her head. She's scared that even thinking about it will be an invitation for the demons to get inside her. She silently recites the books of the Bible in order — *Genesis, Exodus, Leviticus, Numbers, Deuteronomy, Joshua, Judges* — but that doesn't help her sleep either. And she knows better than to try to think of nothing at all. That's another way to be invaded by demons — emptying your mind of all thoughts. This is also called meditation. It's very dangerous because it leaves your mind vulnerable for demons to get in and take over. It takes a lot of concentration for Emily to keep her mind busy at all times, and that's partly why it's so difficult to fall asleep. Sleep itself has become a risk.

She slides out of bed and gets her green sleeping bag, usually used only for camping or for relatives staying overnight, and drags it and her pillow down the hall. She listens at the closed door — nothing. It opens easily and Lenora does not wake up. She's almost disappointed. She would have asked her who was on the phone, and if she ever worries about demons. At the same time, she is relieved that she's asleep; it's strangely comforting.

Emily spreads the sleeping bag out on the floor next to Lenora's bed. She sets her pillow squarely at the top of it, climbs in, and falls asleep.

7

▼

EMILY SITS ON THE LIGHT blue carpet of her floral, ruffled bedroom, with *Circus World* open on her lap. The house hums quietly with its normal sounds — low, mournful music from Lenora's room down the hall, the fridge door opening and closing, a dog barking down the road, the scrape of metal on ice and gravel as her father shovels the driveway. She has a couple of hours before the Thursday night meeting and so she flips the colourful pages of her book.

Her favourite section is about the tightrope walkers. She doesn't understand how they do it. It looks impossible, like walking on air or flying, but Emily knows that no one but Jesus can do that. Instead, they have amazing balance. She reads about the special leather shoes they wear, made specifically so their feet can curve around the wire. Some of them even walk barefoot, clutching the rope between their big and second toes. Emily thinks that would be even more difficult, and would probably hurt. She can't even wear flip-flops on her feet in the summer; they cut the skin between her toes and she hates them.

High wire walkers are also called funambulists.

— Funambulist. Funambulist. Funambulist. Emily practises saying this aloud. She wonders where the word comes from, and hopes she remembers to look it up in the big reference dictionary in the school library. That's what she'll be when she grows up — a funambulist.

She doesn't think Jehovah's Witnesses are allowed to join the circus though, since it's probably full of immoral, worldly people. But she wonders what it would be like to live among the acrobats and clowns and bears and elephants and freaks of nature. Scary, probably. Maybe they would be mean to her because she's just a little girl from a small town who gets good marks and has to read the Bible a lot. Maybe not, though; maybe they would like her because she would be the best funambulist they'd ever met, and people would travel from all over the world to see her walk high above the Earth without a net and she would never, ever fall. She would be famous and maybe even beautiful. Her family would wonder where she was and miss her terribly, but it would be too late. Emily would be used to living in a tent and travelling to new and exciting places every week and signing autographs for her loyal fans. The acrobats and lion tamers and contortionists would fight over who got to sit beside her at the long tables in the dining tent. Everyone would want to be her friend and no one would ever get mad at her, or make her feel like she had done something wrong.

But her best friend of all would be the dog-boy — half-human, half-canine, tragic and beautiful. He would tell her what it's like to live in a cage and have itchy fur and wear a collar and have to bark for the crowds and roll over in the dirt and play dead. He would confess to her and her alone that he never really felt like a dog, because he's really just a boy, one who happens to have some fur, but that he's a normal boy who loves mystery books like she does, and misses his two brothers and three sisters back home, and so she would sneak *Hardy Boys* and *Sherlock Holmes* between the bars, along with a flashlight, so he could read at night and she would never treat him like a dog and beat him like the ringmaster. She would steal the key to his cage and after everyone else was asleep, they would sneak off to the edge of the camp and act out the scenes from the books. Especially the murder scenes. They would compete at who was better at playing dead. Emily thought she would always lose because her weird, twitching eyelid would always give her away.

Just as dawn seeped back along the dirt toward them, they would have to go back to camp, but no one could ever take their secret nights away from them. They would plan to run away together and start their own circus. No one could stop them.

Emily gazes at the grainy photograph of the dog-boy and wipes away a small tear.

A shadow falls across the picture of the furry boy baring his teeth at a fancy-dressed couple, and she looks up to see Lenora leaning in her doorway.

— What's the matter? Your new book too scary for you?

Emily pretends to cough and wipes her face in her sleeve.

— No. It's not scary.

— They what are you crying about?

— Nothing. Never mind.

Lenora would never understand. She seemed to have plenty of friends.

— What are you going to wear to the meeting tonight?

— I don't know. Emily hasn't given it any thought, and usually just grabs the first skirt and sweater or dress she can find, hoping that she didn't wear the same thing to the last meeting. She'd rather be reading than worrying about clothes. Lenora is already dressed and ready to go, in her dark green corduroy skirt and black sweater. Their parents have recently allowed her to wear makeup because she is sixteen now, and she has on green eyeliner that matches her skirt and black mascara. She had to remove the black nail polish though; their mom said it was just too much, too weird, and what would people at the Hall say.

— I'm going to pick out your outfit. I'm sick of seeing you wear the same thing all the time.

— Okay. I don't care.

Emily opens her book again, randomly, to a page about clowns. They're her least favourite part of the circus. They're silly and not funny at all. It's embarrassing to look at them.

— Has Tammy Bales been bugging you at school anymore? Lenora's voice is muffled from within Emily's closet.

— No. She hasn't said anything since that day at the side of the road.

— Good. What a bitch.

Emily gasps. She's not used to hearing her sister swear — other than at Tammy Bales — and never at home. And to say it like it's so normal, and not even take it back. She must have misheard her. She must have said witch.

43

— What did you say?

— Nothing. Forget it. Lenora hands her a red plaid kilt and white blouse.

— Here. Try this.

— I hate that skirt. It's itchy.

— I know how to fix that. I'll just sew in a lining along the waist so you don't feel it. It won't take long.

Emily follows Lenora into her room where she flattens the skirt at her sewing machine and quickly stitches in a strip of white fabric. They go back to Emily's room and she tries it on. It works. The wool doesn't scratch her, and you can't even see the liner. She stuffs her shirt into the waist band.

Lenora frowns and hands Emily her brand-new, black double-wrap belt.

— Don't be such a nerd, untuck your shirt. Emily does and Lenora wraps the belt around Emily's tiny torso.

— I can really borrow your new belt?

— Just this once. There, that looks better. Now you look almost cool.

— Thanks. Emily looks at herself in the mirror. *Almost cool.* She smiles.

— And just leave your hair down, no ponytails or anything.

— Okay. Emily looks at her watch. They don't have to leave for a while yet. She's been waiting for a chance to ask Lenora a question without their parents nearby.

— Who was that girl with you the other day? With the black lips? And the boy in the car with you guys — who was he?

— Nobody.

— But who are they? How come you were with them?

— Just kids from school. Marla and Theo. Don't worry about it.

— But they're worldly. Are you going to get in trouble?

— Ems, just because they don't go to the Hall doesn't mean they're bad.

Emily is confused. Aren't all worldly kids immoral? Because they don't know any better? That's why they're supposed to tell them about the Truth, and what they can do to live forever. Maybe Lenora really is Witnessing to them.

— It doesn't? Are you sure? Are they going to start coming to the Hall with you?

— Yes, I'm sure they're not evil. But Mom and Dad wouldn't understand, so keep quiet.

— Why was Marla wearing black lipstick?

— Because! Lenora throws up her hands.

— You ask too many questions! Because she likes the way it looks.

— Oh. Do lots of people look weird at high school? Are kids mean like in elementary school?

Lenora sighs.

— It's different. Bigger. There are lots of different kinds of kids, from all the different schools. Yeah, there are some nasty ones, but it's easier to get lost in the crowd because it's bigger. And most people don't already know you, so you can start over if you want.

— What do you mean, 'start over'?

— Be someone new. Be more yourself. If the other kids and teachers don't have anything to compare you to, you can, I don't know, be another person. A new version of yourself. Better.

Emily doesn't know what to say. Their parents and the

45

elders are always telling them to improve, to try harder
to please God, but this doesn't sound like the same thing
to her.

— Is it like having an alter-ego?

— Something like that.

— Did you start over? Are you someone else now?
Lenora shrugs.

— Don't worry. I'm the same as ever.

Emily doesn't feel reassured. Black nail polish, worldly
friends, swearing. None of it goes with the perfect Lenora
she's used to — the elders' favourite, straight As, never
getting in trouble. Now she's practically admitted that she
has a double life. The changes must have been so gradual
that Emily didn't even notice, but now it's as though her
sister has turned into someone else overnight.

— Girls! It's time to go!

They head downstairs to go to the meeting. Lenora
puts a finger to her lips.

— Shhh. She grins. Emily looks away and touches the
cold, taut belt.

8

▼

AT THE MEETING, THE MAIN topic is immorality. Didn't one of the elders just give a talk about that recently? Emily knows they are living in *the Last Days*, but why so much about that? Lately it's either immorality or demonism. Sometimes she wishes they'd just teach them more about how to Witness to kids at school, or maybe do some short plays in costume like at the big summer assemblies. She never falls asleep during the dramas. She leans over to her mother and whispers.

— Didn't we just have a talk about immorality?

Her mom shrugs.

— I don't know.

Emily turns her head; her mom's breath smells bad, like the medicine Emily has to take when she has a cough.

There are rows and rows of brothers and sisters in the red, itchy chairs and Emily tries to count them, but loses track after forty-seven, and her dad will get mad if she keeps turning around to look at people. Everyone is facing the front, listening, nodding, looking up the scriptures that Brother Bulchinsky tells them to read. He is as skinny as his wife is fat, and bent at the middle, leaning forward, awkward, in his wire glasses and a light grey suit. Pointy like a safety pin, Emily decides, and tries not to smile.

— Temptation is everywhere. His high, squeaky voice makes Emily look away, embarrassed. It's hard to be afraid when Brother Bulchinsky tells you to be.

— The worldly media — magazines and pop music and television and movies — are full of fornication and adultery. They're trying to tell you it's okay to live without any morals, that sin doesn't exist, but it does. It does. Not just in the big cities, but in our towns and rural areas too. Temptation lurks in fashion and advertising, in PG-rated films, in Satanic heavy metal music. We must avoid these things completely, entirely, with our whole bodies and minds, and keep the demons of immorality at bay. And pray, we must pray . . .

It's as though he is speaking through his long nose, and Emily can't concentrate on his words, only their shrill, nasal sound. That and the smells of the Hall. She wishes they could open a window — so much perfume, hairspray, aftershave — she can hardly breathe. Outside, it's already very dark and the wind howls at the windows and she shivers and wishes she'd brought a sweater. She twists in her seat to check the time. There is still over an hour left of the meeting, and Brother Bulchinsky keeps on whining and bobbing at the waist over the podium.

— Pay attention! Emily massages her forearm where

her father elbowed her, and rubs her hands together to keep warm.

— They are very real, brothers and sisters, and they are always watching us, waiting for us to become weak, to sin, that they might slip in and take over our bodies and minds.

Brother Bulchinsky is talking about modesty now, and avoiding not only sins of the flesh but even thoughts of such transgressions. He is still hunched over, a reflection of the microphone stand bent in front of him. Emily thinks it's funny and tries to draw it but it doesn't turn out the same at all. She doodles a safety pin instead. Brother Bulchinsky's alter ego.

Emily doesn't know what Lenora meant about starting over. Is she one person at school and a different one at home and at the Hall? Emily looks two seats down at her sister. She wears the black felt hat with white stitching — called a cloche — that Uncle Tyler gave her last month. She's staring straight ahead, listening to the talk, following along with the scripture. Lenora looks like her sister, the same as she always does. She doesn't look like a worldly person, like someone who would smoke and swear and hang around with boys in leather jackets and girls in black lipstick.

Brother Bulchinsky asks for a volunteer to read a scripture aloud for the congregation, and Lenora's hand shoots up. He chooses her, and Uncle Tyler brings the microphone over. It's his turn to stride up and down the aisles with the microphone during the question and answer segments. Lenora clears her throat, pauses, then reads the scripture clearly, without stumbling over any words.

Their father smiles his approval, and Brother Bulchinsky thanks her. Emily wonders if she has imagined Lenora's recent swearing.

Fuck you, loser!

What a bitch.

Was it some sort of test to see if Emily would tell on her? Or does she talk that way all the time at school and it just slipped out at home? *What a bitch.* It's stuck, like a song on the radio that she can't get out of her head.

What a bitch what a bitch what a bitch what a bitch what a bitch. She scrunches her eyes shut *What a bitch what a bitch what a bitch what a bitch* and feels like everyone can hear her and what if having a swear word stuck in your head is enough to get you demonized? She tries to focus on what Brother Bulchinsky is saying about abstaining from fornication, but the words all blur into one monotonous drone and her head is so heavy she can't hold it up anymore and she slumps forward into sleep.

9

▼

EMILY TUGS ON HER BOOTS and big puffy blue coat
and plods to the front entrance to wait for Lenora after
school. In the morning, the wind kept pushing against her
chest and she had almost been late, and the air was full of
sharp, angry bits of snow. Emily is relieved that the sun is
back out and the wind has moved on to torment others.
She thinks about what books she'll read over the weekend
and wonders if she'll have to go out in service on Saturday
and Sunday afternoon, or just Sunday. A blast from a car
horn jolts her and her head snaps up to see Lenora waving
her in from the window on the passenger side.

— Come on, let's go!

She climbs in the back seat and tosses her school bag
next to her. Lenora's vanilla perfume has taken over the

air, syrupy and invisible, like how she imagines a Venus flytrap would smell.

— I didn't know you were picking us up, Dad.

— I was rewiring a house near the high school and we finished up early. Thought I'd give you guys a break from the snow. How was school?

— Fine. The same. Emily opens her Trixie Belden mystery to finish another chapter during the few minutes' drive home. When they pull into the driveway and park, Emily jumps out first. Lenora opens the passenger door, and as she climbs out, her black hat falls off and into the snow.

Emily reaches down and snatches it up, then gasps and covers her mouth.

— Your hair!

Lenora's hair is a stark, bleached, white-blond bird's nest on top of head, and the sides of her head are nothing but stubble.

Their father turns around.

— What the h— He cuts himself off and strides toward Lenora.

— Let me get a look at this!

Lenora rolls her eyes.

— I dyed it blonder, big deal.

He grabs her upper arm and pulls her toward the house. Emily has never seen their father's face so pinched and red before.

— You wash that out right now! You look ridiculous!

Lenora laughs.

— You can't wash it out, Dad. It's peroxide. It's permanent.

— It had better not be! He is so loud that their mom comes to the front door and peers out. Lenora is smoothing her hair down over the shaved parts so it looks less like a bird's nest and more like she just woke up.

— Look at what she's done to herself!

They all struggle inside, everyone shouting but Emily.

— Everyone dyes their hair! Even sisters at the Hall! So what!

— So what? So you're grounded until you look respectable again!

— I am not! Mom!

— Jim, just calm down. She sits on the couch and Emily thinks she must be mistaken when she sees her mom actually grin.

— It's really not that bad.

— See? I told you! Lenora smirks.

— Vivian, be quiet. Lenora, you look like one of those drugged up worldly kids at the mall in the city. You're grounded until you fix it.

— Don't tell me to be quiet! The floor seems to shake when her mom bursts up from the couch and stomps toward the kitchen, and Emily puts one palm against the wood panelling, to steady herself during the earthquake her family has become.

Her dad follows her mom into the kitchen and Lenora, who hasn't yet taken off her boots or scarf, dashes back outside, with her long coat streaming behind her like the cape of a teenage superhero. Emily looks in the direction of her parents, who are now shouting accusations and blame at each other, and then out the back door at the path her sister is carving through the snow. She knows this is her chance to do what she has been meaning to do. She zips up her jacket and follows her.

Careful to keep distance between them, Emily ducks first behind the shed, then behind the larger trees, as

Lenora storms into the woods that butt against the field behind their house. Since Lenora is wearing her Walkman, Emily is unconcerned about snapping twigs or tromping too hard in the snow, and as the sun gets heavier and sinks lower, it flickers between trees, and Emily has to squint and rush and hide so as not to lose her sister. She feels like a real detective, a younger Trixie Belden. Sometimes she gets close enough that she can hear Lenora sing tunelessly along to whatever worldly song is churning through her Walkman, and Emily draws closer to try to make out some of the lyrics. Maybe it will be about drugs, and her father will be right; Lenora will turn into one of those scary kids who do drugs and have scars on their faces and live at the mall. Or maybe the song is about fornication, like Brother Bulchinsky warned against the night before.

Then Lenora stops and lifts the foam headphones from her ears, and spins around. Emily ducks behind a tree but trips over a root, falls, and yelps as she lands on her elbow.

— I knew I was being followed. I could feel it.

Emily's elbow stings and throbs, surging with a million little stabs and she's sure it must be bleeding and maybe even broken, but she won't cry in front of Lenora.

— I'm sorry. But I didn't want to stay home. I wanted to see where you were going. Emily shields her eyes with her hand as the sun glares onto the snow and up at her.

— Whatever. Is Dad still mad at me?

— Yeah. They were screaming at each other about who is the worst parent and whose fault your hair is.

Lenora snorts.

— My hair has nothing to do with those narrow-minded control freaks. I did it because I like it and it looks cool.

Emily remembers the bandanna during Family Study.

— When did you dye it?

— A few days ago. Marla helped me.

Emily doesn't remember Lenora being late after school that week. She hopes she isn't skipping school — she'd get in even more trouble than she is over her hair.

— We did it at her place while her mom was still sleeping. She works nights at the hospital as a nurse and isn't all strict like Mom and Dad.

— Was it during your spare?

— What? Yeah, during spare.

Emily scrutinizes the almost-white tufts that stick out from under her hat. She's trying to get used it.

— Do you like it? Do you want to do yours the same? She takes a step toward Emily, who jumps back.

— No way! I mean, it's okay for you, I guess, but I don't want it. She touches her own brown braid as though unsure if it's still there and the same colour it was all day. Lenora doesn't seem as angry at being followed as she had anticipated. She passes her headphones to Emily.

— Here, listen to this song. It's so cool.

A barrage of noise and growls bombards her ear-drums, the singer snarls and shouts amid the thunder of what sounds like a jackhammer attacking a slab of con-crete. She wants to like it, she wants to be like the new sixteen-year-old Lenora, but at the same time, she wants everything to go back to how it used to be. The music sounds terrible, like a catastrophe, the soundtrack for the end of the world. She hands back the headphones.

— Yeah. That's cool.

Lenora laughs.

— It's my new favourite band.

They walk along the main path until it forks and then they turn to loop back toward home. The wind has returned and stirs up the snow in the trees and tosses it into their faces. Emily shivers.

— I like walking out here. I come out and just wander around when I need to think. That and to listen to my music. I never see anyone else out here, it's relaxing.

Emily nods. Maybe she should do that too; every time someone starts to argue or fight in the house, she could leave and just go for a long walk outside in the bush. They're quiet for a while, and then Lenora takes off her headphones and lets them curl around her neck in silence.

— So do you think Mom likes going to the Hall?

Lenora has a way of changing the subject when you least expect it. It makes Emily's stomach hurt and her hands sweat and makes her feel stupid to never see it coming. She probably does it on purpose, to catch her off guard, maybe trick into saying something wrong.

— What do you mean? What are you talking about?

Lenora tosses her head in that way that means she knows something that no one else does.

— Oh, come on! She doesn't even listen half the time. I can tell; I watch her. She just stares into space. And when she does listen, her eyebrows scrunch up and she gets this angry look in her eyes.

Emily has seen it too, she has, but she concocted lots of good reasons on her mother's behalf: she was tired, she had a stomach ache, a toothache, the brother sitting in front of them was wearing too much Old Spice. Doesn't she make Emily and Lenora come to all the meetings and do all the readings? Then again, Emily can't remember the last time she saw her mom reading a *Watchtower* or *Awake!* or one of the many brightly coloured Hall books, unless their dad made them all have a Family Study. But that doesn't mean she's an unbeliever. Of course she isn't; she wants to live forever in Paradise on Earth, just like everyone else at the Hall.

— Of course she likes going to the Hall. She doesn't want to die at Armageddon.

Lenora stops and looks at her.

— Are you sure about that?

And suddenly Emily is not sure. She isn't sure about anything anymore. Her lip trembles and she turns away and runs.

— Shut up!

IT COULDN'T BE TRUE. Of course her mom still cares about everlasting life. Her mom is not falling out of the Truth. Neither is Lenora. No one is.

Lenora catches up to her and they slow down.

— Do you think she's . . . you know . . . Emily is scared to even say the word. She whispers it, as though uttering it aloud would make it true.

— An *apostate*?

Lenora waits a long time before she answers. The wind rushes past them and snaps a branch off a nearby tree. It crashes to the ground and Emily jumps, then shivers.

— No. I don't think she's an apostate. But I think Dad talked her into it, and now she wishes she was normal.

Emily doesn't ask *What about you? Do you wish you were normal too?* Instead, she thinks it's a good time to remind her of the consequences of falling out of the Truth.

— What if she gets disfellowshipped? What if we're not allowed to associate with her anymore?

— Don't worry, she won't. The elders don't know

what she's thinking, and she hasn't done anything wrong. Anyway, she still goes out in service and comes to most of the meetings.

— Yeah. Emily wraps her arms around her middle.

— Once though, a few weeks ago, she told Dad we were going out in service, just her and I, and we went to Uncle Tyler's instead. We rented a movie and she made me promise not to tell.

— Where was I? Emily hadn't been invited. They hadn't wanted her along. Suddenly, doing what she was told didn't seem to be enough for her mom. She shakes her head and kicks at some of the wet leaves in the snow. Could it be possible that she is too obedient?

— You were out going door to door with Dad and Brother Wilde. You guys had no idea!

Lenora laughs it off as they walk back home, but Emily is quiet. They had lied about going out in service. And they didn't want her along. She may have felt guilty, but she wouldn't have told. This must be how worldly kids with divorced parents felt, like they're being pulled in two different directions at once, and wanting to just stay put and not go either way.

In the distance, their house is a grey shape against a greyer sky. Then the kitchen light glints on and their mom is at the window washing dishes.

— Are you going to dye your hair back to normal?

— No way. They'll get used to it. Trust me.

10

▼

ON MONDAY, THE SUN STREAKS through the blinds
into Emily's classroom, leaving stripes of dust suspended
in the air. The bell rings, and the other kids shove their
books away and race outside for recess, while Emily
stacks her books symmetrically on top of one another,
then slides them into her desk. She is the last to leave the
room, relieved to not have to go to the playground today,
and heads to the school library for her volunteer shift
shelving books or taping spines or maybe even helping
open boxes of new books.

The library is in the centre of the round section of the
school, with classrooms all around it. Outside the librarian's office is a chart that lists the volunteers' responsibili-
ties for each of their shifts. Emily loves being a library

volunteer; she rarely has to talk to anyone. Today her job is to shelve the picture books in the little kids' section. She waves to Mr. MacKay through his office window and wheels the cart of books over to the shelves.

As she works, Emily wonders if Lenora will be in a good mood when she walks her home from school tonight, and will tell her about high school and the weird teenagers there and the cafeteria where you can actually buy French fries, or if she'll be angry for some reason and ignore her. Emily has a present for Lenora, from art class last week when they finished their pottery projects. Emily made a clay candle holder for her sister who likes to burn candles, and glazed it shiny black with blood red dripping over the edges — Lenora's favourite colours.

— Don't you want to use a nicer colour than black, Emily? Her teacher tilted her head and put her hands on her hips. Emily shook her head emphatically and continued. The teacher muttered something about "religious kids" and "depressing" and moved on. For once Emily didn't care. Lenora wears a lot of black and red. The candle holder is nestled safely at the back of her desk, wrapped in four layers of silver tissue paper.

As she slides the books alphabetically into their spots, aligning the spines evenly along the outer edge of each shelf, a girl with long braids and bottle-thick glasses walks over to her. Her dress shoes are shiny and wet-looking, and her skirt has big blue flowers on it, blooming and loud. She stops in front of Emily and leans toward her.

— How come you have to stand out in the hallway every morning?

No hello, no introduction, just this question that Emily has been asked countless times — and still she has no good answer. At least this time it wasn't, "What do you do to get in trouble every single day? You're always sent out to stand in the hall! You don't look that bad. You look like a goody-goody!"

— Because.

Emily thinks her name is Agnes. What a terrible name. It looks like the word "acne." Emily tries not to look at the small gold cross on a chain around her neck. Idolatry.

— Are you Agnes, from Miss Wilson's class?

— Yes. You're Emily. Mr. MacKay told me to come and watch you put the books away. I'm new on Library Staff, but I already know the Dewey Decimal system by heart, so you don't need to show me anything. Agnes smiles, and her small, pointy teeth gleam in perfect symmetry. She stares at Emily.

— Oh. Okay. Emily doesn't know what else to say, so she just continues to put the books away. After a few minutes of feeling watched, she breaks the silence.

— The picture books are alphabetical by last name.

— Obviously. Agnes is still smiling at her, but in a way that seems more demanding than friendly.

— You didn't answer my question.

— What question? Emily pretends not to understand.

— Why do you have to stand out in the hall during the national anthem and the Lord's Prayer? You can't get in trouble every single day of school.

Emily's face reddens. She knows that this is her opportunity to Witness to Agnes, to tell her about the Truth, and to offer her some magazines if she is interested. "Interested" is one of the categories at the Hall; if you get a worldly person "interested," you have achieved the first step in turning them into a Witness. Her dad would be so proud of her if she placed some *Watchtowers* at school. He always tells her to be stronger and braver, to talk to her classmates about living forever in Paradise on Earth, about Jesus and the Last Days and Armageddon. Emily never does. She hasn't placed any magazines at school, not even one, and so cannot tick off the box on her very own Service Report. Again this month she will have to write a zero.

— Because.

Sweat sears down her back in rivulets.

— It's against our religious beliefs.

— What religion are you? I'm a Pentecostal. Do you know what that is? Agnes takes a step closer to Emily, who backs up and bangs her hip against the book cart.

— Ouch! Emily pushes the cart between her and Agnes.

— I've heard of it. Your church is just outside of town, on the highway, right?

— Right! Agnes nods so vigorously that her blond braids bounce on her shoulders.

Pentecostals — the worst religion of all. They are from Babylon, and they talk in made-up languages because they are demonized. When they drive past the Pentecostal church on their way to the Hall, Emily's dad tells them not to even look at it out the window. Emily does though, she always sneaks a glance at the Pentecostals. She had assumed they would look different, monstrous, with wild hair and eyes that bulge, constantly howling and maybe even flying. But no — Emily was disappointed to see the Pentecostals parking their freshly washed vans and station wagons, dressed up in three-piece suits and dresses just like them, waving to each other, chatting, some holding hands, strolling into their church.

— So what religion are you, then?

— I'm one of Jehovah's Witnesses.

The elders always tell the congregation never to be

ashamed of their faith in Jehovah God, that young Samuel in the Bible was only four years old when he devoted his life to serving God. At the end of *My Book of Bible Stories*, the only Hall book for kids, it says, *Let's tell as many people as we can about our wonderful God, Jehovah, and His Son, Jesus Christ. If we do these things, then we will be able to live forever in God's new Paradise on Earth.* Emily hopes she sounds proud and confident. Agnes leans across the book cart toward Emily.

— What? I can't hear you.

Emily repeats herself, more loudly, and wonders if anyone else can hear her.

— So you're not allowed to sing? Is that why you have to stand out in the hall? You're not allowed to sing or dance or take alcohol or swear?

— Well, no . . .

Emily is confused; of course they are permitted to sing. They have an entire songbook, purple with gold lettering on the front, called *Singing and Accompanying Yourselves With Music in Your Hearts.* And they dance at weddings, and sometimes drink wine, though *not to excess*, but they definitely aren't supposed to swear.

— We can sing, just not the national anthem. It's against our religion.

— But why?

— Because we are to be *no part of this world*.

— What does that mean, 'no part of this world'?

— It means, well . . . Emily falters. She knows what it means. There are Jehovah's Witnesses, who are in the Truth, and there is everybody else, who are the worldly people.

— It means not taking part in this wicked system of things.

Agnes nods again as though she understands, but Emily can tell that she's bored already; Emily is nowhere near interesting her in learning about Jehovah's Witnesses. Agnes hops from one foot to the other on the other side of the book cart. Her glasses slide down to the tip of her nose. She peers over them at Emily.

— Can you speak in tongues?

— No! That's Satanic!

— No it's not. It's the Holy Spirit.

Emily knows she's wrong, but says nothing. It's pagan, not real Christianity at all; people who speak in tongues are usually just trying to get attention. Her mom says it's either that or they are demonized.

— I've got the gift of receiving the Holy Spirit. I speak in tongues all the time. My mom says that out of everyone at church, I'm the best at it.

Emily nods, turns away, and shelves more books. She's never been this close to a demonized person before, but finds it difficult to actually be afraid of Agnes. Maybe she's faking her gift.

— It's true. I'm the youngest person there who gets the Holy Spirit in my heart but when I start speaking in tongues, everybody listens. Even the old people.

She waits but Emily has no response to this.

— Don't you speak in tongues at your church at all?

Emily shakes her head hard.

— No way!

— No? No one does? That must be so boring! Is your Sunday School teacher nice though? I love my Sunday School teacher, Miss B.; she's the best teacher yet. She never yells or anything. Sometimes she brings us cookies.

— We don't have Sunday School.

— Really? You don't have Sunday School? What do the kids do?

— The same thing as everybody else. Sit and listen.

— But do you understand everything at church, just like the grown-ups?

— I guess so.

Emily isn't sure. Sometimes she doesn't quite get everything the elders say, but she assumes it will be clear eventually, if she pays enough attention.

— Anyway, I don't go to a church, either. It's not called that. It's just a hall. The Kingdom Hall.

— Well, you should come to my church. It sounds way better than yours! The bell rings and Agnes skips away, calling over her shoulder.

— Bye!

Until then, Emily hadn't realized she'd been holding her breath. She exhales and pushes the cart back to the front by Mr. MacKay's office.

On her walk back to class, Emily wonders what an entire church full of Pentecostals speaking in tongues would be like. Terrifying, probably: drooling, shouting gibberish, flailing their arms, then falling to the ground with their eyes rolling back into their heads. Heaps of well-dressed Pentecostals writhing on top of one another in the aisles, their limbs indistinguishable from each other's, as their glasses fog up and their shoes fall off.

Emily doesn't know what makes Agnes the best at speaking in tongues. Is she the loudest? Does she talk for the longest? Does she know what she is saying when she's got the Holy Spirit? How come a little girl is allowed up onstage to do that? She wishes she'd thought of these questions before the bell rang.

She can't ask her parents about speaking in tongues. Emily knows she would get in trouble just for talking to Agnes at school, since being Pentecostal is worse than just being worldly, so Emily decides not to mention this conversation to her parents. But Agnes doesn't seem that dangerous to her.

11

▼

I WAS SCARED. I DIDN'T KNOW what time it was when I woke up and that was enough to terrify me. I was trying to catch my breath, and I felt as though I was late for something, but I didn't know what. There was some sort of fog, thick and churning, all around me, and it was inside of me too, in my mouth, my eyes, my joints, my head. It was hard to move my limbs and my head throbbed and something was attached to my arm.

A white light buzzed above me, unnecessarily loud and cruel, and I winced. I forced my head to turn and look around, but that motion took longer than it should have. Everything was too slow and too loud and it made me angry. The walls were mint green concrete grids and the thick air smelled like ammonia and vomit.

I was wearing next to nothing. Where were my clothes? How dare someone take my clothes? Thinking was difficult; I couldn't focus, and trying made me feel nauseated. My right arm hurt when I moved it. I punched my free hand into the white beside me. Someone began to mutter nearby, but I couldn't make out specific words.

I leaned over the edge of my bed and tugged aside a curtain — two empty beds and the back of a mumbling woman as she lumbered out through the doorway in rumpled grey jogging pants. I blinked and looked again, then nearly fell from the edge of the bed to the cold floor — a row of elders sitting on the bed across from mine, their hands clasped, heads bent in prayer, waiting for me. I closed my eyes tightly and pulled the curtain back around me, and steadied myself on the bed.

I counted to twenty, which seemed to take hours, then opened the curtain again.

No one was there. The clock on the wall said it was 9:15 a.m. A full day had passed since I had started my last exam.

What did they want? Where did they go?

You know what they want. Don't worry, I got rid of them for you.

Where am I?

You owe me. But you should get out of there.

How?

Hurry.

I didn't want her to be mad at me. Without looking at it, I tore the IV from my arm. It dangled next to me, leaking clear fluid onto the floor. I watched a puddle begin to form, and counted forty-seven drops before I noticed the blood dripping from my arm. I shook my head in an attempt to clear it and focus through the haze. I reached for a tissue and my arm took about five minutes to move toward the box. So many beautiful red isobars on my forearm — meticulous, symmetrical, like a map of circuit boards. Crimson dots from inside my elbow spattered the white sheets. I watched them fall, two, three, four, five. My arm got tired and I remembered the tissue.

I dabbed at the blood and it slowed. The sun slashed through the windows, aggressive, jeering, trying to blind me.

I breathed deeply and looked for something to cover up with. People constantly passed by my room but none looked through the doorway at me. Uniformed staff wheeled carts of food, nurses pushed people strapped to stretchers, nervous visitors glanced furtively at their watches. I couldn't walk amid them all, covered in scabs, with my bare ass showing. I considered wrapping myself in a sheet but that would be too obvious. I concentrated for a long time, the insides of my knees against the cold chrome of the bed frame, and then Grey Jogging Pants shuffled back in.

— Hi. She swayed slightly from side to side. Her hair was greasy and flecked with white, and stains dappled her pink sweatshirt. She stood at the foot of my bed, expectant.

I nodded as curtly as I could, and turned my head toward the window, as though looking for something specific in the parking lot below.

— My name is Louisa. She spoke in a slow monotone, rattling a bottle of pills in her pocket.

— What's yours?

I didn't answer.

— My name's Louisa. What's yours?

— None of your business, that's what. I busied myself picking the scabs from my left thigh.

— I can't hear you.

— I don't care.

She peered at something on the end of my bed and straightened up.

— Hello, Emily. What did they bring you here for?

The IV bag was still dripping and the puddle was getting larger. When I didn't respond, Louisa continued to drone.

— I'm here because I have a chemical imbalance in part of my brain. But I feel better since I've been staying here.

It sounded like a line she had memorized and repeated often. My throat constricted with a sudden, dull ache. I bit the insides of my cheeks as hard as I could. It was only the drugs they had forced into me that were making me want to cry, I was sure of it, and I scraped my nails across the lines on my legs. Bits of dried blood chipped off and cuts started to bleed again, and immediately I felt better and exhaled without crying. I still didn't look at Louisa.

— Some of us from the ward play Monopoly every day at eleven before lunch. In the lounge. You should come too.

I shrugged and continued to stare out the window. A man in a white coat got out of a red sports car and walked quickly toward the side entrance. So what if I cut myself once in a while? It was my body, it didn't hurt anyone else. I wasn't schizophrenic or crazy. I didn't belong there.

— Peter keeps winning and Mina says that's because he used be a lawyer at a bank, before he came here. He's been here for three months now, but that's still not as long as me. Peter doesn't talk very much, and Mina is really nice. I'll come and get you for the next game.

I crossed my arms in from of my chest. I could feel my ribs.

— I won't be staying long enough.

Louisa looked startled, as though she'd forgotten that she was talking to someone and was surprised when I responded. She swayed, still rattling the pill jar.

— Do you have any clothes I can borrow? I lifted the edge of my papery gown.

— Like another pair of jogging pants and a sweatshirt? I'm cold. Too much air conditioning in here. It's really cold.

I was relieved to see at least my shoes beside the night-stand. Minus their laces.

— My stuff will be too big on you.

— That's okay. I don't mind. Maybe then I'll feel better, enough to play Monopoly. I smiled at her, desperate.

Louisa grinned. She was missing a tooth in the front.

— Okay then. She pulled a few things out of her drawer and then handed me a pair of yellow fleece pants and a green sweatshirt with wolves on the front. I cringed and turned it inside out and pulled it over my head, gagging at the acrid body odour. I would have to breathe only through my mouth all the way home. I closed my eyes and inhaled and exhaled and tried to focus. I didn't know my way around at all, let alone what the best route for escape would be.

— Emily?

My mother's voice nearly jolted me off the bed. I was too slow. I wanted to disappear. I smoothed the sweatshirt over my hospital gown and opened my eyes.

— You're finally awake.

I said nothing.

— I was here earlier, but you were still asleep. They sedated you after yesterday and I guess you were still out until this morning.

My mother spoke much more quickly than usual, in a strange near-whisper, and she kept glancing around the room. If she saw Louisa, she didn't let on. When my eyes met hers, she looked away.

— Where'd you get that filthy sweatshirt? She heaved a duffle bag onto the bed.

— I brought you some clothes and your toothbrush and some of your books and stuff. Did you see the doctor yet? What did he say? She stopped and stared behind me. Her shoulders sagged and she shook her head.

— Oh, Emily!

I didn't know what she was looking at, and I didn't care. She had purple arcs beneath her eyes and she hadn't bothered to fix her frizzy hair. She walked carefully to the side of my bed without getting too close, as though I was contagious.

She fiddled with the abandoned IV, then gave up. I wanted to explain that I refused to be poisoned with any more mind-controlling drugs, but I was just too tired.

— What happened to your IV?

— It fell out in my sleep.

— Bull.

Again I shrugged. I opened the bag and pulled out a t-shirt and black jeans.

— Emily, let them help you.

— I don't need help.

— But—

— Not theirs or yours or anybody's.

She took a step toward me, then stopped and stepped back again.

Instead of shouting back like the mother I had been used to, she wilted like an unwatered plant, limp and defeated.

— But—

— I'm not staying in here. I'm fine. I'm leaving with you.

— But you're not. You're not fine. She was still staring down at the floor.

— I don't even know why I'm here. Let's just go.

A few moments passed and the hum of the fluorescent lights seemed to get louder, while shrill announcements and rattling carts receded into the distance. She sat down next to me on the edge of my bed.

— You collapsed at school after your exam. They said . . . they said there were marks all over your arms. They said you've been cutting yourself all up. They didn't know what else to do, so they called an ambulance.

Louisa walked into the bathroom and clicked the door locked behind her.

— I don't remember fainting after my exam. And so what, I was tired, I'd been up all night studying. Three nights, in fact. Big deal. I do well at school and you commit me? You're just jealous!

She didn't look at me.

— It's just a few days. They have to do an assessment.

— You're trying to sabotage me! You don't want me to go to university because the elders will get you in trouble.

— That's not true, Emily. I wish you didn't have to be here either. I don't know what else to do. It's for the best.

— For the best? Nothing's wrong with me!

— I know nothing is wrong with you. But . . .

— But what.

— You've been injuring yourself. It's not normal.

— No one is normal. Let's just get out of here.

— We can't. She exhaled loudly.

— We have to be careful.

— What do you mean, careful?

I knew exactly what she meant, but I didn't care, I said it anyway.

— Because of Lenora?

She didn't move. She sat very still for a long time, and I watched the big, old industrial clock tick with hesitant, unnerving jerks, as though unsure it was doing it right.

Then the bed began to shake slightly. My mother's upper body was quivering.

— I'm sorry. I just— She inhaled harshly, trying to stop crying.

— I guess I just did everything wrong with you guys. I thought it was right, I wanted what was best for both of you, I really did, and it all ended up wrong.

I didn't know what to say to her. It would have been better if she'd said that she hated me, that everything was all my fault. For what happened to Lenora, to Uncle Tyler, for what happened to me. Being there, in the psych ward. The nuthouse. It was all my fault. I knew that was the truth, but she was blaming herself. And that made it even worse.

— It's not your fault.

This made her cry even harder.

— But it is. And I'm sorry.

I let her cry. I passed her a tissue but I felt very far away, as though I were watching this happen on a stage far on the horizon. Why now? Why was she finally saying all this stuff? Why not before?

— Are you going to leave the Truth?

— Oh Emily. Of course not. I mean, I don't know. It made so much sense at first. And I was so in love with your dad. I was. I just. I don't know really. He changed. Everything changed. He was so focused on the Hall and the readings and trying to get in good with the elders and get more responsibility, he just withdrew from me. From us.

She paused and I didn't say anything. I just let her keep talking.

— I thought that if I got more involved with the Witnesses too, it would bring us closer together.

— Did it work? Once I started, I couldn't stop asking cruel questions.

She sighed and shrugged.

— For a time, yes. But then he just got more and more distant, like he was just playing a role. I don't know. Maybe that's what everybody's marriages are like.

— Where's Dad today? How come he didn't come here?

— You know he's Full-Time Pioneering again this month. He can't bring himself to ever skip a day. Someone might tell the elders on him or something. She tried, and failed, to laugh.

— What about when he's done?

— By that time, visiting hours will be over.

Part of me wanted to cry, but I couldn't. It was as though all her tears had supplanted and negated the need for my own. We were both exhausted.

— Are you going to come back tomorrow?

— If you want me to.

We both attempted smiles that ended up contorted, lopsided grimaces. She left and I collapsed back on the bed.

Even though I couldn't explain it, something between us had changed, if only for a moment.

Louisa emerged tentatively from the washroom, as though she'd been listening at the door for my mother to leave. I handed her back her sweatshirt and pants and pulled the curtain all the way around my bed and tugged the blanket over my head.

I trembled under the scratchy, coarse covers. I didn't know what had happened to me, what was real and what people were making up, and I was scared of my own mother. I didn't want to experience any more of her raw, confusing unhappiness. It made me panic. I felt like I could sleep for days.

Can you tell me a story? Like you used to?

You give up too easily.

Please?

Fine. Just this once. Once upon a time, we could fly.

12
▼

ON SATURDAY MORNING, EMILY GOES to the hard-
ware store with her father. She hardly ever gets to go
because he usually picks up his supplies when she's at
school, so she jumps at the chance to tag along and visit
the toy section. She assumes he doesn't want any talking
in the car, which is fine with her, so she reads from *Circus
World* on the drive into town.

The shop smells old and dusty and it's cluttered,
but Emily still likes it. You never know what you might
see there — a hard-to-find Star Wars action figure, doll
clothes so old that the hippie outfits are becoming trendy
again, and sometimes they even stock live tropical fish.
Just as she reaches the farthest corner of the store, the pet

section, someone bellows at her dad. She heads back to the aisle with the coils of cords and wires to see who it is.

— Ah, well, will you look at that — it's Jim Morrow! Didn't recognize you there, buddy!

— Hello, Mr. Patton. How are you keeping?

It's Carli and Sally's dad, from next door, though he doesn't live there anymore. Emily stops at the end of the row, pretending to inspect some rolls of red and blue wire.

— Call me Carl. And maybe I should call you Brother Jim, eh there, Brother Jim, how's the Lord these days? Mr. Patton laughs long and loud and looks around to see who else is listening. The other customers smirk or look away.

— Almost didn't recognize you there, Jim, without your tie on, and without that briefcase full of *Watchtowers*!

A teenage boy with thick glasses and long hair snickers from behind the cash register. Emily's dad's face turns red. He narrows his brown eyes, and Emily's stomach knots and burns. She looks down at her hands and picks at the hangnail on her thumb. It feels good to tear off bits of dry skin there. It bleeds a little bead of crimson and she pops her thumb into her mouth.

— I'm just joking with you there, Brother Jim, don't be sore. How's that wife of yours?

Emily wonders what they would look like from high above, if she were a funambulist. She puts one foot perfectly in front of the other, over and over, along the crack in the tiles on the floor until she is standing next to her father. From a hundred meters above them, she would see tall, skinny Mr. Patton, with his half-bald head and his lopsided red nose, leaning toward her father and swaying with laughter, and her dad too, stocky and not as tall, putting his hands in his pockets and angling his shoulders away.

— Fine. We're all fine. He turns his back to Mr. Patton and nods sharply.

— Let's go, Emily. They don't have the cables I need.

EMILY CAN SMELL HER MOM'S instant coffee when they get home. Even though she would rather stay home all day and watch cartoons and read, she is going out in service with Uncle Tyler. Lenora is supposed to come too, but she overslept and promises to go on Sunday instead.

In the kitchen, her mom sits slumped at the table and Uncle Tyler leans against the fridge. The kettle screeches and Emily jumps. Her mom rubs her temples, sighs, and turns off the burner.

— Okay kiddo, looks like it's just you and me today, let's go.

Uncle Tyler's coat and suit jacket are slung over one shoulder and his tie is loosened. His hair curls over the collar of his shirt. Emily frowns. She knows that people from the Hall already think his appearance is inappropriate; their parents argue, debating whether or not they should tell him what the other brothers and sisters say about him. He might get in trouble with the elders if he doesn't start being more careful, but he doesn't care.

Emily has packed her Hall purse with her Bible, the most recent issues of *Awake!* and *The Watchtower*, and some back issues, which they can place with interested people for free. The new issues are two for a dollar, which is called a contribution. She has also hidden a Trixie Belden mystery under her Bible. She stayed up late reading it under her blankets with a flashlight, and she wants to find out what happens next. Uncle Tyler won't tell on her; he's not like that. She pulls her coat on and hops from one foot to the other, excited but nervous at the prospect of an afternoon with her uncle. She knows that going out in service with him is not going to be like when she goes door to door with her dad, who's always so serious, mad at her, or disappointed that she isn't better at preaching to strangers. Lenora is way better at it; her voice never shakes and her face doesn't turn bright red.

But going out in service with Uncle Tyler makes her feel like she is in trouble in a different way. She knows her dad didn't want her to go. Her parents argued about it the night before.

— I don't trust that he'll be a good influence on the girls, or that he'll set the proper example, Vivian.

— Of course he will. Just because he's young and likes to joke around doesn't mean he doesn't take the Truth seriously. They'll be fine. It'll be good for them to spend some more time with their uncle.

Emily is disappointed that Lenora isn't coming, and jealous that she can stay home whenever she wants — Emily never has any choice in what she can do — but secretly she's glad she'll get Uncle Tyler all to herself. He's never in a bad mood and, more importantly, he understands her. For example, if they're supposed to call on a house where one of her classmates lives, he'll let her wait in the car instead, lying down in the back seat with her book, or they'll skip that address entirely. He never tells her that she should be stronger or try harder or Witness more at school; he just lets her relax.

Even though he seems to always be on the verge of getting in trouble, she's missed him lately. Things are more fun when he's around, like at the meetings when he gives her silly notes when her parents aren't looking. Once, last year, he made her give him her Hall purse at the break.

Besides her Bible, *Watchtower*, and songbook, she had also snuck another Trixie Belden mystery with her, and she didn't want to get caught. Not that she would read it at the Hall; only in the car on the way there, or afterwards. She just couldn't put it down. Sometimes, while her dad would chat with the elders after a meeting, she'd sneak out to the cold unlocked car and read her novel by the interior light, with the door ajar. But she trusted her uncle, and she handed over her Hall purse. He told her not to look in it until after the meeting, and she didn't, but she was unable to listen to the brothers' talks at all for that hour, since she was busy squirming in her chair, trying to guess what he put in her bag. It turned out to be a treasure map that he drew himself — a map of the car, with an arrow that pointed to the sun visor. When Emily pulled that down, she found a note that said to look under the floor mats — three of them concealed only twigs and pebbles and gum wrappers but under the fourth was a note telling her to look where "there were no mittens." It didn't take her long to find the bag of chips — dill pickle, her favourite — in the glove compartment.

EMILY'S MOM IS STILL IN her housecoat. Her hair is even bigger and fuzzier than usual, and she stills has smears of yesterday's dark blue eyeliner under her eyes. She's staying home with Lenora while their father is out working on another house. She makes sure Emily has her hat and mitts with her, but fortunately doesn't check her bag. When she stirs her instant coffee, the spoon clangs like a bell, shrill and loud.

— How come you're not coming, Mom? Emily knows she won't get in trouble for asking a question like this, because her uncle Tyler is here and she never gets in trouble in front of company.

— I'm not feeling well. I'll take Lenora out tomorrow, don't worry. She takes a long slurp and looks at Uncle Tyler.

— I thought you were getting your hair cut yesterday. Look at it, it's way too long. Emily's mom frowns, chews at her lip.

— Sister Bulchinsky was going on about it after the meeting the other night to anyone who would listen. It's embarrassing.

Uncle Tyler runs his fingers through his curls, stretches them out.

— Almost enough for a ponytail. What would Sister Bulchinsky say then?

Emily's mom sighs and shrugs.

— Everyone says it's immodest. Don't cause trouble. Try to set a good example for your nieces.

— Relax, would you? I forgot. I'll get it cut this week. He winks at Emily.

— Let's hit the road, kiddo.

Her uncle likes cars, and has had a different one every year or two, mostly older ones that he and his friends fix up, and his latest one is unlike any she's ever seen. The front half looks like a car and the back looks like a pickup truck. It's called an El Camino. Uncle Tyler keeps it spotless and shiny and she squints her eyes at the bright blueness of it. He starts the car, puts on his sunglasses, and turns up the radio as the car crunches down the driveway. They lurch onto the road and the tires squeal. Emily cringes and turns to look back. Her mom is shaking her head between the panels of green floral curtains.

Uncle Tyler turns the volume up and nods his head to

the music, driving faster than her father would. In fact, he's nothing like Emily's dad. He's younger, and is more like a big brother than a grown-up like her parents. He's more like Lenora, someone Emily looks up to, but they both do things that make her insides clench up and then she can't sleep very well. Neither has done anything so bad that the elders have reproved them, but small things that she knows mean something bigger, like Lenora having worldly friends, or her uncle growing his hair long. One of them is not so bad, but lots of them added together turn into trouble.

Uncle Tyler drives with one hand on the steering wheel and drums on the seat to the music with his other hand.

— You like The Cult, kiddo?

Emily doesn't know what to say. Occult means the devil, Satan, Jehovah God's biggest enemy. If you are interested in the occult, you can get demonized, just like people who use Ouija boards, just like Brother Richard's house.

He turns the radio down slightly.

— Hey, relax, I'm just kidding. I know you don't listen to this stuff. I'm just teasing. Forget it.

Emily looks out the window. They pass the street the Kingdom Hall is on.

— We're supposed to go that way. She points back toward the street that they missed.

— I know. I thought we'd go for some ice cream first. We have lots of time before the service meeting.

The service meeting is always short, only about fifteen minutes, and is usually held at the Kingdom Hall, though sometimes it's at a brother's home, in his kitchen or rec room. Today it's at the Hall, and the elder will go over the main points to use when they go door to door, and then they'll organize who goes in whose car. Some brothers and sisters don't have cars of their own, or their cars are in such poor shape that it isn't appropriate to use them in service. They'll also find out which territory they're going to be working in today. Emily knows it is wrong, but always hopes for a territory as far from her school as possible.

Emily's dad hardly ever lets them go for ice cream when they go out in service, except maybe once in the summer, and only after they were done, after they'd marked their hours down on the time slips.

They aren't allowed to listen to the radio out in service either, unless her dad has to check the weather, but no music. No worldly music, that's for sure. Her uncle's music is loud and fast, maybe even heavy metal. At one of the Thursday night meetings last month, the elders explained that if you play these songs backwards, you hear messages from the devil. They tell you to kill your mother, or commit fornication, or do drugs. Some kids in the States killed themselves after listening to Black Sabbath. It's called backward masking, and if you listen to it, even by accident, you can become demonized. Black Sabbath and Judas Priest are the worst of all.

— You like this song, kiddo? It's called 'Rain.' Uncle Tyler hums along.

— *Here comes the rain . . .*

— It's okay, I guess. She lets her breath out carefully. It doesn't sound Satanic, they're only singing about the rain, and Jehovah makes the rain, and all natural things, so it must be all right.

— Actually, your sister loaned me this tape. She's a big fan. Her uncle looks over at her.

— Really?

— Really. She has pretty good taste in music.

Emily didn't know that Uncle Tyler and Lenora hung out together without her, trading tapes and skipping going out in service. And talking about her probably, since she wasn't invited.

— What do you think of her new hair-do? Wild, huh? She's turning out to be pretty cool.

— I guess so. Emily looks out the window, seeing nothing.

— Hey. Cheer up. What's the matter?

— Nothing. She turns away.

— Are you sure?

Emily forces herself to look over at Uncle Tyler and smile. It feels ridiculous and plastic. How can he even believe her?

— Yeah. I'm okay.

They pull into the Dairy Queen parking lot.

13

▼

EMILY BREATHES AS DEEPLY AS she can, holds it as she counts to ten in her head, then exhales, as Uncle Tyler turns onto Willow Street, toward the Kingdom Hall. The caramel sundae sloshes and heaves like a swollen, polluted river in her stomach. *Please Jehovah, don't let me throw up in Uncle Tyler's car. In Jesus' name, Amen.*

She exhales loudly a few more times, and the nausea passes. When they reach the Hall, the parking lot is empty.

Her uncle smiles, his sunglasses still on. With her parents, Emily has never missed a service meeting. This is unlike other Sundays, the pattern is wrong. Ice cream in the middle of the day, a fast car, loud music, an empty Hall.

— I guess we missed the meeting. Uncle Tyler's voice fills the car over the radio. He doesn't sound worried.

— You said we had lots of time.

— My watch must be wrong. His car doesn't have a clock on the dash like Emily's father's car does.

— Don't worry, you won't get in trouble. I'll tell your mom it was my fault. She can give me crap about it, I don't care. I'm used to it.

Emily cringes at the almost-swear. Substitute swears are just as bad as actual ones, they mean the same thing and everybody knows what you're really saying.

— But how will we know which territory we're supposed to be in today? There is no way he can know that; Uncle Tyler is not an elder, not even close. He's too young, first of all, but that's not it. There are other reasons Emily cannot quite identify. He's not worldly, he's baptized, but he's not like her father, serious and strict and always studying the books and magazines from the Watchtower Society. He isn't like other men at the Hall, who rarely even smile, who have secrets and committees, wives and kids. Uncle Tyler doesn't seem to care what other brothers and sisters do, although they all keep watch over one another. No one is ever left out.

They can't just pick any road to start on, another car of Jehovah's Witnesses would likely already be there, or could have been there last week. The door-to-door schedules are carefully planned by the elders; they keep track of everyone's time sheets and who is assigned which territory. You can't call on someone too often, or they won't listen and will be even less interested.

— We don't need a territory today, I have some back calls we can make instead. It'll be okay. We won't get in trouble.

— You have back calls?

— Sure I do. I'm not as bad as your parents think I am, you know.

Emily's stomach starts to improve, the ice cream stops sloshing, and her face isn't as hot.

— Are they studying?

— What? Uncle Tyler looks out the window at the names of side roads.

— Is who studying?

— Your back calls. Are any of them studying with you?

Uncle Tyler laughs as he pulls into a long driveway on River Road, toward Pine Shore Trailer Park. No, he is coughing. He hacks into his fist, turning red, clears his throat, then responds.

— No. They're not studying. Not yet, anyway. Soon, probably. They're definitely interested. You can tell your dad that; pretty soon they'll be studying the Truth.

Studying is the next step toward becoming part of the Truth, becoming one of Jehovah's Witnesses. After they study the literature — the various magazines and books like *Is There a Creator Who Cares About You?* or *The Truth That Leads to Eternal Life* — the new Bible students start coming to the meetings, although they aren't allowed to raise their hands to answer any of the questions yet. After studying for a year or so, the new people are eligible to get baptized at one of the district assemblies or the summer convention. Once you're baptized you are a Jehovah's Witness forever, unless you get disfellowshipped. Lenora got baptized when she was just fourteen years old, which is young to be baptized, but Lenora is smart.

Emily hasn't personally known anyone who has been disfellowshipped, though she has seen one or two of them come to the meetings once in a while. You can become disfellowshipped if you commit a grievous sin and aren't repentant. A disfellowshipped brother or sister is cast out from the congregation, and no one is allowed to talk to them, not even their own relatives. If they continue to come to the meetings at the Kingdom Hall, they must sit at the back, alone, and not speak to anyone. Everyone whispers and then are shushed, because you must treat them as though they are dead. It says so in the Bible, in I Corinthians: *Remove the wicked from among yourselves.*

Her uncle shuts off the car near the first block of trailers. Emily tries not to be nervous. Deep breaths slow her heartbeat back to normal, but things don't feel right. The sun glares against the wet snow and hurts her eyes. She squints, picks up her Hall purse, and gets out of the car.

Uncle Tyler forgets his briefcase in the El Camino.

Emily has only been to the trailer park once before, last year, and it was not like going door to door on a regular street. The people are louder, the dogs run loose, toys are strewn on lawns, and kids stare at them, or worse, climb trees and throw chestnuts at them.

The park is brown with muddy slush, with rusted skeletons of bikes left outside in winter. It has snowed lately, then melted, then snowed again, which always makes a mess. Emily walks carefully behind Uncle Tyler, avoiding slush and dog poop, wondering why this place is called a park. There are no swings, no picnic area, and it's far too cluttered. None of the trailers have wheels; they are there for good.

Uncle Tyler knocks on the door of trailer number seventeen. There's no sound from inside. Emily shivers and wonders if they'll have any kids she can talk to, maybe a boy her age who has a lot of Lego sets, or even video games. Not very many kids from the Hall have video games, but she's played a ping-pong game, and *Pac-Man* at Uncle Tyler's place.

Someone pulls the curtain aside from the window, then a man with a big blond moustache flings open the door.

— Tyler, my man, how's it going! He wears tight black jeans and a t-shirt that says Styx in orange letters.

He shouts into the trailer over his shoulder.

— Hey Jeff. Rise and shine, Sleeping Beauty, Tyler's here! He shakes his head at her uncle.

— The lazy bastard. And who might you be, young lady?

Emily looks up toward her uncle. He nods.

— Emily.

— This is my niece, Emily, my sister's kid. I'm taking her out in door-to-door service this afternoon.

— Right on, I get you. He bends down toward Emily and extends his hand.

— I'm Michael. Come on in out of the cold.

Michael's living room furniture is green and scratchy and dirty dishes cover the coffee table, along with an assortment of beer bottles and ashtrays. Emily tries not to look at the mess. She sits on the edge of the couch, her Hall purse at her feet. She can still smell it though, cigarette butts and stale beer, and gags. She doesn't want to hurt Michael's feelings, so she covers it up with a cough, and decides from then on to breathe only through her mouth.

— What've you been up to, man?

— Not much. The usual. Uncle Tyler shifts around on the couch next to Emily and settles in.

On the walls are posters of various worldly bands, like Trooper and Queen and Kiss. Some hang crooked. Emily looks at the floor, a yellow shag rug, in dire need of a vacuum. That's what Emily's mom would say: *in dire need*. At home, Emily's mom vacuums every day, and it is Emily's job to go after her and pick up by hand any bits of lint missed by the vacuum. She crawls across the rug in the wake of the vacuum, pick pick pick, gone are the little white bits of lint, while Lenora sneers in the doorway, spitting words as though they are rotten, words like "demeaning."

— Don't force your OCD on us, Mom!

Sometimes when their mom isn't looking, Lenora will toss bits of lint from her towel or a tissue onto the rug. Lenora doesn't tell Emily what OCD means.

— Hey. What's up? A man stands in the living room doorway, rubbing his eyes.

— Jeff. What's up.

Jeff leans against the door frame in a slouchy red bathrobe. His feet are bare and hairy.

— Emily, that's Jeff.

Jeff waves. Emily nods.

— Emily's my niece.

— They're out performing the will of God today. Why don't you see if Tyler can ask God to cure your hangover?

They laugh. Jeff moans.

— Shit, man, seriously. Don't talk so loud. Hurts.

— Where did you two go last night? That new place over the border?

— Yeah man, Tool Box, very cool, good music, and live shows too.

Uncle Tyler coughs again, jerks his head toward Emily.

— You guys still have my old Atari hooked up?

— Sure. Michael stands up.

— You like *Pac-Man*, Emily?

She nods.

— It's in the bedroom. Want a drink? Pepsi or orange juice?

The bedroom is a mess and the orange juice has pulp, which makes Emily gag again. She can't see any of the floor beneath the piles of clothes — t-shirts, jeans, boxer shorts, socks. Wood panelling lines the walls and the room smells like dirty laundry. Michael turns *Pac-Man* on and gives her a folding chair.

— Have fun, Emily. He closes the bedroom door behind him. Emily wonders whose room she's in.

Pac-Man absorbs Emily's attention, and she does not feel guilty that she's playing video games instead of helping her uncle, or instead of going door to door. She forgets they've missed the service meeting as the little yellow head swallows everything in sight, and her points accumulate until a hand cramp forces her to take a break. According to the white plastic clock on the wall, she's been playing for an hour and ten minutes.

Laughter brims from the trailer's living room, and Emily wonders what could possibly be funny. Not the *Last Days* they currently live in, not the knowledge of impending Armageddon, which will bring an end to this world and its wicked ways, which is what Uncle Tyler should be telling them. Some of the books published by the Watchtower Bible and Tract Society have pictures of Armageddon in them — lava and rocks raining down from heaven, everyone running and cowering, the ground cracked open, swallowing people whole, bolts of lightning, bodies in pieces. It is Emily's job to let as many people as possible know about Armageddon, so that they have a chance to learn the Truth, and survive, even live forever.

After Armageddon, God will make the entire world into Paradise on Earth, and even the dead will be resurrected. Emily doesn't know anyone who's died, not really, just some really old brothers and sisters from the Hall, but no one who was a relative or a friend.

Most of the books have pictures of Paradise in them too, which is always outside in the sun. There are usually mountains in the background, several types of trees and flowers, children playing with lions, lots of other animals (some not even from the same continent), baskets of fruit, and people hugging each other. They hug because they were dead before, and the picture is after the Resurrection, and everyone is overjoyed to see each other again.

Everyone from the Truth who is dead will be resurrected after Armageddon, even people who were good and pure but died before Jehovah's Witnesses existed. God knows who they are and will decide, just as He chooses who survives Armageddon. Then they will have a chance at eternal life in Paradise, with no more war, disease, greed, pestilence, or even bad weather. Emily is not positive about the bad weather part — all those trees and flowers and fruits would need rain, but all the pictures show Paradise as very sunny.

There are, however, some exceptions to the Resurrection. People who murder themselves, which is called committing suicide, will not be resurrected. Killing yourself is worse than killing another person, though Emily is unsure why. She thinks it should be equal to the murder of an enemy or an attacker, since there is still only one life lost, but it's not the same. She will ask her father, he will know that, as well as about the weather in Paradise, if it is always summer, or will there still be winter, and what about thunderstorms.

Emily can't hear what her uncle Tyler and Michael and Jeff are discussing in the other room. Music blares, and there's a strange smell. It's like cigarette smoke but sweeter, and unfamiliar. Emily wonders when they will leave and try Uncle Tyler's other back calls. She turns off the Atari, then the light, and steps into the hall.

The smoke in the living room is thick, and Jeff coughs. When her uncle sees her, he jumps off the couch.

— Emily, oh, there you are. How was *Pac-Man*? I was just coming to get you.

— It was good. I got my highest score ever. What's burning?

— Nothing, nothing, everything's fine. That's some special incense that Michael has, it's to make the room smell better, kind of like an air freshener, that's all.

— Oh. Emily thinks that her mom once told her that incense is pagan, and therefore to be avoided. And it's definitely not improving the smell of the trailer anyway.

— Well, it's time to go, kiddo. More work of the Lord to do.

Michael and Jeff laugh as Uncle Tyler straightens his tie and puts his suit jacket back on. They do not get up to walk them to the door.

— Do you still have those *Watchtower* back issues in your bag, Em? I forgot mine in the car, and Michael has read the ones I left him last time, right?

Michael grins.

— Sure, man. Hey, don't forget that Cure tape you wanted to borrow.

Emily gives Jim the magazines and he thanks her and waves goodbye from the couch. Outside, they squint against the sun's glare.

— Are we going to see your other back calls now?

Her uncle checks his watch.

— Well, it's three o'clock, we have time for one or two more, I guess.

They drive for a long time, out into the country, and into the little village near the lake.

They stop at a dingy bungalow with an empty driveway.

— It doesn't look like anyone is home.

— Well, let's see. Uncle Tyler takes his briefcase out of the car.

No one answers the door. They drive the twenty minutes back into town, and her uncle says nothing, just sings along to the songs on Michael's tape.

He pulls up in front of Emily's house.

— So long, Em. He drops her off and doesn't come into the house to see her parents, or stay for dinner. Emily doesn't get a chance to ask him if Michael and Jeff will be coming to any of the meetings with him, but she already knows the answer.

14

▼

AFTER A FEW WEEKS, THE air warms and the snow turns to grey slush. It's Wednesday, so there is no meeting and Emily tries not to feel so relieved. She trudges up her wet driveway without Lenora, dragging her boots through a set of tire tracks. Both of her feet are cold and tingly and thoroughly soaked.

She tried to wait for her sister; she walked home as slowly as she could, twisting to look behind her every twenty-five paces. Lenora wouldn't have shown up even if she had waited in front of her school for an hour; she rarely does. Who will yell at her more this time — her mother or Lenora? Which one is worse depends on their respective moods. Her mother is unpredictable: she might sigh and shake her head, then mutter at Lenora, saying who does she think she is, ignoring Emily altogether, which she prefers, or she might accuse Emily of covering for her sister and send her to her room until her sister reappears. Lenora will most likely refuse to have anything to do with her.

Emily is tired of the pattern. It's unfair that she gets caught in the middle of their arguments, especially when they have nothing to do with her. From now on, things will be different. Emily will stay out of it. When they do get mad at her, she will do whatever it takes to fight back the tears. She'll be more like Lenora, who never cries, even if they slap her — *spare the rod, spoil the child* — or ground her for weeks. She just clenches her fists, tosses her hair, and forces a laugh. Ha. She tells them they'll regret it, just wait, they'll be sorry.

Lenora will probably accuse her of trying to get her in trouble on purpose. Then she won't speak to Emily for days. That's worse than her mother's temper, which at least passes quickly. When Lenora ignores her, Emily feels like brick walls have risen up from the ground and surrounded her. Imprisoned and desperate, she first jumps up and down, which proves futile, then she pounds her small fists. No one can hear her, and no one but Lenora can let her out. What she's been locked out of she doesn't entirely know, but she's well aware that without her sister, she will miss something important.

Emily stops in her slushy plod up the treed driveway. On the other side of the pine trees, next to the house, someone has parked an unfamiliar red car. Their grey four-door isn't there, so Emily knows her father is still at work. As an electrician, he doesn't work fixed hours. He's always home in time for the meetings at the Hall, but on other nights he may be home at four, or not until nine. It depends on the job.

She stops and looks in the window of the unfamiliar Mustang. The seats are black and clean, and the dashboard is uncluttered, but scattered on the passenger seat is an assortment of cassette cases. The only footprints begin at the driver's side and trail around the house toward the backyard. Solitary footsteps in the snow must be followed, Emily decides. She stretches her legs to match the steps, as she plunks her small boots into each of the larger imprints.

— Fee fi fo fum . . . She lurches from side to side and stomps into the boot marks, which lead to the back porch and disappear into the house. She is a giant. She will crush the worldly people who pick on her, like Tammy, like Josh Hansen from school, like teachers who sigh when she tries to explain that she must miss art class if they are going to draw Santa Claus. Her teacher last year, Miss Robin, was like that — always annoyed when Emily told her what she wasn't allowed to do, what was forbidden for Jehovah's Witnesses. It's hard enough to put up her hand in front of the entire class and say, "I'm supposed to leave the room during Christmas activities; it's against our religion," and even worse when the teacher throws up her hands and says, like Miss Robin did, "Is there anything that's not against your religion? How about snow? Can you draw a snowman instead? Or is that a sin too?" The other kids' laughter surged like a tidal wave and filled the room with their snickers and stares. Though she fought it as hard as she could, hot red shame flooded her face and everyone could see. She bit her lower lip until she tasted metal and salt, no way would she let out the strangled sobs, and so she choked a little, then drove the white crayon into the black construction paper so hard she snapped the crayon in half.

Bam, goes her humungous foot on Miss Robin's head, and she grinds in her heel. *Bam*, again, and this one is Josh Hansen and his crooked teeth and ugly mouth calling her *Joho loser* over and over during every recess, and now he is in a million pieces. *Bam*, even harder, she smashes Tammy Bales into a pulp and keeps right on going, naming each of her classmates one by one, *bam bam*, her giant feet do not miss anyone and she crushes them all in a snowy frenzy until she reaches the back porch.

She doesn't even feel her icy feet anymore and nearly forgets that she is following mysterious footprints like a detective.

Tense and alert, Emily opens the back door quietly, and doesn't let it slam shut. There is a stranger in her house, a visitor, someone with a red car. A car she's never seen before in the Kingdom Hall parking lot. The elders discourage two-door cars, because they are awkward for groups of people going door to door. They don't say that they're forbidden, but no one ever gets one. She wants to find out who has the rebellious car, but she can't let her mom notice the absence of Lenora. She'll just have to be silent and hurry past the kitchen. Maybe her mother will just assume that Lenora is with her, already upstairs or in the bathroom, and leave her alone. She decides that she should learn how to make her footsteps sound like two people.

Quickly though, she realizes that none of her methods matter this time. No one could have heard her come in anyway. Loud music blasts from the kitchen — worldly music, along with the sound of her mother singing. Emily's muscles stiffen. No, it's not just her mother's voice; it's a duet. Someone else sings along, and it's definitely not her tuneless father. Even during the songs at the Hall, she can see her father's lips move, but she never hears his voice.

Emily thought that Lenora was the only one in the family who listens to worldly music, though usually just through headphones, so as to avoid their father's objections. As far as Emily knows, her mother owns only a box of music theatre albums like *Oklahoma!* and *West Side Story*, which she never listens to. The only records her father even has are 45s of moose calls. He listens to them just before hunting season, and practises mimicking the guttural grunts. Lenora says that they sound like someone struggling, unsuccessfully, to go to the bathroom.

Emily can't make out the words, but her mother's powerful vocals surge through the house — loud, louder than any of them are allowed to be at home.

— Stop, stop, stop. Emily's mother gasps, choked with laughter. Something, possibly her mother, thuds against the wall.

— Start that part over again, I love that verse! Come on, play it again!

— Okay Viv, okay, just hold on — I dropped the pick.

Emily takes off her boots, careful to keep them on the rubber mat and not get any snow or mud on the carpet. She hears the refrigerator door open and close, then the clank of bottles.

— Thanks. The other person's voice is muffled, as though he has something in his mouth, but sounds familiar. Before she even begins to guess, the window-rattling guitar screeches up again.

— *So where were the spiders . . .* The pair sing in the kitchen and Emily hangs her coat on the gun rack. She has no choice but to walk by the kitchen doorway to get to the stairs to her room.

Emily hates to sing. Like her father, she moves her lips accordingly, with little or no sound sneaking past them. At school, music is the only subject in which she doesn't get an A. She hopes her mother doesn't force her to sing with them. She doesn't always know what, at any given moment, her mother will do next.

As she runs past the kitchen, the music stops in the middle of a line. The last guitar note hums through the speaker and fades away.

— Hey Emily! How are you, kiddo?

She turns back to see that it's her uncle Tyler.

— Hi. She tries, and fails, to smile as he hides a beer bottle behind his back. She doesn't let on to them that she's seen it. He wears dark blue jeans that look too small and a black sweatshirt with the sleeves pushed up to his elbows. His strawberry blond hair is longer, shaggier than when she last saw him. He still hasn't gotten it cut.

— Say congratulations to your uncle. He just bought that fancy new car today.

Emily nods at her uncle. He hasn't been at all of the meetings lately, at least not the Sunday morning ones. Missing meetings is always a sign of either defection to the World or serious illness. When she asked her parents last week if Uncle Tyler was sick, her mom and dad both answered at the same time.

— That's one way of putting it. Her dad raised his thick eyebrows and shook his head.

— He's fine. Her mom glared back at him.

Emily hadn't known that her uncle could play the guitar. She didn't know anyone who could play an instrument, for real, other than a couple of kids at school who played the piano during music class. Emily did know that her mom could sing though. Sometimes she wonders if that's the only reason she goes to the meetings at the Kingdom Hall anymore. While she may look angry — likely at her, Emily assumes, or Lenora — during the brothers' talks, when it's time to sing one of the meeting's three songs, she opens her purple and gold songbook, and jubilantly belts out the lyrics, resounding and beautiful. Her voice is clearer, louder, and better than any of the other sisters' in the congregation. Sometimes her parents fight about that.

— You're being immodest, and showing off.

She just rolls her eyes and ignores him.

Her mother's long dark curls bounce in every direction and are splayed across her face. She pulls back her hair and secures it with an elastic band, takes a long sip from her bottle of beer, then starts to gather up the dirty plates and bottles. She walks slowly and deliberately across the green and yellow linoleum and into the laundry room, and doesn't say a word to Emily. No questions about Lenora, no yelling, nothing. She doesn't even look at her.

— I didn't know you could play the guitar. Emily doesn't know why Uncle Tyler has never mentioned it before. Why is everyone keeping secrets from her? Maybe she should start having some secrets of her own.

— Sure, I play a bit of guitar, here and there, nothing much, just for fun. He winks.

— Want to try, Em? Come here! He reaches toward the table to set his drink down while lifting the guitar strap over his head. He misses, and the beer bottle clatters to the floor, splattering the foamy, brown liquid everywhere. Emily squishes her eyes closed as her mom strides back into the kitchen.

— Darn it, Tyler! Her hands grip her hips and she glares.

— That's going to reek for hours!

— No, thank you. I have to do my homework.

Her mom scrubs the floor with a cloth, and her uncle, looking unsure what to do with his hands, puts his guitar back on and strums a few chords.

— Turn the amp off, Ty. Jim's going to be home any minute. Help me clean this place up.

Emily turns away from the doorway and goes upstairs to do her math homework.

In her pale blue room she sits on the edge of her perfectly made bed and picks at her hangnails. She can't concentrate on her fractions. Blood pools on her left index finger and she licks it away absently, listening to her mom and Uncle Tyler downstairs. They aren't singing anymore, but she can't make out what they're saying, amid the sounds of running water, dishes clattering in the sink, and chairs being slid back into place. Emily gets up and hides the candle holder in her top dresser drawer under her tights, though there is still no sign of Lenora. The back door rattles shut, and from her bedroom window, Emily watches her uncle walk toward his car. Before opening the door, he pauses, pats the hood, and grins, then climbs in and drives away.

— Bye. She sighs deeply, her nose pressed up against the glass, fogging it up.

15

▼

AFTER A WEEK OF FITFUL sleeping alternated with saccharine, perfunctory counselling and keeping my hands away from sharp objects, they let me out. My parents pretended I'd never been in the hospital and that was fine with me. The house, the Kingdom Hall, and the town itself were like prison cells and all my energy went into planning my escape: researching universities, filling out forms, creating a budget, getting a summer job. These were things considered normal, even commendable for most teenagers, but for me, it was forbidden, and therefore covert. It was sedition.

I got a job in a local greenhouse, and planned to work as much as possible all summer to supplement the student loans. One night I came home to my father standing on the front porch, a manila envelope clenched in his hand. When he saw me on my ten-speed in the driveway, he started shouting.

— And just what is this? He waved the package over his head.

— Who do you think is going to pay for you to run off in September? You think you're so much smarter than everybody else, but I've got news for you, you're not going anywhere, you hear me?

He got louder and louder as I rode past and into the backyard. He jogged behind me.

— Answer me! Who do you think you are?

He grabbed my shoulder and I fell off the bike into the gravel. Jagged bits of stone dug into my palms and stung like wasps. I ignored the pain and untangled myself from the spokes, then snatched my envelope from his hands.

— I'm not asking you for any help. I'll pay for school myself. I brushed the stones from my hands and arms and knees. My left shin was gouged and bleeding.

— Oh no, you won't. You have no idea what you're doing. You're not moving hours away to a city you barely know, living with . . . with . . . strangers!

I noted that he didn't say "worldly people" or mention the Last Days. He didn't have to.

— We can talk about you maybe commuting to the community college part-time or something—

— I've made up my mind. I'm going.

I knew better than to stay and argue. Commute to community college! He just didn't want me to miss any meetings; he didn't want to look bad in the beady eyes of the elders. That is, he didn't want to look any worse. I folded the envelope and shoved it into my pocket, then got back on my bike and rode for a couple hours in the dark, veering far onto the side of the road when a car passed. Every so often I would stop and run my fingers along the edges of the envelope, afraid to open it. What if I didn't get in? What would I do then? I couldn't stay there, in that town, with the elders circling me like predators, waiting to pounce on any moral misstep.

Under a streetlight near a truck stop, I finally opened the letter.

Dear Emily Morrow:

Congratulations. We are pleased to accept you into the Faculty of Arts and Science . . .

Beyond that, the letter didn't register. I yelped and danced on the side of the road, high on my own sense of impending freedom. I thought of nothing else for the rest of that summer. Gradually, I boxed up the items that mattered to me and stashed them at Uncle Tyler's, to be shipped to me later in the fall. And then I got on a bus and left.

THE BASEMENT APARTMENT was in the west end of the city, a half-hour's walk from school. The landlady, Maria, lived upstairs and liked me because I was quiet and didn't smoke and/or have a pet.

— You're a good girl. Maria came down to visit, smiling, a week after I moved in.

— Here, take this, for protection.

She thrust a small clay Virgin Mary at me, then a six-inch bleeding Jesus on porcelain cross. He had long hair and sad eyes and was caked with a layer of dust. I was supposed to hang them on my door to ward off evil, or to remind me of my sins, or both. I had grown up afraid of these types of pagan idols. Replicas of Jesus and Mary adorned many of the front doors and porches in my neighbourhood, and I couldn't quite break the habit of averting my eyes every time I walked past them.

I held them stiffly in my fists.

— Thanks.

Maria nodded and smiled.

That was the first time I'd ever touched a cross. It actually felt disorienting, illicit. I had no idea what to do with the figurines. I didn't feel obligated to refuse the gifts and launch into a patronizing explanation about the beliefs of Jehovah's Witnesses, but I still surged with reflexive panic at accepting false idols. I smiled back at Maria, who clearly had no idea of the spiritual quandary she had instigated, and she crossed herself with a pudgy hand and smiled. Then she let her grey and white cat, Damascus, back inside, and a streetcar rattled up the road. I looked down at my new talismans: Jesus' left foot was chipped.

I started university with thousands of others, bought my books, and unpacked. I majored in English Literature because I couldn't think of anything else I really enjoyed. There were just so many options, it was overwhelming. Sometimes I even missed the facade of simplicity that my upbringing had offered — with so much being forbidden and off-limits to me, choices were few, and therefore simple, and without agony. Maybe someday I could open a bookstore or become a librarian. Growing up under the constant threat of Armageddon, I had never much considered adulthood or career options, and was in no hurry to do so now. My classes weren't that much more difficult than those in my final year of high school, just slightly more interesting.

The only part of first-year university I didn't excel at was social life. I avoided the ridiculous-looking Frosh Week activities, which was easy since I didn't live on campus, and I didn't say much to my classmates. In a city, anonymity was easy. I didn't want people to know who I was, where I came from, how I grew up, or anything about me. I didn't want friends. Just like I did as a kid, I craved invisibility.

Sometimes I stayed home in my pyjamas and watched television all day. It mostly blared the news. Bombings in the Middle East. Starvation in east Africa. Rock stars shooting themselves. Missing children who turned up bloated in rivers. So many different forms of death. I would mute the volume, and it was even more ominous without the narration. All this destruction reminded me of images from issues of *Awake!* and *The Watchtower.* Calamitous portents. At overtired, anxious times like these, scriptures would lodge themselves in my head and drone over and over. Better to just get them out of my system, I thought, and so I chanted verses I'd memorized years ago.

Nation will rise against nation, and kingdom against kingdom; and there will be great earthquakes, and in one place after another pestilences and food shortages; and there will be fearful sights and from heaven great signs.

I even remembered that the quotation was from Luke chapter twenty-one, verses ten and eleven.

It was time to get a job and distract myself. There were lots of telemarketing and restaurant positions available, according to the newspaper I got on the corner. I had experience in neither and that didn't impress any of the managers I called. I started to lie to the bars, telling them that I had bussed tables in a diner back home. It could have been true, I told myself, trying to justify it. I had a lot of these silent arguments, convincing myself that they were not actually lies if they could have perhaps been true.

Finally, after hours of enquiries, a pub near the university was interested, particularly after I told them I was a student there.

— Can you come by for an interview tonight? At seven, before it gets busy? Ask for Kameela.

— Sure. Of course. Thanks a lot.

For the next couple of hours, I practised carrying drinks. I filled the two glasses and two mugs I owned with water, put them on a plate and carried them around my apartment. It was harder than it looked and my wrist began to ache. I sloshed water onto the plate and then the floor a few times, and mopped it up. I would have to practise a lot more before doing this for real. I went into the bathroom and smiled into the mirror.

— What'll it be? My attempt at a friendly drawl sounded like I had a speech impediment. My grin looked cartoonish, like someone had pasted it onto my face.

— What can I get you? I cocked my head and tried to look inquisitive.

I wasn't very outgoing, but I wanted the job, and I knew you had to be friendly to get tips. I couldn't be quiet and nervous like I was in class or I wouldn't have the job for very long. I needed something to help me gain — or at least fake — confidence.

I took a deep breath, closed my eyes, then exhaled and opened them. There was an unopened box under my bed. It was one of the boxes Uncle Tyler had sent me from back home, where it had been sealed for years. My hands began to shake. For the next half-hour, I pulled the box out from under the bed, then slid it back. The thought of opening it felt wrong, like stealing. I paced, unsure if I could bring myself to do it.

Don't be such a coward. Just open it.

Are you sure? You don't mind?

I gritted my teeth and got a steak knife from the kitchen and slit the seams and pulled open the box. It was full of familiar items and their smells — cheap vanilla perfume, musty t-shirts — made my face flush and palms sweat. I rummaged until I found something that would work.

The label said *Blood Red.*

I pulled off the lid and carefully applied two coats to my lips.

— What's your poison? I winked at the imaginary table of frat boys. Better. I practised a few more times, in borrowed Blood Red boldness, until I felt like I could do it.

I had rarely dealt with drunk people before. I didn't know if there would be fights, spills, or worse — vomit. The very thought of that nearly panicked me into calling back to cancel my interview. But the alternative — hours of phoning strangers and trying to sell them things they didn't want or need — had even less appeal. I just hoped I'd be lucky and no one would ever throw up during my shifts.

I chose a plain black skirt and a white blouse to wear to meet Kameela. What I used to call my Hall clothes would now be for job interviews.

16

▼

THURSDAY IS ANOTHER LIBRARY shift, and Mr. MacKay
says he doesn't need her, that she should go outside and
get some fresh air instead, but Emily doesn't know what
to do with herself during recess. In a section of the playground near the doors by their classroom, some girls
are making snow angels. They study and compare each
attempt to see whose is the neatest, most perfect angel.
Any with smudged edges or different-sized wings are dis-
qualified. Agnes the Pentecostal is winning. They would
let Emily play if she wanted to, but she's not allowed to
make snow angels. She tries to remember why, to practise
explaining it in her head to a worldly person, but she forgets the exact reason. It has something to do with idolatry.
Or maybe Christmas.

A snowball fight ricochets across the soccer field, as warring boys hurl clumps of ice and snow at each other, fistfuls that probably contain stones, twigs, dog pee, or worse, and anyone near the field is a potential target. Emily stays by the doors, huddled in the alcove, trying to turn the pages of her Trixie Belden mystery without removing her gloves.

— Hey!

Emily does not look up. Boys rarely direct their shouts at her.

— Hey you! Josh Hansen lumbers toward her. He's a year older than her and several inches taller. Last year he was suspended twice for fighting, and each time he gave the other kid a bloody nose. Emily tries to hide the book, sick of being made fun of for reading at recess. It fits halfway into her pocket, and her arm, if she holds it still, covers the rest.

— What?

— You Emily Morrow? His shadow blocks the sun's glare and he rests his bare hands on his hips.

— Yes.

— Is Lenora your sister?

— Yeah, why?

— Because.

Josh squints at her, and takes a step closer, demanding, expectant. Emily stumbles back, butting against the door. He smirks.

— When did your sister decide to go punk?

— Punk? What do you mean?

— My brother says she's the hottest punk in school. Josh laughs.

— Are you going punk too?

— No! And Lenora isn't either!

Emily knows her sister, she does. But she dyed her hair and doesn't wear it normal and long anymore, and she came home late the night before, way after dinner, and refused to say where she'd been. *Out* was all she told her parents, and she didn't even respond when they yelled at her for half an hour, finally grounding her for a month. It's like having two sisters, and wondering where the other one went.

— You know who my brother is?

— No. And I don't care either. Emily's heart beats fast; she breathes hard to keep up with it, and wonders why the bell hasn't rang yet.

— He's the biggest skinhead in town.

Emily doesn't know what a skinhead is, and doesn't want to.

— So?

— So? Josh mimics her and steps even closer. Theo said he tested her, to see if she's a real punk or just a stupid poser, like you.

He glares at her, like he's waiting for an apology, or an explanation.

— And he said she is. Your sister's a real punk. She passed the test.

The bell rings and the alcove swarms with kids shouting and shoving and teeming to get inside.

— I bet they're gonna do it too. They've been going out long enough. Theo doesn't screw posers, he told me. So there! Josh pushes her against another kid, cuts in front of the line, and goes inside.

— Sorry. Emily stumbles and her book falls from her pocket and lands in the snow.

THAT NIGHT EMILY WAITS UNTIL she's alone with Lenora to ask her about what Josh said. After dinner, she knocks on her sister's door.

— What is it? I'm busy.

— It's only me. Emily tries the door; it's locked.

— Let me in. It's important!

Lenora sighs loudly, unhooks the latch, and opens the door. She flops on her unmade bed and flips through a glossy magazine.

— So what do you want?

— I have a question.

— Yeah, so? Can't you ask Mom, instead of always interrupting me?

— No.

— Fine. What do you want to know?

Emily pauses, making sure she gets the word right.

— What's a skinhead?

— An asshole. Why? Lenora opens a bottle of royal blue nail polish.

— I'm telling! You swore!

— No you're not. You're not telling anyone, or I'll tell that you were reading a worldly book out in service last time, while Dad was at a door and you were in the car.

Emily doesn't know what to say. She was very careful to put the book back in her bag when her father left the house and walked down the driveway toward the car again. She didn't think Lenora, dozing off in the front seat, had noticed.

— Yeah, that's right, I saw you. You think you're all smart hiding your stupid mystery books, but I saw you.

Emily doesn't say anything.

— Still gonna tell on me?

— No. But what's a skinhead?

— I told you.

— Besides that.

— Okay, okay, I'll tell you. They're like the punks but they all look pretty much the same, with shaved heads, big boots, jeans, and black t-shirts. Most of them are racist jerks, but not all of them.

Emily knows what racist means from the meetings at the Kingdom Hall; Jehovah's Witnesses are not allowed to be racist, because Jehovah God created black people and white people equal. In their congregation, however, there are no black brothers or sisters.

— Now do you understand what a skinhead is, or do I need to draw you a diagram?

— So Theo Hansen is a skinhead? Was he the guy in the car that time? When you guys picked me up? Is he a racist?

Lenora quickly looks up from painting her nails and smears some blue on the knuckle of her thumb.

— What do you know about Theo Hansen?

Emily grins. She finally has Lenora's attention.

— I don't know. His stupid brother Josh goes to my school and was talking about you today.

— About me? What does some little grade school kid have to say about me?

— He said you were going punk.

She pauses, waiting for Lenora to deny it.

— He said that his brother tested you.

Lenora says nothing.

— He said you passed.

— Whatever.

— He said you two are going out.

This part seems the most impossible of all, and she wants, more than anything, for Lenora to deny it.

Lenora begins another coat of nail polish.

— Well, what did he mean? Why did he say you were punk? What was on the test? She drops her voice to a whisper.

— Is he really your boyfriend?

Lenora continues to ignore her.

— Come on, tell me!

Despite a few more minutes of Lenora's silent treatment, Emily doesn't give up. Lenora has finished her nails and blows on them.

— Was it hard?

— Was what hard?

— The test.

— Ems, come on, do I look like a punk rocker to you? Do you even know what that means?

— Yes! No! I mean, I know what it is.

— Fine. I'll tell you. But you have to promise you won't tell anybody. I mean it, and if you do, if I even think you might have told Mom or Dad or anyone, I'll tell them you were reading your worldly books out in service. Got it?

— I promise. Now tell me!

— This is what happened. A few weeks ago at school I wore my white sweater and at lunch I spilled grape juice on it. I didn't have anything else to change into, so Marla, whose locker is next to mine, loaned me an extra t-shirt. It was a Misfits fiend skull shirt, a real one from New York City, not a stupid copy—

— What's a Misfits . . . Emily trails off.

— Never mind. It's a band. It was a band t-shirt, that's why you're not allowed to tell.

— That's it?

— Pretty much.

Jehovah's Witnesses cannot have posters of rock stars

hanging in their rooms or wear t-shirts of bands, because that's idolatry and is a sin. There is but one true God, and though they are allowed to watch television and listen to the radio, they must not worship humans. Emily loves Han Solo, and Chewbacca too, and has a tiny picture of them, torn from the newspaper, hidden under her mattress.

— But what was on the test?

— You're such a geek. It's always about books and tests with you. Okay, I'll tell you, but then you have to get out of my room and go away, get it?

— Okay, if you tell me. Emily wonders how hard the test was, and if she would be able to pass.

— I was walking down the hallway on my way to French class, by myself, and Theo started walking next to me, real close, like he knew me or something.

— The skinhead?

— Yes, the skinhead, the biggest skinhead in school, even the teachers are scared of him. But he's not a racist. Anyway, he said to me, 'Smash the heads of little girls and hang 'em on my wall,' like he was trying to freak me out, pretend he's a serial killer or something.

— Is he demonized?

Lenora laughs really loud.

— I won't let a guy like him intimidate me, so I looked him right in his big green eyes and I said, "Skulls," from the first album, *Walk Among Us*. Any more questions?' And then he smiled. I'd never seen a skinhead smile before, honestly, and he kept walking with me, all impressed that I got it. He was still grinning like an idiot until I said, 'Actually, it's "Hack the heads off little girls," not "smash."' That got him, so he called me a bitch and stomped away.

Emily stares at Lenora. She doesn't understand. Maybe she's just trying to scare her. She narrows her eyes and looks, really looks, at her sister. Platinum hair, blue finger-nails, crimson lips. Her Hall clothes are the same but even the plain grey dress looks somehow immodest. She squints and Lenora becomes even more unfamiliar and indistinct. What happened to her sister? She wants to yell for her to stop it, to just stop being so weird and different and new, and just go back to normal. She can still see glimpses of her sister sometimes, just enough to know that she's still there, and that makes her even more frustrated, like she's hiding from her on purpose. That's when she decides not to give Lenora the candle holder she made especially for her. She'll give it to her uncle Tyler instead. She climbs off the bed and backs away from her.

Lenora looks up and grins.

— That's how I knew Theo liked me. Now get out of my room.

17

▼

THE NEXT DAY, EMILY DECIDES to play by herself, alone in her room. She doesn't want to be around anyone else.

On the bed in front of her, she lines up her stuffed animals in a row: Toaster, Zig Zag, Raggedy Ann, a pink bear named Rosie, Barbie, and assorted dolls. They are playing At the Meeting.

Emily stands at the foot of the bed, in her father's suit jacket, sleeves unevenly rolled, with his black and silver striped tie knotted awkwardly around her neck, Bible in hand. She is conducting the meeting. She is the elder.

Each member of her congregation has a tiny *Awake!* magazine on its lap. Emily likes the *Awake!* magazines better than *The Watchtower*; the articles are not just about the Bible, but discuss animals or food or other countries, and they're more interesting, though she feels guilty thinking that. It took Emily two hours to make all the miniature booklets. She wrote the titles and drew the pictures by hand, etching black lines where paragraphs would go, and painstakingly writing out the Watchtower Bible and Tract Society address in New York in tiny printing on the back of each copy.

— Attention please, could I have everyone's attention. She uses her deep, serious, elder-like voice. She wishes she had actual chairs for each of them, but making the magazines was hard enough. The real Kingdom Hall is a plain rectangular building, perched on the outskirts of town, surrounded by its parking lot. Inside are rigid lines of red chairs, perfectly aligned and spaced before each meeting. Her blue and white bedroom, with its floral curtains and ruffled bedspread, looks nothing like the Hall. Her math textbook is the stage, and she stands on it, imagining the podium and microphone.

At the real meetings, the podium is only for the brothers' talks, which take place on Thursdays and Sundays, though it is not just the elders who speak. Any brother who is old enough can be assigned a topic on which to give a short speech at the Thursday meeting; they don't even have to be baptized yet. The elders create what Emily assumes must be an elaborate schedule of subjects and names and dates. You get a month's notice when it's your turn, and you never know your topic until then, which must be terrifying.

When a young brother presents his first talk, everyone is excited and pays attention, whispering about his performance, shushing one another, while they all wonder what kind of marks the elders will give him. Some of the elements they score are comprehension of material, enthusiasm, volume, and gestures. With each brother's subsequent attempt, the elders focus on different points, usually the ones on which he'd previously scored "Needs Improvement." Emily's mom says you can always tell when a brother is being marked on "Gestures." He'll extend one hand jerkily toward the congregation at regular intervals, every ten seconds, then immediately clutch the podium again, like a tic. Sometimes it's hard to actually pay attention to what he's saying, because you get lulled into his rhythmic hand movements. The gesture may or may not be relevant to what the brother is saying, and Emily's mom often mumbles her own critiques.

— There go the hand spasms again. Must be Gestures tonight.

There is also a table and chairs set in the corner of the stage, next to a large vase of fake flowers. The table and chairs are for the sisters' talks. They don't stand alone at the podium. The sisters are assigned a partner, and their presentation is in the form of a conversation, or a short skit, like at school. You have a lot more creative license, Emily's mom says, than the brothers do. In their sketches, one person can pretend to be the reluctant worldly person who is won over by the Truth and agrees to a home Bible study at the end, or it can be a discussion between two sisters to clarify a particular point. Lenora has done a couple of talks now — one with Debbie Vincent, who is a few years older than her, finished high school, and now Auxiliary Pioneering, and one with their mom. In that one, her mom pretended to be a worldly person who was going to give permission for her daughter, dying of leukemia, to get a blood transfusion, and Lenora was the Witness who explained why it was wrong and talked her out of it. Their talk was supposed to be set at a hospital, and they wanted Emily and Lenora's father to walk across the stage in a white coat with a stethoscope around his neck, to make it more authentic. He refused, saying that was going too far.

— Don't make a mockery of the Truth.

— You're no fun at all! Lenora slammed her door and their mom just shook her head. They rehearsed every night for two weeks. Even without the doctor's cameo appearance, she scored "Very Good" on all her points.

AHEM. EMILY BEGINS HER talk, looking down upon her small congregation of silent followers.

— Tonight we are going to talk about Armageddon and the Great Tribulation. Please turn to page four and pay close attention.

Outside, her father scrapes the shovel through icy snow and rasps a path from door to car. Good. Her father is outside, her mother is in town getting groceries, and none of them know where Lenora is. She doesn't want any of them eavesdropping on her playing At the Meeting. She might get one of the scriptures wrong and her dad would correct her, or Lenora would make fun of her. It's much better to have the house to herself and be alone. She licks her lips, smoothes her hair, and resumes her sermon.

— Armageddon is when Jehovah God will destroy all the worldly people and only people in the Truth will be saved. It will be very frightening. What are some of the ways He will put an end to this wicked system of things? Emily surveys the row of creatures on her bed.

— Yes, Brother Zig Zag?

— Lightning?

— That's right, Brother Zig Zag, God will use big bolts

of lightning and fire to kill the worldly people. Good for you. What are some of the other ways? Brother Toaster?

— Giant boulders of hail?

— Very good! Definitely there will be monstrous hailstones. Even worse than that, Jehovah will also use earthquakes and diseases that make your eyes burn out and your arms fall off too. Molten lava will rain down from heaven, giant boulders will stone to death the unbelievers, and lightning bolts will split the trees and the buildings. But we must be very brave and strong and even happy when Armageddon and the Great Tribulation come, because afterwards there will be Paradise forever. Do you have a question, Sister Raggedy Ann?

— Um, yes I do. Her voice is a tiny squeak.

— What is the Great Tribulation?

— Ah yes, brothers and sisters, the Great Tribulation will be very, very tough for everyone. It will be a time of extreme hardship and persecution. It's when God will test us by making terrible things happen, so He can find out who has good faith and who is secretly bad. All Jehovah's Witnesses will be tortured in various ways, and some brothers and sisters might even die.

Emily pauses. She isn't sure when the Great Tribulation is supposed to happen, if it's before Armageddon or after. Her gold *My Book of Bible Stories* doesn't mention it, though there is a picture of Jesus leading an army of white horses into the fires of Armageddon on Earth. She thinks it must be before that, while all the worldly people are still alive.

Emily wonders how God will kill Tammy Bales when He destroys the world at Armageddon. Will she be melted alive from the fire and lava? Her face and clothes and arms would dissolve into a gooey heap and she'd be gone, and no Resurrection for her. Or maybe she'll be crushed to death by massive hailstones, all of her bones broken and smashed, splintered, and protruding through her torn, bleeding flesh. Perhaps she'll be struck by lightning, split in half by an angry bolt thrust down from the hand of God. She'd be sliced in two, and everyone would be able to see her liver and bone marrow and dangling veins.

— Some people will get diseases like leprosy and curse God and die. Other people will be tested like Abraham. Who remembers what happened to Abraham? She surveys her obedient congregation.

— Yes, Sister Barbie?

— God made him tie up his son and sacrifice him with a big knife for no reason, and just as Abraham was about to cut his throat open, God said he could stop.

— That's right, Sister Barbie! Good for you. He passed God's test.

Downstairs, a door slams, and she can hear her mother put the groceries away. She wonders if she will call her down to help, so she stops for a minute, but her mom says nothing.

Emily starts when the phone rings. Her mother answers it, then tells someone that Lenora isn't home. Emily exhales and straightens her suit jacket. She is too hot inside it, but the elders never take off their suit jackets during a meeting. Not even in the summer.

Emily rearranges her congregation on the bed, seating Rosie and Zig Zag next to each other. They are married, she decides. She shoves them against each other. Then she straightens Barbie's clothes, and tugs her skirt down.

— That shouldn't be above your knees, Sister Barbie; you'll get in trouble. Emily gives her a dirty look and walks back onto her math textbook to resume the meeting. Her elder-voice booms through her room; she smiles at how authoritative she sounds.

— Attention everyone, attention. The break is over, take your seats please.

She clasps her hands in front of her and rocks on her heels. She gazes down at her charges, all staring straight ahead like they're supposed to. What she has to say next is going to be difficult.

— I have bad news, my little brothers and sisters. It is unfortunate to have to say, but today I must disfellowship a member of our congregation . . . Emily trails off. She doesn't exactly know what she is supposed to say next. She's never heard anyone get disfellowshipped before, and isn't sure how the elder would put it. She takes a deep breath and considers how they talk about the more difficult topics at the Hall.

— We must all be clean and pure before God. When someone sins again and again and doesn't care, they must be removed. They have to get disfellowshipped. That means no one can speak to the person who is cast out, not even your family. It must be as though they are dead. If they repent, they are allowed to get reinstated, but until then, they must sit in the last row at the Hall and not talk to anyone or put their hand up at the meetings.

Emily breathes quickly, as though there is not quite enough air in her room. It is scary to think of someone getting disfellowshipped, but she must go through with it, because someday it could happen to someone in their own congregation and she must be prepared.

— Does everyone understand?

Emily runs over and nods the heads of all her dolls and stuffed animals.

— Good. She steps back onstage.

— Sister Rosie, you are hereby disfellowshipped. It is for adultery. That's God's will.

Emily knows what adultery is; it's when you are married and you have fornication with someone who is not your husband or wife. She pats Zig Zag on his head.

— Don't be sad, Brother Zig Zag. Maybe she'll be repentant and get reinstated before Armageddon. Emily picks up Rosie.

— Begone! She throws her against the other side of her bedroom, and hears a click as one of Rosie's plastic eyes hit the far wall. She slides down onto the pale blue carpet and is still.

— You're bad and must be punished! Emily straightens her tie, stomps over to Rosie, picks her up by her foot, and opens her sock drawer. She shoves Rosie into the back corner next to her tights with holes in them and slams it shut.

From the kitchen, her mother calls her to set the table for dinner.

— Coming! Emily forgets to stop using her elder voice.

— The meeting is over.

After she puts her toys back in their usual places, she tries to undo her dad's tie. She can't get it off; the knot is too tight. Her fingertips burn from trying.

— Hurry up, Emily!

Emily shrugs the jacket off and onto the floor, tucks the rest of the tie under her t-shirt, and goes downstairs, hoping her mom won't notice and be mad at her for taking one of her dad's Hall ties.

— Why are you wearing your father's tie? Emily's mom hands her a stack of plates from the cupboard.

— I was playing.

— Playing what?

Emily shrugs.

— Playing dress-up?

— Yeah.

— Dressing up like a man?

Emily's face goes red. It would sound even weirder to tell her mom that she was pretending to be an elder.

— Who were you dressing up like, Emily?

— I don't know.

But Emily doesn't want to lie; she is afraid of Armageddon and the Great Tribulation, and she has lied enough lately. She decides that would rather tell the truth than risk leprosy or giant hail.

— I was pretending to be an elder. Like at the Hall. Emily doesn't look at her mother as she sets out the cutlery, evenly spacing the spoons and the knives and the forks.

Her mom coughs and when Emily looks at her, she smiles.

— What on earth for? Don't you have any homework to do? Don't you want to play outside or something? We'll be going out in service all afternoon tomorrow — you should have some fun while you can.

Emily shrugs. She was having fun. She likes making little *Watchtower* and *Awake!* magazines for Zig Zag and the others, and she likes to conduct meetings for them.

— Come here and let me untie that before your father sees you.

Her mom grins at her and pulls her toward her, ruffling her hair, for the first time in what feels like forever.

18

▼

TWO GUYS AND A YOUNG woman were hunched over
a table in the corner. At regular intervals, one of them
would look over their shoulder when they thought I
couldn't see them, then say something to the others. They
seemed to take turns looking at me. I didn't want to serve
them but I was the only waitress working that afternoon.
Like most days, I hadn't slept much the night before and
it was hard to focus. Worse, the customers never seemed
to stay in one spot after they ordered their drinks, and so
I had to try to remember who wanted which beers and
then figure out where they were.

I wove through the clusters of students and faculty
members to deliver three pints to the table that was
watching me.

— It's about time.

One of the guys, in a baseball hat and a t-shirt that was a little too tight, shook his head and paid. I gave him his change and he didn't tip. I stood next to the table and said nothing. I looked at him and he looked at me.

— Aren't you even going to apologize? We're dying of thirst over here.

I bit the insides of my cheeks and ignored him, while I cleared an empty glass from their table.

— Hey, didn't you hear me? Are you deaf?

— Easy, Rob. Calm down. The girl looked at me and cringed.

— It's okay. It's no big deal, really. I know it's busy.

— Sure it's a big deal. Beer is always a big deal! The one called Rob laughed, then stared at my hands. My grip tightened on the empty glass. If she were in my place, Lenora wouldn't stand for this. She would look him right in the eye, and smash the glass over his head.

— Oh my God! Are you okay? The blond girl stood up and leaned toward me.

The glass had shattered in my hand. I looked at it, then at her, then back at the shards. My tray was covered in sharp sparkles of glass.

— It must have already been cracked. Are you sure you're all right?

I nodded to them and made sure there was no glass left on their table, then strode across the dirty carpet and cleaned the tray off behind the bar.

— You get all the glass cleaned up over there?

— What?

It was the bartender, Grant. I wished he hadn't noticed.

— The pint glass you just broke. His slow voice was thick with sarcasm.

— Did you clean it up?

— Yeah. The glass was just on my tray. It was cracked. Be careful how you put them through the dishwasher.

— Whatever.

After that, my hands started shaking.

When I delivered their next round, the guys ducked under the table, cowering from my approach. I distributed their drinks with exaggerated care.

— Look out! She's dangerous!

I tried to smile, but I could feel my face contorting into something grotesque. My nostrils flared. I concentrated on collecting their empty glasses, careful not to clench them too hard. And to touch each one at its base, nowhere near where their germ-filled mouths had been.

The girl wasn't laughing at me. In fact, she looked a little embarrassed by her friends. Her head was lowered and she looked up at me from under long blond bangs.

— Don't worry about it, okay? It's totally fine. Not your fault.

— Thanks. She leaned toward me across the damp, sticky table.

— By the way, don't think this is weird or anything, but I think you have terrific posture.

— What?

— Your posture. It's unusually good. I notice things like that.

— Okay. Um, thanks.

— Are you a dancer? A gymnast? Do a lot of yoga?

— None of the above. I turned back toward the bar. Some people were even stranger than me.

Twenty-seven paces back to the waitresses' station where I returned the empty glasses. Kameela, my supervisor, was glaring at me. Her name meant "almost perfect" in Hindi, a fact she never hesitated to point out, to anyone.

— Emily, I thought we discussed this. What are you doing?

She had her hands on her hips, leaning against the bar. As far as I knew, I hadn't screwed up any other drink orders.

— Nothing. Working. What?

— The gloves. I said no. They look ridiculous. Take them off.

— You did? When?

— Yesterday, Emily. It was during your shift yesterday, remember? Don't try to pretend you forget. I'm not stupid.

— No. I faltered, unsure what I was saying no to.

— Now. You look like a freak. You're embarrassing the pub.

— But—

— I don't need another monologue featuring bacteria and viruses and tiny centipedes crawling through your skin. Are you stoned or something? Just serve the beer and count your tips. It's not that hard.

I told her that if I got sick it would be the pub's fault, but she didn't care. Kameela didn't take me seriously. It's a mistake not to worry about things you can't see. Every shift, I could feel microscopic insects crawl around in my stomach, laying eggs, excreting toxins, and I just couldn't bear it; I'd sneak off to the bathroom, gagging, and wash my hands again. One night, I had washed my hands twenty-seven times during my shift.

I peeled off my left glove and stuffed it into my pocket. I fingered the soft bracelet I always wore on my left wrist. Somehow, it made me feel better.

— Oh my God! What's wrong with your hand?

I still didn't answer. I put the other latex glove in my pocket too.

— Do you have leprosy or something? Grant laughed at Kameela's question.

— I told you she was a freak.

I tried to roll my eyes at them, cool and aloof, but my eyes narrowed and I was furious. My hands didn't look that bad. It was just dry skin. Pink in places. A bit raw from all the washing.

— You know what, Emily? Kameela used her high, fake-nice voice that I only ever heard her use with me.

— It's really not that busy. Why don't you take the rest of today off? Hopefully whatever happened to your hands will be healed up by your next shift.

I put my gloves back on and settled up with my tables. The table in the corner didn't order another round. The blond who liked my posture gave me her card.

— Seriously, you should come by and check it out. I think you'd be ideal. First lesson's free. She waved over her shoulder as they swayed between tables and out the door.

I WOKE UP ANGRY. AN AMORPHOUS rage zipped through my entire body. It darted up my arms then down my legs, careened through my stomach, inflated my chest, then curled my hands into fists. I squirmed between my sheets, kicked away my blankets, and dug my fingernails into my palms. The clock radio said 5:14 a.m. I lay on my back panting, seething at the ceiling, tingling and electrified. I couldn't get back to sleep.

It wasn't the first time that this singeing fury had

jolted me awake. It happened more and more often, and not because of dreams or nightmares, but more that feelings I'd denied or suppressed for so many years were now determined to seep out. After so long, it was unavoidable. They'd shoot out my pores or fingertips like tiny lightning bolts. I felt unpredictable, out of control, as though if I left my apartment I might start screaming at someone shovelling their walkway or buying a newspaper, or I might suddenly hit the mailman as hard as I could. I was constantly on edge, always too aware of my own emotions. I had to talk myself into going outside, and hope I wouldn't lose control if I left the apartment.

I was paranoid again, like I had been back home, as though someone was scrutinizing and judging me. Although I was alone, it reminded me of being at the Kingdom Hall. While the elders preached peace and empathy from the podium, everyone sat and speculated as to who would be the next to be disfellowshipped. Glances darted from behind folded *Watchtowers*, and every nudge implied knowledge of someone's wrongdoing. A cupped hand at an elder's ear was a conspiracy. Rumours and traitors were rampant. The whispers were ceaseless. There was always bloodlust.

Were you next?

Yes.

Were you scared?

There was a long pause and I thought she'd gone away.

I need you to do me a favour.

I didn't respond. I didn't even want to know what the favour was. I shook my head and got out of bed. I paced from one end of the apartment to the other. I opened windows. I closed them. I scratched at my forearms. Saying no could push her away and I didn't want that, but I was afraid of what she might ask me to do. I was afraid of not being able to do it.

I don't know. What is it?

Find him.

Find who?

You know who. He's here. Find him.

Then she was gone. I tore the sweaty sheets from my bed, balled them up, and tossed them into my laundry basket. Night was fading to a lighter purple, and the sun would soon make this less real.

What was I supposed to say to him? Was I supposed to make myself known, or just figure out where he was, then wait for her to tell me what to do? Did she want me to get revenge? If so, how?

I paced for a while, then shrugged. At that point, I had nothing much to lose. Starting at the beginning seemed to make the most sense.

I called Information and got the numbers for the Hansens back home. There were three. I tried not to remember the last time I'd called Theo's house, so many years before, the night that felt like a giant boulder had slid across the sky and covered the sun forever.

The first one rang and rang and no one picked up the phone. As I dialled the second number, I tried not to think about what I was doing lest I panic and hang up. On the tenth ring, a groggy voice answered and I told her I was trying to reach Theo Hansen. My hands were hot and damp and my voice quavered.

— Who's calling?

I coughed to gain some time.

— Pardon me?

— Who is this? And why are you calling at the crack of dawn?

— I'm an old high school friend of Theo's. I'm . . . uh . . . I'm organizing a reunion, and I wanted to invite Theo, but I've lost touch with him.

— Pretty weird time to call about a party. What did you say your name was? She sounded more alert now.

— Mary. I cringed. It even sounded like a fake name.

— Well, Mary, sorry to disappoint you, but I don't have his current number. Last I heard, he was working in some record store in the city, but he doesn't call home anymore.

Here. He was here.

— Hello? You still there?

— Sorry. I tried not to choke.

— I'm still here. Thanks. And sorry for calling so early. I work weird hours.

— Yeah. If you find him, tell him it's okay to phone his old mother once in a while.

Mrs. Hansen hung up and I lay back down on the cool, bare mattress, the currents of anger replaced with the hot buzz of adrenaline. Whatever she wanted me to do with him, I would do it. I would stalk the streets of the city until I found him.

19

▼

— YOU HAVE TO HOLD STILL. Lenora yanks a strand of Emily's brown hair for emphasis.

— I am! Just quit pulling so hard!

— Do you want me to finish this, or do you want to go to the meeting with only one braid done?

— Okay. Emily pouts, her eyebrows furrowed and face scrunched up, insistent.

— I'll stop squirming. Emily doesn't know anyone else who knows how to do French braids, not even their mother. All the most stylish and best-looking kids at school and at the district assemblies have French braids, and Emily has wanted them all year, and Lenora has finally agreed to do them for the Thursday night meeting. She just didn't know that it would take this long or be this painful.

— Good, because I have to start over. The first one's no good.

Emily howls and stands up, shakes her arms and legs, then sits back down in front of Lenora.

— So has a worldly guy ever called you on the phone?

Emily watches Lenora grin in the mirror and pull up her black bra strap.

— Maybe, maybe not.

— I won't tell anyone! I bet they have. What boys?

— Shut up! Don't be so loud.

— Sorry. I won't say anything, I promise.

— I don't know if you can keep a secret.

— I can!

— Swear? To God, even?

— Lenora! You can't say that!

— Fine. Promise forever or else?

— I promise. Forever. Or else.

Still holding Emily's half-braided hair, Lenora leans in toward her ear. Her breath tickles the hairs on Emily's earlobe and she gets goosebumps.

— Yes. Worldly guys have called me.

— Really? Who?

Lenora laughs.

— I'm not telling you that! One guy in particular, at the moment.

— Does he like you? Lenora shrugs, then smiles again.

— Probably.

— Is it Theo? What are you going to do? Does he know you can't go out with him?

Lenora laughs again but this time it's a stabbing, mean laugh.

— Whatever.

She parts Emily's hair with a sharp comb, and divides it into sections using the pointed end.

— Ow! You don't have to stab me in the skull!

— I do if you want this to look good. Or would you rather look like Carli and Sally?

Emily is both repulsed and fascinated by the twins next door. A chain link fence separates their backyard from Emily's, and the two yards could be different planets. The Morrows' yard is mowed and tidy, with a swing set and a garden shed. In the twins' yard, an old refrigerator with no door leans against a tree, with thick weeds surrounding it, while rusted bicycles — or parts of bicycles — lie in wait to trip and scrape the careless. There are mounds of garbage bags that no one takes to the curb, and rusted barrels that Emily is afraid to look into, as well as two broken slides, deflated pool toys, and lawnmowers that no longer function, or so she assumes, since the weeds and grass are well past Emily's knees. Occasionally Carli and Sally invite Emily over to their side of the fence for a game of hide and seek, and she usually goes, given the abundance of hiding places, but only if her mom isn't looking, and not without fear.

— Okay, I think I've got this now. Lenora tugs another chunk of Emily's hair into the braid. Emily cringes but stays quiet, feeling bad about Carli and Sally, and confused about Lenora and worldly boys, but getting used to the yanks and pokes and the throbbing of her scalp.

Lenora stops working on Emily's hair and paces around her red and black room flexing her fingers and cracking her knuckles.

— You owe me for this. It's painful work, you know.

— It hurts me too. But it'll look really good, right? Emily stretches halfway out of the chair, trying to see her hair in Lenora's full-length mirror on the back of her door.

— Sure. Just hold still.

— If you can do it without pulling so much, I'll stay out of your chair. From now on.

— You better stay out of my chair. Or I'll never do your hair again.

— I promise!

— For real?

— Yes!

EVER SINCE EMILY WAS A toddler Lenora had her own chair, a big brown vinyl recliner in the living room, which she'd claimed as her own. Their parents thought it was strange and inappropriate that a child could command her own chair, the way fathers or grandfathers do, but Lenora always got her way if she howled loud enough. She would sit in that recliner, legs outstretched, reading her Bible study books for hours. Their father reasoned that if claiming the chair would get Lenora to read *Watchtower* publications regularly, then so be it. She would also do her homework there, watch television, and, eventually, gossip on the phone. Only recently has the teenage Lenora spent more time locked in her bedroom than sprawled in the recliner.

— Want to see something?

— What?

Lenora pulls at the collar of her shirt, stretching it to expose a purple blotch on her collar bone.

— I have a hickey.

She leans back on her hands, smug. She winks at Emily, who wrinkles her nose and turns away.

Emily doesn't exactly know what a hickey is, though she knows it is something you get on your skin, like a birthmark, but it's from immorality. Their next-door neighbours, the Pattons, have hickeys.

— See this? Carli had once asked, pushing up her left sleeve. Emily had tried not to look at the birthmark on her arm, on the inside of her elbow. It looked like a fist-sized lump of raw hamburger. Emily didn't know how she got that, if she was born with it or if it grew after a long sleep filled with nightmares. She was afraid to ask; the answer might be horrible, that a dog had chewed her arm up, or a machine, or she might tell her it was a disease, a contagious one. The birthmark, however, was not what Carli was telling her to look at.

— See what?

— This. Carli pointed to a bruise on her shoulder.

— It's a hickey. Cool, huh? Derek gave it to me. She pulled her sleeve back down.

— Want one?

Derek was the oldest Patton brother, and still lived at home. His hair was long and stringy and he had tattoos all over his arms and even his neck, and he sat for hours on the front porch, smoking and swearing at the dogs, heavy metal screeching from his tape player. Her mom said that Emily should stay away from him — don't stop and talk if he asks a question, just keep walking.

— No thanks.

Emily cringes. She feels weird, guilty, as though she's done something wrong.

Lenora pauses and sighs. She just stands there smiling, not even doing her hair anymore.

— Let me see the back.

Lenora angles another mirror in front of Emily so that she can see the back of her head in the mirror on the door. She reaches up, amazed at the shininess and intricacy and perfection of her very first set of French braids.

— Don't touch! You'll wreck it. Hold on. Lenora gets a bottle of hairspray from her dresser and sprays it all over Emily's head.

— Yuck. Emily coughs.

— Stop! The aerosol is thick and sticky, and smells like bug spray. She spits some into a tissue.

— Okay, you're done. Go away.

Emily stands in front of the mirror and turns from side to side, admiring her hair. She looks at Lenora.

— I don't think you should be getting hickeys. You're going to get in trouble.

— Whatever.

— It's immoral.

— I don't care what you think. You don't even know what 'immoral' means.

— Yes, I do.

— So what does it mean?

Emily doesn't answer. She knows it's wrong, *sins of the flesh, fornication*, she's heard it all at the meetings before, but she can't explain exactly what it means. She decides she will look up "fornication" in the big dictionary during her next library shift.

— See? You don't know.

Lenora doesn't look at her as she studiously applies blue eyeliner beneath her green eyes.

— I mean it. You're going to get in trouble.

— Oh yeah? For what?

— Saying stuff like that.

— No, I'm not. Because you promised to Jehovah that you wouldn't tell. And you aren't going to break a promise to God, are you? And risk being destroyed at Armageddon? I don't think so. Now go away.

Confused, Emily goes to her bedroom. Lenora has been baptized for two years now, and until now, has never talked about immoral stuff. It could be a trick, something to get Emily in trouble. She decides not to tell, in case that's exactly what Lenora wants, but she's still angry and frustrated.

She gets dressed and is ready for the meeting early. After twisting around in front of the mirror to admire her hair a while longer, Emily decides to get back at Lenora for the story.

She sits in Lenora's recliner for ten minutes before anyone notices. Her mom, sipping from her usual lidded coffee cup, shakes her head.

— You're asking for it. Lenora's not going to be happy, and I don't have time to break up fights. I have to finish getting ready for the Hall. We're leaving soon.

Emily doesn't care, there's nothing Lenora can do. She sits with her arms folded in front of her chest and her legs straight out, barely reaching the footrest.

With a rush of air, Lenora flounces into the living room.

— What do you think you're doing?

She taps her blue painted nails on the armrest. Emily says nothing, just hums to herself, and looks straight ahead like no one is there.

— Get out of my chair.

— No. It's my chair too. It's everybody's chair.

— No, it's not; it's mine. Now get up. Lenora leans into Emily's face. Emily can feel the wet air from her mouth.

— Now! Lenora's face reddens and her eyes narrow.

— Gross. Emily turns her head away.

— Say it, don't spray it.

Lenora clears her throat.

— This is your last chance. She counts to three.

As Emily sits rigid and stares at the window across the room, a warm gob of slime hits her cheek and slides toward her chin. She wipes it on her sleeve and looks at Lenora.

— Pig. She doesn't get up.

Lenora stomps out of the living room, and the bathroom door slams shut. Emily squirms and grins in the chair, trying not to laugh out loud. Victorious, she folds her arms behind her head and closes her eyes. While Lenora sulks in the bathroom, Emily pretends she is at the beach, lying on a towel under the warm sun, the waves quiet behind her.

As she stretches, languid, taking up as much space as possible, there is a sudden tug, hard, on the side of her head. Lenora pulls her right braid.

— This is your last chance, for real this time. Get out of my chair!

Emily doesn't budge. There is a flash of silver near the corner of her eye, and something cold against her ear. Then the swish and clang of steel jaws, the unmistakable snap of the scissors.

Emily laughs.

— I'm not scared of you. She pushes her chin out further.

— This is my chair too.

— You asked for it. Lenora yanks her hair again.

Emily hears one quick snip, and something lands in her lap. She looks down and there, lying motionless across her knees, is her limp, amputated braid.

20

▼

IT HAD GOTTEN COLD, JUST after the first snowfall of the season. My breath wisped like I was smoking and I tried to ignore it, tried not to see the swirling shapes and faces. That happens when sleep abandons you. You see things, glimmers and flickers, elusive forms darting in and out of your periphery, but you can't quite focus on them before they scurry, unseen, into corners. Memory becomes pliable and elastic, and you stop believing that time moves from point A to point B. Beginnings and endings are less significant. By that frozen day, things had begun to overlap, to occur out of sequence, and I struggled to fit them all back together again, to scrabble at the pieces I had collected and hoarded. I tried to shove them back together in the right order, but by then I couldn't remember their chronology anymore.

I could see her face when I exhaled, so I put on a scarf, but that made my face wet and even colder. The corner of my left eye twitched for an impossibly long time, strange and disconcerting. A tiny heart beating way too fast, about to explode. A microscopic bird, trapped and panicked, beneath my eyelashes. I leaned against a mailbox and closed my eyes until the pulsing stilled. I counted eleven deep breaths.

— Are you okay? A woman pushing a stroller stopped, reached her arm toward me. I pulled away.

— I'm fine. I resumed walking and winced. I called back over my shoulder.

— Thanks.

Though they were too small for me, I wore her eight-hole Doc Martens. They were tight when I put them on that morning, but I had convinced myself that they would stretch as I walked. I wanted them to fit, I wanted them to be mine. They'd been in one of the boxes I stashed under my bed, along with various t-shirts and skirts, countless mixed tapes, old photos, and dried-up makeup. My dusty shrine of decade-old fragments.

The two-page list of record stores was in my pocket. I fixed my gaze beyond my breath and watched the street signs and building numbers. The first shop, Sound Effects, was easy to find. Electronic music blasted through a rush of warm air as I pushed open the door. The girl behind the counter peered briefly at me from beneath her blue bangs, said nothing, and went back to the magazine she was reading. The rest of her hair was a yellow tangle piled on top of her head and she wore what looked like a dog collar around her neck. The store sold gleaming keyboards on small platforms, shelves of microphones, various cords, and expensive devices with a lot of knobs on them. I wandered down one aisle and back up the other. There were a few bins of CDs and tapes and records, but I recognized none of the bands. The repetitive song that had been playing slowed, then stopped. No one else was in the store. My arm itched and I rubbed it through my coat.

— Looking for anything in particular?

The girl stared at me like I'd been shoving tapes down my pants or something, her one eyebrow slightly raised, expectant.

— No, not really.

The music resumed with a deep thumping. My eye started to twitch again and I tried to ignore it. I hoped she wouldn't notice and think I had some weird, contagious infection. I walked up to the counter with what I hoped resembled confidence.

— Um, I was just wondering, is Theo working today?

— Who?

— Theo. When's he in again?

— Nobody named Theo works here. You mean Tommy? Lots of girls come in looking for Tommy . . .

— No. I guess I have the wrong store.

She smirked.

— You sure?

— Yeah. I'm sure.

— Whatever. Good luck.

What had I expected? That he'd be there, in the first store on my list? I shook my head and went back out into the cold and kept walking. On to the next. It got easier to ask after the first few times, but I didn't know what I would say to Theo if I found him.

What am I supposed to say to him?

Pick up where I left off.

What does that mean? Can't I just say 'give me back my sister'?

For the next few hours, the blisters on my heels throbbed and swelled, and finally broke raw and bled through my socks.

I didn't know what she meant. What was I supposed to do with him? I thought she wanted revenge. I thought she wanted me to cut his brake cables, or get him fired from his job, or make his life hell in some way. But pick up where she left off? What did that mean? Be his girlfriend? Is that what she meant? Was it a trap?

I started to take my frustration out on the bitter record store employees, like a guy in tight black jeans and a ring through his eyebrow.

— Are you sure no one by that name works here?

— Yeah, I'm sure. I'm the assistant manager, okay?

I stomped out, sighing loudly, as though personally affronted. I heard him laugh as I left. I turned around and swung open the door.

— Go to hell!

I continued, refusing to let frustration slow my progress. My list was arranged in what I thought was a reasonable route through the city. The next stores were in a west end neighbourhood, farther from downtown, less commercial, and hopefully full of the kind of places where Theo would work. I wanted to reach a few of them before they closed.

I walked for another hour, crossing railroad tracks and passing abandoned buildings, until I was in a different area entirely. Pedestrians were fewer and there were more industrial and automotive businesses than retailers. My rage had waned and my pace slowed. The inside of my left forearm was still sore. At the next red light I pushed up my sleeve to find out why it stung so much. What I saw made my stomach churn.

A mess of jagged scratches, sticky and raw where the scabs had torn off and stuck to the sleeve of my sweater. A network of lines, deliberate intersections, scrawled desperately — a message.

One series of marks looked like numbers, and I twisted my forearm around and squinted. 53235. I didn't remember etching these digits, nor did I know what they meant. Or what she was trying to tell me. A palindrome. The origins of the word *palindrome* were Greek: *running back again.* Beginnings and endings that were the same, and could be repeated, over and over, to infinity. I shivered.

I stopped looking at the addresses and walked as fast as I could. I just wanted to stop thinking, to be conscious only of my body. I ran, and my lungs ached with searing cold and my feet burned with blisters. I didn't even realize I was crying until I stopped moving and rested with my hands on my knees and my head between my legs. I stayed that way until I could breathe normally again.

I wiped my face with my scarf and a taxi driver slowed down and honked his horn.

— Fuck you! I screamed.

He kept going. That may have been the first time I'd ever said that, to anyone, ever. I started to laugh, almost silently at first, then out loud — not that my swearing was funny, but the sheer release was mania, it was adrenaline, it was addictive. I had to say it again and again, and the words became contagious, infecting each other and multiplying, and even if I had tried, I couldn't have stopped them.

— Fuck you! I howled over and over into the desolate

street. My scarf was undone and my hair whipped across my face. I must have looked like a crazy person, screaming obscenities and laughing my head off, but I didn't care. It was liberation. It didn't matter what anyone thought of me. There were no Ministerial Servants to decide if I was accepted or not, no elders to admonish me, not even any family to punish me anymore.

I walked on, deeper into the unfamiliar neighbourhood.

The wind was icy and the city was huge. It was just before dusk, when the light is exhilarating, when it gleams gold and silver against tall buildings and bounces off windows and cars like an excited, living thing. The walls and storefronts glimmered as though underwater, the sun glazing them from afar. It was my favourite time of day. It was the only time when I could be invisible again, when I could stop thinking and just look.

I pulled off my glove and pressed the bracelet against my cheek.

I was falling backward into her.

Ten years of obliterating memory, of nothing but school and homework and Bible study and planning my way out. Shock is a great eclipser, and can last years.

But as soon as I left home, I remembered everything — a flood, a typhoon, a volcano — Lenora the natural disaster.

By then I was on the second page of my list, and no Theos worked in any of the stores. I was lost, and couldn't find the next one on my list. Where I expected The Record Keeper, there was a gas station. The light began to fade into grey, and my determination soon followed. I didn't know where I was but I didn't want to go home. I was a failure. All day I'd tried so hard, and with what result? My blisters oozed, I was lost, on the verge of frostbite, and I hadn't found him. I slumped against the wall in the doorway of what looked like an old warehouse. Everything started to hurt at once: my clawed up arm, my aching feet, my empty stomach.

Suddenly the door behind me swung open and gouged my back. I yelped.

— Oh my God, I'm sorry! Are you okay?

A tall woman with her hair in a bun stood over me. I nodded.

— Are you sure? She adjusted the gym bag on her shoulder.

— Yeah, I'm fine.

She got into a white car parked on the side of the street and drove away. I stood on the sidewalk, rattled back into reality, and looked at the sign over the doorway I'd been whimpering in.

I grabbed the post next to me. It had become harder and harder to distinguish what I'd dreamed from what I'd imagined, and what had happened from what was happening. I unzipped my coat, threw my glove on the ground, and pulled a rumpled business card from my pocket.

Academy of Circus Arts.

I breathed in, and I knew what I had to do, whether I found Theo or not.

I pulled open the door that had just scraped my back.

A wall of bright light and heat and echoes stopped me, and I stood still. There were trampolines, trapeze rigs, acrobats, dancers — noise and movement everywhere. I pulled off my coat and let it drop. High above me, suspended between poles and ladders, was a thick cable. A thin man stood poised in the centre of it, as though suspended, majestic, in mid-air. A funambulist.

I pushed up my sleeves, put my hands on my hips,

and smiled, until someone tapped me on the shoulder. I blinked and tried to focus on the blond woman next to me. It was the young woman who'd complimented my posture at the pub.

She stared at me, then frowned.

— Your arm is bleeding.

21
▼

TYLER, WHAT ARE YOU trying to prove? Don't you know that people are saying all sorts of things about you? Emily's mom is hissing questions through her teeth as though she doesn't want to ask but they slither out anyway.

Uncle Tyler shrugs. He's going to the Tuesday night meeting at the Kingdom Hall with Emily and Lenora and their parents. It was their father's idea that he have dinner with them — roast beef — even though he doesn't seem to like Uncle Tyler very much. Hardly any of them spoke during the meal, and as soon as they were finished eating, Lenora dashed up to her room and their dad retreated to the den. Emily and her mom and Uncle Tyler sat for a while longer. Weeks have passed since their last argument about his hair, and he still hasn't gotten it cut.

— Look, it's just hair; it's not such a big deal.

Her mom shakes her head.

— It's a big deal to the elders. It's not just about your hair, either—

— It's hardly even long, give me a break. It's barely past my collar.

Any hair that goes beyond the collar of a brother's Hall shirt is considered long, and therefore worldly.

Emily opens her math book and pretends to do her homework, which is already done. She runs her fingers through her chin-length bob. Both of her braids, sadly reunited, are hidden in a shoebox under her bed. Lenora said that it looked better like this anyway, but only because it was her fault she had to get it all cut off in the first place.

— Look, the elders have said a few things, unofficially, to Jim — and they wanted him to counsel you. I asked him to let me do it, but if you're not going to listen to me, it's going to get blown way out of proportion. They think that if you're letting your appearance become worldly, then you must be behaving that way too, blah blah blah, so they're going to start watching you more closely. If they haven't already.

— What's that supposed to mean?

Emily looks at her uncle, then at her mom, then back at her uncle.

— Emily, it's time for you to go upstairs and get ready for the meeting. You can wear whichever dress you want.

Emily doesn't respond, and keeps her head hovered over her textbook.

— Tyler, I don't know what it means. You know how the elders' wives are, always watching what everyone else does and then telling their husbands. Things can get out of control really quickly. If there's anything you're doing that you shouldn't, if you're associating with worldly friends too much, stop now before they find out.

Emily wants to tell her mom about Michael and Jeff, that Uncle Tyler met them out in service, that they're interested in learning the Truth and will probably start attending the meetings soon, and that they won't be worldly for long. She doesn't, not yet, and she bites the insides of her cheeks, and slowly packs up her homework, waiting for her uncle to tell her mom about them himself.

— You're overreacting.

— I wish I was. You know how rumours fly around the Hall. Once they start, there's no stopping them, and before you know it you're being publicly reproved or hauled in front of a Judicial Committee.

Uncle Tyler shifts in his chair. Emily clears her throat.

— Tell them about those guys that you're almost studying with. Tell the elders about them, and then they can't be mad, right?

— What? Who is she talking about?

— No one. Forget it.

— But why? They seemed interested. They took the magazines and talked to you all afternoon.

— Yeah, well, they're not interested, okay? And Viv, relax about my hair. It's just stupid gossip.

— I know. But stupid gossip is dangerous. Just cut your hair to appease them. Trust me, it'll make life easier.

— Fine. I'll do it this weekend.

— Fine.

They get up and start the dishes and Emily goes upstairs to change into her Hall outfit. She's disappointed her uncle didn't mention his back calls, and she can't understand why people don't help themselves better when they're getting in trouble. He and Lenora just make it worse. It would be so easy for them to just get along and do things right, but they don't. It's like they want to get in trouble.

She stares into her closet. She has no idea what to wear. Emily doesn't care very much about clothes, or hair for that matter, not like Lenora, who plans out her outfits and alters her tops and skirts to fit her better, or to look cooler, by adding extra zippers or rows of black velvet ribbon. *I use clothing to express my individuality*, Lenora explains, but Emily doesn't really understand. Who cares? She doesn't want anyone to look at her anyway.

As usual, her sister's door is closed, but Emily knocks.

— It's me. Can you help me get ready? I don't know what to wear.

Lenora rarely passes up an opportunity to dress her sister, and Emily hopes this time will be no different.

There is no answer to her knock. The water goes on in the bathroom and Emily sighs — one of her sister's epic showers. She goes into Lenora's bedroom anyway and closes the door softly behind her. Maybe she can get some ideas from her sister's closet.

It's a mess, with piles of dirty clothes on the floor of the closet, shirts and pants and dresses falling from hangers, reminding Emily of slabs of meat dangling from hooks in the window of the butcher shop. She winces and wishes she hadn't thought of that. There are black t-shirts, jeans, kilts, and second-hand cardigans all jumbled together. Not like her own closet, which is neatly organized — shirts first, then sweaters, dresses, pants, skirts, and everything that is the same colour together. It's easier to find things that way. She sees nothing she wants to borrow and every-thing would be way too big on her anyway. The shower still hums and sputters in the bathroom.

She glances around her sister's dark and messy room and wrinkles her nose. It smells like her vanilla perfume, candle wax, and unwashed laundry; she should open a window once in a while. School books are scattered on the floor, makeup is strewn across the vanity, and bottles of nail polish glint chaotically across her desk. Her bed, unlike Emily's, is rumpled and unmade, and her outfit for the night's meeting is strewn across the blankets. There is a black skirt and a red turtleneck sweater, a pair of black tights and a matching black bra and underwear set, ready to put on when she comes back from the bathroom.

Emily can't imagine what it must be like to wear a bra. Her own chest is flat, and shows no signs of changing, which is just fine with her. She turns sideways in the mirror and runs her hands over her chest; so far so good. But she can't stop looking at Lenora's bra — it's a grown-up thing, complicated with hooks and lace, beautiful and dangerous. She can't believe their mother let Lenora get a bra like that, so ornate and decadent, and — as the elders would call it — immodest. She's seen her mother's bras in the laundry before, plain and floppy and white or beige and sometimes pink but never this fancy. It's an exquisite three-dimensional sculpture. Emily picks it up and runs her fingertips along the lace trim on the cups and straps. Something flutters in her stomach, papery wings, fear, envy, almost pleasure, and her pulse leaps to keep up. She holds it across her outstretched palms like a treasure, or an injured bird, and listens again at the door. The water still runs, and her mom and Uncle Tyler chat and laugh downstairs. She has time.

As fast as she can, she pulls off her blue sweater and tosses it onto the end of Lenora's bed. She slides her arms under the bra straps and pulls it to her chest. Reaching behind her, she tries to fasten the hooks but can't quite reach. There are two of them, and all she has to do is hook them together, but she can't see what she's doing, and it's too frustrating. How does Lenora do this every day? It must take a lot of extra time. No wonder Lenora is always late for the meetings and for school.

Her arm starts to tense and cramp up from the awkward angle and she gives up. She'll just pretend it's done up properly, and leaves the back open between her shoulder blades. Taking a deep breath, she turns to face the mirror. Her eyes widen, and her stomach aches but in way that feels good, and without meaning to, she squeezes her legs together, which also feels good. She looks funny, like she's playing dress-up, which she is, but it's exciting. At the same time, her face starts to go red, because she suspects she's doing something quite wrong. Before reaching for her sweater, she takes one more long look. When she is old enough, she is going to get a fancy bra just like this.

— Oh my God! You pervert!

Lenora, wrapped in her thick yellow bathrobe, stands in her doorway and shrieks. One hand is over her mouth and other is on her hip. Emily turns purple, she feels sick, she cannot look at herself or anywhere. She flings the bra to the ground like a poisonous snake and grabs her sweater all in the same motion.

— What's going on up there? their mother yells from the bottom of the stairs.

— Nothing! they shout back in unison, and Lenora slams the door and, feet wide apart, arms folded across her chest, she stands in front of it.

— What were you doing?

Emily, fully clothed again, stares at her sister's red and black flecked carpet and says nothing. She can hear Lenora smirk without looking.

— Answer me. Why were you trying on my bra? Are you some kind of kinky weirdo?

— No!

— Well, why then? Do I have to get Mom up here? Or Dad?

— No! Emily tries to push past her and run away but Lenora shoves her back onto the bed.

— Did you like it?

— Like what?

— Wearing my sexy bra?

— Gross!

— Liar.

— Let me go!

Emily's throat snaps shut with a dull ache. She doesn't want to cry in front of her sister; she fights and fights and closes her eyes and turns her head but it's too late.

— I'm sorry. Let me go.

— Not so fast. First, put it back where you found it.

The room is blurry through her tears and too hot and it smells and she wants out so badly but knows that's impossible now, and it's all her own stupid, stupid fault.

She doesn't look at the bra, but picks it up by its strap with two fingers and holds it as far from her body as possible and drops it onto the bed.

— Second, I won't tell on you if you keep a secret for me. Oh, and I hope it goes without saying that you will not ever even mention the very existence of that bra to Mom or Dad, right?

Emily nods so hard she thinks her head might launch from her neck and bounce against the far wall.

— Good. Now go get changed for the Hall and then I'll
tell you some stuff. Now that I know you can never, ever
tell on me about anything!

Emily can still hear her laughing as she closes her own
bedroom door. She throws herself onto her bed and cries.
What was she thinking? Of all the ridiculous, embarrassing things in the world to do, she had to do that. She
wishes so hard that she could take it back and erase it
from reality forever.

— Hurry up!

She can't feel sorry for herself for long though, they'll
be leaving for the meeting soon, and Lenora is calling her.
She quickly opts for her beige corduroy skirt and leaves
on the same blue sweater, tugs on some tights and heads
back to Lenora's room.

— So guess what.

Emily shrugs and still can't meet Lenora's eyes.

— What?

— Uncle Tyler's in big trouble.

— What are you talking about?

— I know things.

— You do not. He's not in trouble. He just has to get
his hair cut.

Lenora laughs again. Emily wishes she didn't always
make Lenora laugh without meaning to.

— What's so funny?

— You. You're so naïve.

— What's 'naïve' mean?

— Stupid.

Emily tries to ignore her. Not because of the insults,
but because she doesn't want to hear any more about
Uncle Tyler, or Lenora's secrets. They don't make her feel
special or privileged like a secret should; they just make

her feel nervous and nauseated and like she's done something very wrong herself.

But Lenora isn't finished.

— His hair is the least of his worries.

Emily's eye is itchy. She tries to resist, but the burning twinge is insistent. She rubs her eye, but that's not enough. She rubs it again, then plucks out a bottom eyelash. It stings, but in a good way. Then she pulls out another, and that feels so good that she plucks out another, and another and another. Four, five, six, seven. She counts eleven eyelashes before Lenora yells at her.

— Stop it! That's disgusting! You already have a big bald patch under your other eye. You look like a freak.

Emily sits on her hands on the bed near Lenora. Lenora stands up and twirls around the room, doing a fake dance to no music. Emily wonders if she's wearing the special bra under her turtleneck. She hopes not, and doesn't look anywhere but at her face or the floor. Lenora sways her hips and waves her arms.

— I know someone who saw him somewhere he shouldn't have been.

She dances back and forth across the room. Emily says nothing and doesn't move. If she doesn't know, then none of it can be true.

Finally, Lenora sits back down beside her.

— All right, I'll tell you.

— Tell me what?

— Why Uncle Tyler's going to get in big trouble.

— He's not! He's going to cut his hair, he promised.

— I already told you, it's not about his hair. That's just an excuse.

— It is not! Stop it!

Lenora stands up again, looking down at Emily, who

still sits on her hands. She tries hard not to move. If she stays as still as she can, everything will stay the same, and no one will get in trouble. Not Uncle Tyler, not Lenora, not her. Nothing will change. She closes her eyes.

— He was seen in a nightclub. Drunk. In Buffalo.

Emily opens her eyes.

— He was not! You're making it up!

— I'm not. I swear to God. Think I should tell the elders? Lenora smirks.

Emily runs to the bedroom door and looks into the hallway before closing it tightly.

— Be quiet! What if they hear you?

— I have another secret.

— So what?

— Don't you want to hear it?

— No.

— This is a good one, Ems.

— No. Just shut up! I don't want to know anything else.

— I'm in love.

Emily makes a gagging noise and pretends to throw up in a pillow.

— With who? With Theo?

— None of your business. But it's the real thing. And someday we're going to get out of this town. Escape. Together.

Emily's never heard her sister talk like this before and it frightens her. Where is she going to escape to? Without noticing, she plucks out a few more eyelashes.

Lenora pauses when they hear footsteps on the stairs, and then leans in toward Emily's face. Emily closes her eyes again and wishes she could go temporarily deaf, so she doesn't have to hear any more secrets.

— Listen to me.

— No.

Emily lunges toward the door but Lenora grabs her arm and pulls her toward her face.

— Do you know what 'in drag' means?

There is a loud knock at the door and they both jump.

— Girls! Your mom says you have five minutes before we have to leave.

Emily and Lenora look at each other. Lenora responds in a silly high voice.

— Okay, we'll be right there, Uncle Tyler!

22

▼

AGNES THE PENTECOSTAL IS COMING over. Emily didn't tell her parents that Agnes is a Pentecostal, but that's not the same as lying, not exactly. She can't tell her parents every little thing that happens to her or every thought that comes into her head. Besides, Agnes isn't like other worldly kids; she doesn't swear or cheat on tests or steal candy from the corner store. She just reads and talks about Sunday school and mystery books. They've done lots of shifts together at the library and she is the closest thing to a worldly friend that Emily has — or any kind of friend, for that matter. She told her parents that she's been Witnessing to Agnes at school, that she might want to come to a meeting with her someday, and they agreed to let her come over to play. It was sort of true, since Agnes has been asking her questions about Jehovah's Witnesses, like why don't they celebrate Christmas or birthdays, and whether or not Emily has to knock on doors and preach to strangers. She answers as best she can, then changes the subject to Trixie Belden mystery books, which they both read, or how Mr. MacKay the librarian smells.

Emily checks that her shirt is tucked in, that her hair is combed, and then picks at one of the scabs on her index finger. Agnes has never seen her bedroom or met her parents before. She hopes that she doesn't find them weird and tell everyone at school that they're freaks, just because they pray before they eat and don't have a Christmas tree. Emily reassures herself that they can't be any stranger than the Pentecostals. It's the first time Emily's parents have ever allowed her to have a worldly friend over, other than the next-door neighbour kids, the Pattons, who used to just come over whenever they felt like it, because their mom worked all the time and their dad had run off.

Her mom is making homemade macaroni and cheese for them for dinner and Emily hopes that Agnes likes it. Emily walks back and forth from the kitchen to the living room, where her father sits on the couch in jeans and a plaid shirt, reading the latest issue of the *Watchtower* that was in yesterday's mail. She stops to look out the window and see if Agnes is there yet. Her mom is dropping her off at 4:00 and will pick her up at 7:30.

— Stop pacing, Emily. You're making me nervous. Her mom grates cheese on top of the casserole and slides it into the oven.

— She'll get here when she gets here.

— I know. Where's Lenora? Emily hopes her sister doesn't say anything strange or mean to Agnes. Hopefully she'll have a lot of homework to do and will leave them alone.

— In her room, as usual. Being anti-social.

Emily isn't sure what she should do with Agnes when she finally arrives — will she want to play a game, like checkers or Snakes and Ladders, or will she prefer to dress up her dolls in different outfits, or maybe go outside and swing on the tire swing? What if she thinks Emily's toys and games are boring? What if she doesn't have fun and never comes back? What if Emily never has a proper best friend? Gravel crunches in the driveway and she watches a grey sedan pull up to the house. Agnes climbs out of the car and blows her mom a kiss goodbye. Her mom honks the horn and waves. Agnes is wearing a white blouse tucked into a green and orange tartan skirt with white tights. She looks like she could be on her way to the Kingdom Hall. Emily thinks it would be nice to have a friend her own age there to sit with during the meetings sometimes, instead of just her family. She jumps when the doorbell rings, and stands there, then looks at her mother.

— Well, answer the door, Emily! Her mom sounds exasperated.

Agnes stands on the porch and pushes her glasses up her nose. She smiles and adjusts her backpack.

— Hi.

— Hi Emily. Agnes stands on her tiptoes and looks past her and into the house. Emily wavers in the doorway.

— Aren't you going to ask me in?

Emily reddens and stammers.

— Of course . . . come on in.

Agnes takes off her boots and sets her bag down. She clasps her arms together.

— Thank you for having me over.

— You're welcome.

— Hi Mr. Morrow.

Emily's dad smiles and waves from the couch then looks back down at the magazine on his lap.

— My mom says I should thank your mom too.

— Okay.

Emily hopes her mom doesn't say or do anything embarrassing. Agnes follows close behind her into the kitchen.

— Mom, this is Agnes.

Emily's mom sets her mug down next to the stove and shakes Agnes the Pentecostal's hand up and down, hard, for far too long.

— Hi Agnes! Welcome to our happy home! How are you on this fine day?

Emily cringes.

— Mom . . .

— Fine thank you, Mrs. Morrow. Thank you for having me over.

— Oh, you're most welcome.

— Do you need any help with dinner?

— No, no, you kids go play. We're going to eat in about an hour.

Emily gives Agnes a quick tour of their house and then they go to her bedroom. Agnes perches right at the edge of the bed, as though sitting farther back toward the pillows would be unsavoury. She folds her hands in her lap. Emily isn't sure what she is supposed to do next, and Agnes is quieter than she is at school.

— Do you want to play checkers?

— Okay.

Emily sets out the board and arranges the pieces. They click and clack like her father's knuckles when he cracks them. Agnes moves her red piece forward. Emily considers her first move and slides a black disc forward. Agnes hops her red piece over it and captures Emily's black one. Emily frowns. Agnes leans forward over the checkerboard.

— Can I ask you a question?

— I don't know. I guess so.

— What happened to your father's hand?

Emily didn't think Agnes had noticed his missing fingers, something Emily is so accustomed to that she doesn't even think about it.

Emily doesn't answer right away. She waits a few moments, twisting her hair around her finger and counting the tiles on the board. Sixty-four. She takes her turn and then Agnes takes hers and quickly snatches up two more of her pieces.

— He was in an accident. When he was little. Emily doesn't look up.

— What kind of accident?

Emily isn't very good at the strategy necessary to win at checkers. She keeps unintentionally setting herself up for Agnes to take two of her pieces every turn. Each move she makes leaves exposed vulnerabilities she didn't even know she had.

— Just an accident. In a thunderstorm.

— What happened? Did his hand get mangled in a machine? And they had to amputate to free him?

— I don't know.

— Really? You don't know? Why not?

Agnes takes her turn and overthrows another black piece.

— He doesn't like to talk about it.

— Was it a car accident? Was anyone else hurt?

That's the part they're not allowed to talk about. Years ago, when Lenora was younger, she asked a lot of questions too. Her father clenched the side of the kitchen table so hard you could see the bones in his good hand almost tearing through his skin. He told Lenora *Never mind*, to stop asking so many questions, and she persisted, *But why, what happened?* until finally he picked up his half-full dinner plate and threw it against the far wall. Emily was very small, but she still remembers the spaghetti inching down the yellow floral wallpaper below the clock, like earthworms on the sidewalk after a storm. He didn't speak to any of them for a week after that, and their mom has since made sure they know it's one of the things they're not allowed to talk about.

Emily doesn't look up at Agnes. She doesn't want to have to lie outright, so she shrugs instead and finally takes one of Agnes' red pieces. Emily is relieved when her mom calls them down for dinner.

They sit down at the table and her father is in his chair and Emily's mom sets the casserole and salad on the table before taking her seat. Lenora's chair is empty. Music drifts from upstairs, but no one tells Lenora to turn it off.

— Bow your heads.

Emily's father prays. She sneaks a look at Agnes. Her eyes are scrunched up tight and she clasps her hands in front of her. She hopes that their prayer doesn't seem too strange compared to what Agnes is used to. She doesn't know how the Pentecostals pray, if it's always the same set of memorized lines like the prayer at school, or if they make it up from scratch every time, so it's genuine.

— Our Lord and God in heaven, we thank you for this meal and all that we have . . .

Emily tries to focus but keeps peeking out her left eye to see if Lenora is waiting in the doorway or has somehow appeared in her chair. She doesn't want her parents to yell at her in front of Agnes. Her stomach is so tight she doesn't know if she'll even be able to eat.

— Give us the strength to always keep faith in you even when persecuted, that we might please you and live forever and see our loved ones again after the Resurrection.

He pauses for a minute and Emily isn't sure if he's lost his train of thought or what.

— Please forgive all of our sins, as we are imperfect and make many mistakes we don't mean to.

He clears his throat and continues.

— Please continue to bless us in our weakness and forgive us, in Jesus' name, Amen.

— Amen. Emily and her mom murmur in unison.

— Amen! Agnes chirps so loud her father starts.

Emily exhales loudly.

Her mom serves them the macaroni and cheese with a big wooden spoon, and Emily can tell that her smile is fake. She is only being nice because they have company. She must be mad at Lenora again. She sits down and rearranges her cutlery several times while the rest of them begin to eat.

Emily's dad swallows a couple of mouthfuls, then clears his throat and sets his fork down. None of them are used to having unfamiliar people over.

— So, what did you two get up to today?

— We played checkers, Mr. Morrow. I won every game, didn't I, Emily?

— Yeah—

— Don't talk with your mouth full, Emily!

— Sorry. Emily apologizes to her mom but wishes she hadn't snapped at her in front of Agnes. She stares at her food and moves it around on her plate while her father asks Agnes polite questions about school. Emily and her mom eat in silence.

When they are nearly done, Lenora bursts into the room like a hurricane, her long black and red plaid shirt billowing around her. She plops several spoonfuls of macaroni and cheese onto her plate and doesn't seem to notice a couple of sticky noodles drop to the floor. Then she shakes a bottle of Tabasco sauce over it all, so it's speckled with red. The chair rattles as she drags it across the floor and she sinks down heavily.

— Your macaroni and cheese is really good, Mrs. Morrow. I've never had it homemade like this before.

Lenora seems to notice Agnes for the first time.

— Who on earth are you?

— Thank you, Agnes. I can give you the recipe to take home if you like.

— Um, this is my friend Agnes. From school.

It's embarrassing that Lenora even asked, and Emily coughs, then kicks her sister under the table.

— Ouch! What'd you kick me for?

— Nothing.

Lenora turns to Agnes, swallows her food, and grins.

— So, are you worldly?

— Lenora . . . Their mom is using her warning voice.

— It's a valid question. I mean, 'bad association' and all that. Right?

Emily doesn't look up, just keeps moving her food around, her head close to her plate. Agnes turns to Lenora.

— I don't really understand the question. What do you mean?

— I mean, are you going to start coming to the Kingdom Hall with us? Or is Emily wasting her time?

— Shut up! Emily turns bright red and can't look at anyone.

Agnes looks from Lenora to Emily, then back at Lenora.

— What do you mean?

— What do I mean? Emily isn't allowed to hang around with worldly kids. Unless she's converting them. Right, Dad? Isn't that how it is?

— Lenora.

He looks at her with that sharp, long look that means *you're in trouble*, but Lenora ignores him.

— I know you're Jehovah's Witnesses and stuff, but I have my own religion.

— Well, that's good to hear that you read the Bible. Their dad tries to take the conversation away from Lenora.

— What religion do you belong to?

— I'm a Pentecostal. Agnes smiles and crunches her lettuce.

Their parents exchange a look between them and Lenora laughs.

— Wow. Hard-core. That's like the thrash metal of Christianity!

Emily doesn't know exactly what that means, but knows enough to recognize that her sister is making fun of Agnes.

— Shut up, Lenora!

Agnes, however, openly ignores Lenora, which impresses Emily.

— Can I ask you a question, Mr. Morrow?

— Sure, Agnes. What is it?

— It's kind of a personal question, so I hope you're not offended.

Emily sucks in her breath quickly and swivels her head toward Agnes, then coughs, trying to signal her to be quiet. Even Lenora has stopped eating and watches her, waiting to hear what she'll ask. The room goes silent and Emily can hear the clock tick louder than it ever has, every second, she counts six of them before anyone speaks.

— How come you're missing two fingers on your left hand? Was it from an accident?

Emily's face burns, her mom drops her fork, and the clatter echoes. Lenora blows a low, slow whistle between her dark red lips.

No one speaks. Her father folds up his napkin and sets it gently onto his plate. Then he looks at his deformed hand, turns it palm-side up, then back again, as though seeing it for the first time.

— There was an accident. I was just a kid. I don't remember very much.

He doesn't seem to say this as much to Agnes as he does to himself, but Agnes persists.

— I think you went to school with my dad. Cal Vandergroot? Do you remember him?

— I don't think so.

— Are you sure? He remembers you.

He says nothing more, just stands up and walks out of the kitchen, still looking down at his hand. His footsteps recede as they reach the top of the stairs. The bedroom door snaps shut.

They finish eating in silence.

— Would you like some help with the dishes, Mrs. Morrow?

— No, thanks. Go outside and play or something. You have about an hour until your mom will be back.

In the living room, Emily asks Agnes what she wants

to do. She avoids looking her in the eye. She wishes she'd just go home early.

In the yard, they take turns on the tire swing. Agnes climbs on top of it, swaying and holding on to the rope.

— Push me harder!

Emily does, then stops her and stands in front of her.

— Why did you ask my dad about his hand? I already told you he was in an accident a long time ago.

— I think there's more to the story than that. Don't you?

Emily shrugs.

— And why did your sister say all that stuff? She's weird.

— I know. She wasn't always this weird though. She's a teenager.

Emily says this almost proudly, as though teenagers are rare and exotic creatures, as though it explains everything. Agnes gets off the swing and grins and points behind them.

— Let's go way back there by the bush.

Without waiting for a response, Agnes jogs toward the woods at the rear of their lot, through melted patches of snow and muddy grass and slush. Emily bites her lip and looks back toward the kitchen window. The sun is starting to set, and she isn't allowed to play far from the house after dark, but she doesn't see her mom at the curtains. Knowing her dad will be mad at her about what Agnes said, she doesn't want to go inside either.

— Wait up!

Agnes is fast and plunges into the trees while Emily flails behind her, snapping twigs and trying not to fall. There is still enough light to see flashes of Agnes' white-clad legs as she weaves between oak and poplar and maple trees. Unlike Agnes, Emily picks her way carefully, watching that she doesn't step in any mud or trip over a log. She's surprised; she always thought Agnes was so prim.

Ahead, Agnes stops and bends down to the ground.

— Look what I found!

She catches up with Agnes, who holds something in the air with both hands. Emily comes closer and screams. She backs away from Agnes.

— Don't be scared. It's just a plain old garter snake. It won't hurt you.

She moves toward Emily, still holding out the snake. It tenses and twists in her grip. A real, live serpent.

— He must be confused by the warm weather this week. Maybe the snow melted wherever he was hibernating, so he woke up early. Poor little guy!

Agnes coos and smiles at it, like it's a kitten or a puppy, and Emily covers her mouth when Agnes leans in to kiss it.

— Put it down!

It writhes and twists, trying to get free, and Emily backs away. She's never seen anyone touch a real snake before. After what feels like hours, Agnes the Pentecostal tosses the snake into the undergrowth behind her.

— Scaredy-cat!

— I am not!

— You are too! You looked like you were going to cry!

— Snakes are disgusting, that's all. I wasn't scared.

Agnes smirks.

— Last month a real live snake handler came to our church. He was from Tennessee.

— What's a snake handler? Where's Tennessee?

— In the States somewhere. He talked funny and had a gold tooth, right here. She points to her upper left incisor.

Emily's stomach churns and she cringes; Agnes touched her own mouth after holding a filthy snake.

— What was he doing here?

— He tours North America with his copperheads and rattlesnakes and comes to Pentecostal churches in every town. It's an honour.

Agnes nods her head up and down. Emily wonders if this snake man is like their District Overseer, who tours the region, giving talks at all the different Kingdom Halls.

— But what does he do with the snakes?

— He puts them around his neck and holds them up and lets other people take them.

— What for?

Agnes pauses.

— You know. For faith.

— Like a test?

— Yeah, testing your faith. Like in the Bible.

— Do they ever bite?

— Sometimes. But he's a holy man. God is stronger than the devil and the snake handler won't die from the venom. It's like in the Bible, when it says, 'They shall take up serpents . . .'

— So he brings real live poisonous snakes into your church? Emily wonders if it's Satanism.

— Yeah, real live rattlesnakes. I wanted to hold one, but my mom wouldn't let me. She was scared, just like you!

— I don't believe you.

— It's true! I might even be a snake handler when I grow up. I'd be really good at it.

— Where does it talk about that in the Bible? Emily knows the Bible very well, and she can't think of any scripture that tells you to tease deadly snakes.

— It's in Mark something. Chapter sixteen, I think. Look it up in your own Bible, there's one in every room in your house.

— I will. But I still think you're making it up.

— I never lie! Lying is a sin!

— What's the scripture then?

— 'They shall take up serpents, and if they drink any deadly thing, it shall not hurt them . . .'

— That doesn't sound right to me.

— Well it is. You want to know something else, a secret?

— Not really.

Emily has had more than her fill of other people's secrets.

They pause and nudge the slush with their toes and finally Emily speaks.

— What, then?

— I'm not allowed to say.

— Don't then. I don't care.

— Promise you won't tell? Especially not your parents?

— Okay.

Emily's stomach feels weird, like before she puts up her hand to give an answer into the microphone at the meetings.

— My dad told me something about your dad. He knew him when they were still kids.

— He did not. My dad said he didn't even remember your dad.

— He did too! He said they're exactly the same age and went to the same school.

The bare branches rattle and Emily shivers.

— Well, don't you want to know the secret?

— I don't care.

— You can't ever say that I told you, okay? Promise?

— I said I don't care if you tell me or not. Emily shrugs and wishes she'd never asked Agnes to come over to her house.

— Well, I think you should know.

Emily bites her lip. Agnes doesn't slow down.

— It's your right.

— What is?

— To know the truth.

— But I do. I already know the truth.

— No, you don't.

— Yes, I do.

— Then how come I know stuff that you don't? And it's not even my family!

— You do not.

— I do too.

They both look at each other. A nearby branch rustles and a huge owl rises out of a tree and flaps off, screeching, into the dusk. Emily shivers again.

— My dad said that your dad killed his little brother.

Agnes takes a step closer to Emily, her hands on her small hips, chin thrust forward, and the wind stops blowing, the trees are still, and everything stops, even the birds, waiting for Emily to say something.

— That's a lie! He's an only child.

— It's the truth. He used to have a brother. When your dad was ten and he was seven.

— You're a liar!

The macaroni and cheese turns into a hard lump and it pushes against her stomach so hard she almost falls down, but she grabs a tree instead and lets it hold her up.

— I'm not lying. My dad told me. Ask him yourself. That's how he lost his fingers. I swear to God.

Emily's eyes burn. Agnes just stands there, watching her with her round, hard eyes that look like a crow's.

— He did not.

Emily can only whisper. She doesn't know what's true anymore and what isn't.

There is a car horn in the distance, and soon after, Emily's mom calls them.

— Come on. We better go.

— Maybe I'll let you be my assistant snake handler someday, unless you're too chicken.

Agnes runs back toward the house and Emily trudges in the slush far behind. She doesn't say goodbye, and the car door slams in the distance. The sun dips behind the trees and disappears.

23

▼

I WAS READY TO BEGIN. The light, hot and metallic, buzzed and glared above the bathroom mirror.

In one hand I held a small, worn photograph, and in the other, a roll of tape. The edges of the picture were soft and curled at the corners, as though dropped in a puddle then left for years in a dark drawer. Two teenage girls in black pouted against a row of dented metal lockers.

I set the photo face up on the counter beside the sink.

The tape stretched and crackled when I tugged it, dangling sticky sinews of glue. I tore off the end, and the serrated edge of the dispenser gouged the side of my thumb, leaving a neat row of bloody dashes. I gritted my teeth against the sting.

— One, two, three, four, five . . . I tried to count each

tiny cut before they oozed into one solid line. The blood was about to drip onto the picture but I moved it in time. A tiny red splash landed on the bathroom counter. Red on white. By then, I was used to seeing my own blood, but this time it disoriented me, as though I were spinning backward in time. The bathroom seemed to tilt and I grabbed the sink to steady myself. I stumbled and blurred, my stomach muscles clenched, and I sucked in as much air as I could. Eyes closed. Don't look. Don't look down.

I cranked the cold tap and held my thumb under, counting to thirty, then twisted the tap off. My left hand throbbed from the icy water but it quelled the sting. I bandaged my thumb and continued my new ritual.

This time, I avoided the dispenser's metal teeth and wrenched off a gooey length of tape, looped it, and stuck it on the back of the picture. I pulled my sleeve over my hand and pressed the photo against the wall to the left of the mirror.

Her hair was bleached and parted on the side, one half shaved to her scalp and the other side teased up high and sculpted down across her left eye. I remembered shouting matches between Lenora and our parents over her hair, her torn clothing, her black and blue nail polish, her loud music. The arguments eventually all seemed the same, and after that melded into one.

Her hair had been shorter than mine, but I'd get it as close as I could. I took a deep breath, picked up the scissors, and hacked a bit off one side. It fell to the floor, and as difficult as it was, I resisted the urge to clean it up. I glanced back toward the photograph, and she peered out, unsmiling, sophisticated, her dark red lips a half-pout, half-sneer. Marla was at her side, in black leather pants and a red shirt with a plaid vest over it. She was grimacing and giving the finger to whoever had taken the photograph.

— I can do this.

It became an incantation. I practised the pouting sneer. I looked like someone who had unwittingly swallowed something rotten. I tried again, reminding myself it wasn't me in the mirror anymore. Better.

In the drawer to the left of the sink, beneath the picture, was my brand-new lipstick. *Vixen Red*. Almost identical to *Blood Red*, but new, not dried and crumbling. It would have to do. I smeared that across my lips and my stomach fluttered.

— I can do this.

The clippers buzzed alive when I flicked the switch and I quickly sheared off the hair above my right ear. It felt strange; I wasn't used to the prickle of air against my scalp. The gel was wet and shiny and easily shellacked my hair down and to a point over my left eye. Then I sprayed it in place, solid and sleek. That was the easy part. The rest of my damp hair then needed volume and height. I sprayed a mound of mousse onto my palm and smeared it into the rest of my hair, then began to tease it into tangles with a fine-toothed comb. I pulled fistfuls of it straight out from my head and ran the comb backwards through the clumps until they were ten times their usual size. It took seven back-comb strokes per section to get it right.

— Comb that bird's nest down! I could hear my father shout, as I achieved the kind of look that could scandalize a Kingdom Hall full of devoted, gossipy Witnesses. I smirked and made my hair even bigger.

It wasn't difficult. The hard part would be getting it back to normal later, but I tried not to worry about that. I closed my eyes, held my breath, and coated the entire thing with a thick layer of hairspray. I checked the picture: pretty close. I reapplied the Vixen Red, sneered, then pouted.

My skin erupted into goosebumps. The resemblance was exact.

I stood up straighter and pushed my chest out against the red flannel shirt. I watched myself undo the first button. Something — excitement, blood, danger, pleasure — surged and tightened between my thighs. I undid two more. My face flushed.

Under my plaid flannel shirt, I wore her black lace bra.

I unbuttoned the rest of my shirt and let it drop to the floor. Again, I didn't fold it and tuck it into a dresser drawer; I didn't tidy up at all.

Where did you get all this stuff? Bras, bustiers, garters, thongs . . .

None of your business.

Did you wear it under your Hall clothes to the meetings? Your dirty little secret?

Questions I hadn't dared to ask ten years earlier. I stared at the pouting punk rock girl in the mirror. One bra strap slid down my shoulder, and I left it like that. Every bit of my skin tingled. The setting sun streamed red into the bathroom, dousing it with a hot, pulsing eeriness. I turned off the light.

I unzipped my jeans, tugged them off, and kicked them toward the shirt. More black lace. The throbbing between my legs increased. I slid my cool fingertips over my exposed nipple and it hardened. A moan slipped between the crimson lips in the mirror. I hardly recognized myself. I sneered, then grinned.

Four steps to the bathroom door. I counted steps like

the blind. Funambulists, too; they had to know without looking how far to walk. One. Two. Three. Four.

In my bedroom, I kept the black lace on. Explored the warm, slippery folds and tasted my fingertips. Briefly, I cringed. Freak. Disgrace. Aberration.

No. I blocked out the guilt and treated it as an invader. Pictured it as fist-sized black lumps that I dashed to the ground from way up on the high wire. Inhaled and exhaled and started again. Looked at my half-off bra like someone else might. Pictured a tall, hard, boot-clad Theo above me: kissing my neck, licking my stomach, sliding downward. I moaned again. I bucked against my palm until all the colours in the world exploded and flooded me.

I lay damply on my bed in the darkening light, feeling a mix of pleasure, exhilaration, and shame. As my breathing slowed to normal and the pink blotches on my chest faded, so did my elation. Guilt overwhelmed me and quickly ignited into disgust.

I had gotten turned on by wearing my sister's underwear.

The phone rang. I started but didn't get up from the bed. I tore off the flimsy black bra and thong and threw them across the room. One, two, three, four, five rings until the voicemail kicked in. My number was unlisted, and very few people even had it. Probably just a wrong number or another telemarketer.

One. Two. Three. Four. Five. It rang again. A few minutes later, a third time. My heart beat faster, as though I was being chased. I pulled on my bathrobe, walked slowly into the living room, and stared at the slate blue phone. It didn't ring again.

53235. An indelible transmission — my pinkest, deepest scar. A fragment flitted back and that was enough to finally decode it. The coordinates of a scripture, etched into my skin forever.

Vengeance is mine, and retribution.

I tightened the belt on my robe and wrapped my arms around myself. Paced the nine steps across the living room, and nine steps back.

I told myself to calm down. It was probably just Kameela or someone from work wanting to trade shifts. I wanted to stop being ridiculous and just check the messages, but I couldn't separate what I'd just done from the phone calls. I felt like I'd been found out, like someone had been watching me the whole time. I shivered. It was almost entirely dark in my small apartment, and I switched on a lamp. In the bathroom, I splashed cold water on my face. Then I went back to the phone and quickly punched in my password, 53235. The monotonous voice told me I had three new messages.

I recognized her voice immediately and my mouth went dry. I held the receiver away from my ear but I could still hear her.

— We've been frantic trying to find you. Why didn't you give us your number? We had to get it from the school. I've barely slept for weeks . . . please call us at home . . .

The next message was the phone number. As if, by some miracle, I had forgotten it.

I hung up in the middle of the third message. Strode into the bathroom. Touched my hard, sticky hair. Looked at the picture. Looked back at myself.

This is me. This is me. This is who I am.

I narrowed my eyes, bit the insides of my lips, and took a deep breath. I could do it. I wasn't afraid of them. In the living room, the phone sat in the centre of a small table, cold and menacing, poisonous. I stared at it for so long it seemed to move on its own, sliding slightly to the left or right every time I looked away.

Finally, I stomped over to it and grabbed the receiver, almost surprised that it didn't leap from my hand and smash itself on the floor.

I listened to the message again, this time all the way through.

— We've been so worried. We don't understand why you won't even talk to us. First Lenora, now you. It's not fair! This is no way to treat your parents. Please call us back this time.

Her voice cracked and there was silence, but she didn't hang up. After some rustling, she came back on the line.

— At least, if you won't call us back, mail the pictures of your sister. Why would you take them? Why would you do that? It was the only thing we had left. How could you take them all?

She was shrieking by then, howling *How could you* over and over.

But they were mine; that was why I took them. The photos didn't belong back in that house, because she didn't want them there. She wanted me to have them.

I had no choice but to take them, to take everything of hers. They didn't deserve her then and they never would. They weren't good enough for her. Only I was. Only I understood. Only me.

My mother paused, then asked another question, her voice wavering.

— Why do you say Lenora on your voicemail? Why do you say *Leave a message for Emily or Lenora?*

This is me. This is who I am.

24

▼

LONG AFTER AGNES HAS GONE home, Emily's mom wakes her up to tuck her in and say good night. Her breath is terrible, sour and bitter at the same time, and she keeps leaning in too close to Emily's head. She scrunches up her face. Her mom sways over her for a moment, then plunks down on the edge of her bed.

— Agnes seems like a nice girl. Is she going to come over again?

Emily turns toward the far wall and doesn't answer. After a few moments, she shrugs.

— What's wrong? Are you still upset about Lenora? Don't worry, I told her she's not allowed to embarrass you like that again. It wasn't very nice.

She starts to make up a silly song in a silly voice.

— Not nice at all! Not even one bit. Mean old big sister! Not nice—

— Stop it!

— Okay, okay! Jeez. Everyone around here is so sensitive! No fun at all.

— I'm serious.

— I can see that. Very serious. She rearranges the blankets around Emily, pulling them up to her chin.

— Is there something you want to tell your old, boring mom about? A girl talk? We could pretend we're at a slumber party.

— No.

— Come on, Emily, it's okay. You can tell me.

— Go away!

Her mom doesn't leave. She stays on the edge of the bed humming a tune Emily doesn't recognize. Emily sits up and shakes the blankets off.

— I want to know what happened to Dad's brother.

— Your dad's brother? Wow.

Her mom stares at something, or at nothing, on the far wall for a long time before responding.

— Why did you tell me he was an only child? You lied. Dad too.

Her mom says nothing, just presses her lips together and keeps looking at the wall.

— I want to know what happened. All of it.

— There was an accident. A car accident. When they were kids. That's it.

— I mean for real! Tell me the truth!

Her mom stands up and Emily stands on her bed and they face each other.

— That is the truth. There was a car accident, and his little brother died. Your father's fingers got smashed in the metal of the door and they had to amputate them. That's it.

— I think there's more to it. More that you're keeping secret.

— Well, you read too many of those mystery books. It was a terrible accident and your dad's brother died right beside him. He doesn't like to talk about it.

— Are you sure that's all there is? There's nothing else?

— Yes. That's it. Now go back to sleep.

Emily doesn't know why, but she believes Agnes more than her own mother. They're lying to her. Somehow, for some reason, he killed his own brother, like Cain and Abel. She gets back under the covers and turns toward the wall until her mother clicks the door closed behind her.

THE NEXT MORNING, LENORA KEEPS running to the bathroom and gagging, then flushing the toilet. She isn't coming to the Sunday meeting. No one forces her, but Emily knows she's faking. Lenora never gets sick; she has a stomach of iron, so Emily doesn't know why their parents believe her. It's not fair that Lenora gets to stay home by herself.

Emily strides over to the bathroom door and puts her ear against the wood. Lenora moans and mumbles something she can't quite hear. She's so dramatic. She should be an actress like their mom used to be.

— Jehovah knows when you're faking. It's the same as a lie!

Lenora flushes again and Emily shouts even louder.

— He'll know if you're not at the meeting today! Lying is a sin and sinners will be destroyed at Armageddon!

It's her job to lead Lenora back to the Truth. To show her the right path. To be the way and the light. Not to follow her into wrongdoing. Even though she's too young to be baptized yet, she can still be a shepherd and help the lost sheep, just like the elders. She nods then, up and down, knowing that Jehovah is watching her at that very moment. The more she nods, the more she convinces herself she's right.

— That's enough, Emily. Her mom pulls her away from the bathroom.

— God doesn't take attendance like your teacher at school. Leave your sister alone; she's not feeling well.

Water runs in the sink, drawers open and close, and a few minutes later Lenora creaks the door open and slouches in the bathroom doorway. Her hair is greasy and tangled and she isn't even wearing any makeup. Her hands are unsteady, and she puts them into the pockets of her slouching, yellow bathrobe. Her mom feels her forehead, pauses, then checks it again with the back of her hand.

— I think I have the flu.

— You don't have a fever. Maybe it was something you ate. Sleep it off.

She pushes Lenora toward the stairs. Without looking at them, Lenora plods upstairs, clutching the banister as though she can't walk without it.

— She's faking!

They go back to the kitchen and finish eating their cereal while Lenora's small stereo thrums angry music down through her floor. Their mom frowns as she puts her Bible in her Hall purse.

— Tell your sister I said to turn her music off.

— Okay.

Emily takes the stairs two at a time, planning to tell

Lenora that what she's doing is wrong, and that she must repent and not commit any more sins for a while, before it's too late.

At her door, the music drones and she can feel the vibrations through the door against her palms. She stands like that, mesmerized, her hands flat on the door and her forehead resting against it. The singer's voice is slow and deep. *Mournful*, Emily thinks, *like he's lost something*. The low, dark sound of the music matches his vocals. Before the next song begins, a weird sound strains from the room. It's a muffled gasp or a choke.

Emily raises her hand to knock, but puts it back down. She doesn't know what to do. Maybe Lenora has something stuck in her throat and needs help.

— Lenora?

She doesn't answer. Emily puts her ear against the door, but hears nothing except the music. During a quiet part of the song, she hears it again.

Lenora is crying.

She draws back as though burned. Lenora doesn't cry. *Only babies cry. Don't be a crybaby.* Emily sways and leans against the wall in the hallway and closes her eyes.

— Mom says to turn it off! She yells this and runs down the hall, into her own room, and dives onto her bed. She stays there until they call her to leave for the meeting.

AFTER THEY HANG UP THEIR coats in the cloakroom and find seats, Emily doesn't know what to do with herself. They're twenty-five minutes early for the meeting because Emily's dad is a Ministerial Servant now, and has to work his monthly shift at the Literature Desk, selling back issues of *The Watchtower* and *Awake!* or copies of *You Can Live Forever in Paradise on Earth* and *Your Youth: Getting the Best Out of It.* All the brothers and sisters in the congregation of course already have their own copies of each of the books that the Society publishes, but they buy extras to place with people they meet out in service or to give to worldly people they're studying with.

Without Lenora at the meeting, Emily has no one to talk to, so she walks around the Hall, trying to look purposeful, like she is going somewhere specific. She strides back to the cloakroom and checks her pockets, as though she forgot something. Brother Davies comes in, stomps his boots on the mat, and nods at Emily. She nods back. In the main room, her mom is chatting with some other sisters, and she doesn't want to interrupt. Instead, she shuffles down a short hallway and into the smaller back room where they hold the short Service Talk before going door to door, or where mothers take the babies when they cry during the talks in the main room. It's also where the elders draw the brown tweed curtains across the windows and hold private meetings, like the ones they have with wayward sheep. When this happens, everyone whispers about who is in trouble with the elders and why, and will they be *disfellowshipped*, or *publicly reproved*?

Bookshelves line two of the walls from floor to ceiling, and she runs her fingertips along the dusty spines of the books, breathing in their mustiness. She counts how many across each row, fifty-two, then forty-seven, then twenty-two of the thickest books. She tries to calm down, but can't. How could they let Lenora stay home, how could they actually believe her stomach flu excuse? She just wanted to stay home and talk on the phone to her worldly friends. Or worse, to worldly boys. To Theo. Emily bets if they call right now, the line will be busy. She goes back to the Literature Desk.

— Dad, I need to use the phone.

— What for? Who do you need to call?

— I think we should call Lenora. You know, to make sure she's all right.

— Is that what you mother said?

Emily shrugs.

— She's probably asleep. Don't worry, she'll be fine.

— But—

— What can I get you, Sister Bulchinsky?

As her dad retrieves some *Watchtowers*, Emily stomps down the hall and returns to the back room. She stares at the shelves of books without seeing them. She can't even concentrate to count any more of them. Why can't they see that Lenora is lying? Why don't they pay more attention? Why can't they make her be good before it's too late? What if Armageddon were to start tomorrow?

— All alone in here, Little Sister Morrow?

Brother Wilde bulges in his too-tight green suit, full of niceness he doesn't mean.

Emily smiles a too-tight little smile and turns back to the books, peering closely as though searching for a particular one.

— Interested in those 1950s *Watchtower* volumes, Emily? Times sure were different back then, yessiree.

Emily shrugs.

— I haven't seen your sister yet this morning. Brother Wilde waits for an explanation.

She shrugs again.

She doesn't care that he's an elder; she doesn't answer

him. He shakes his head and sighs and it sounds like he's deflating.

— Well, Satan sets all sorts of snares, you know that, don't you, Emily? Keep your faith in Jehovah strong and you will prevail over evil.

Emily digs her fingernails into her palms. She wants badly to shout, *So will my sister*, but she doesn't.

— I'll pray for Lenora, Emily.

Emily nods without turning around.

— I haven't seen your uncle Tyler at the last couple of meetings either. Is he sick too?

Emily starts to count the books again, even though she's already done that row. Why can't he leave her alone? She doesn't know why they aren't at the meeting, she doesn't know why they want to get in trouble, she doesn't know why everything is all wrong lately.

— Thirty-seven, thirty-eight, thirty-nine . . .

Brother Wilde pulls a chair up to the bookshelf next to her, blocking the rest of the row. His aftershave makes her eyes water.

— I understand you and your uncle went out in service together a couple Sundays ago. Did you enjoy that?

— Sure.

She bites the insides of her cheeks rhythmically, first the right one, then the left, back and forth, until she tastes blood.

— Which territory were you in? Do you remember the streets?

— I forget. *Please forgive me for lying, Jehovah, I just don't want to get anyone in trouble, in Jesus' name, Amen.*

— Did you two place any magazines that day?

Emily shrugs and looks at her feet. Her black shoes have scuffs on the toes.

— Your uncle hasn't filed his Service Report in a while, that's all.

— A couple back issues, I think.

— Is that right? Great. And you don't remember where? I didn't see you two at the service meeting that day, so we couldn't give you a territory.

— We did back calls.

Brother Wilde smiles and nods.

—That's great. I didn't know Brother Tyler had back calls. Did you help your uncle Witness to them?

Emily cringes, remembering *Pac-Man* and loud music and a table covered in beer bottles.

— A little bit.

— Did they have any kids your age to talk to? Maybe you showed them your favourite part of *My Book of Bible Stories*?

Emily likes "Daniel in the Lions' Pit" best. Even though he is good, the king has Daniel thrown into a dungeon of hungry lions, but God doesn't let any of them hurt him.

— No. It was just two guys.

Brother Wilde shifts in his chair and leans closer to Emily. She looks at him. His face is shiny and his eyes are too small for his head.

— Two men? Were they brothers?

— I don't know. Maybe.

Emily hadn't thought of that. Somehow she knew that Brother Wilde would think that was better.

— Probably they were brothers. I think they had to share a room, so they must be.

— They did? How do you know that, Emily?

Brother Wilde stands up but doesn't move the chair. Emily backs up a little bit. She can't tell him that she was playing video games instead of Witnessing to them. Brother Wilde would tell her dad and she'd get in big trouble.

— I had to go to the bathroom, and it was through the bedroom.

— I see. Brother Wilde nods.

— Out there at that trailer park, Emily? Is that where the two men live?

— Maybe. Emily doesn't want to lie any more than she already has.

— I think so.

Brother Wilde smiles and pats her shoulder. Emily flinches.

— Well, just remind your uncle to file his Service Reports when you see him. And tell him to get well soon.

Emily nods but feels like she's done or said something very wrong.

IN THE CAR ON WAY HOME, Emily is silent, but not because of her father's No Noise in the Car rule. She is reliving her conversation with Brother Wilde.

— You're awfully quiet, Emily. Don't tell me you're getting sick too. Emily's mother looks back at her over her shoulder.

— No.

— What's wrong then?

— Nothing. Emily stares out the window.

Her mom twists to face the back seat.

— Tell me what happened.

It's her fake, sing-song voice, the one for when Emily's upset or she's making fun of someone at the Hall.

— Nothing happened! Her shout startles even her. Emily is breaking all her father's Quiet Rules, but she doesn't care.

— It's not fair that you let Lenora stay home again!

How come you don't make her go? How come you don't make her do what she's supposed to do? You let everybody gossip and whisper about us!

— Emily! Be quiet!

Emily cries and pounds her fists on the car door, on the seats, on the windows, everywhere. Her father pulls over to the side of the road and her mom chants, "It's okay, don't yell, it's okay, don't cry" over and over without looking at her.

— I told you to simmer down!

Without even undoing his seat belt, her father reaches into the back seat and slaps her face. The world goes hot and dark. Her teeth rattle and she can't catch her breath. Her cheek stings. She wants to reach around his head from behind and gouge out his eyes with her fingernails.

— Are you okay, sweetie?

Sweetie. She's so phoney. Everybody she knows has become so fake, like they've each been replaced by a stranger.

Emily digs her nails into her arms as hard as she can and grinds her teeth the rest of the way home. Her father drives far faster than usual, and as soon as they're home, he strides into his den and slams the door. Emily's face still stings and she paces around the house, faster and faster, and can't make her blood stop buzzing and zipping through her veins.

Emily's mom pulls her into the bathroom and after she dabs Emily's red cheek with cold water, she tries again.

— What's really wrong, sweetie?

— Don't call me that! And I already told you!

Emily pushes her away and goes straight up to Lenora's room. Her door is locked.

— I know you're not sick. Open the door!

Lenora doesn't respond.

— You're a faker and a liar and God knows it and so does everybody else at the Hall! She pounds on the door again and again until she hears her sister's muffled voice.

— Go away.

— No! I'm not leaving until you tell me the truth!

Lenora turns on her stereo.

— I'm not lying for you anymore!

Emily screams and punches the door. The pain in her hand is even worse than when her father hit her, but somehow feels good. She sits in the hallway and hits the wood floor as hard as she can, over and over. She howls and hurls herself in front of Lenora's bedroom. She cries there, prone, for what feels like hours.

Lenora doesn't come to the door. No one tells her to stop or to go to her room. No one does anything. Emily's hand begins to swell and soon it is almost double its normal size.

In the empty kitchen, she takes an ice pack out of the freezer and places it on her knuckles. She hears the car start, then through the kitchen window, sees her father, alone, turn onto the highway and drive away.

25

▼

EMILY MISSES SCHOOL ON MONDAY and when she's back on Tuesday with a cast on, her classmates crowd around her, markers in hand, shouting questions and trying to be the first to sign it.

— What happened? How did you break it? How many bones are broken?

Emily shrugs. She can't tell them the truth; it's too embarrassing. It would be much more glamorous to fall from a tree's highest branch, or crash her bike into a motorcycle. If they find out what she really did, everyone will think she's even more of a freak. She bites her lip and responds.

— I fell.

— Calm down, class. Everyone will get a turn to sign Emily's cast.

Mr. Laurence smiles at her. She looks away, hating to be singled out; it's bad enough that she has to stand in the hallway every morning during the national anthem and miss Christmas assemblies. She cringes but dutifully holds out her arm for her classmates until it aches. There are lots of "Get well soon!" comments, and some of the girls draw flowers in orange and red and yellow. Some people just write their names in small, quick letters without speaking to her. Emily knows they don't really want to sign her cast, and they don't look at each other. One of the boys, Robbie, takes his time drawing some funny-looking blobs, then grins triumphantly.

— What is it? Emily lifts her left arm up and tries to peer at the underside of the cast.

— I can't tell what it's supposed to be.

Robbie smirks.

— It's what we learned in health class yesterday!

He laughs and runs back to his seat. Emily was absent for health class because she had to get her cast, but she has a pretty good idea what he means. Her mom had sat her down one night before bed and told her all about reproduction between a man and wife. Gross. Emily had just nodded and said okay even when she didn't understand everything, and both of them seemed glad to get the conversation over with as quickly as possible. She'll have to colour over Robbie's diagram before her parents or the teacher see it.

After geography is recess, and Emily is silently rehearsing the prayer she'll say about lying when Mr. Laurence comes over to her desk and asks her to stay in. He must have seen the dirty picture, and Emily will get detention for letting him draw such a thing on her cast, even though she couldn't have stopped him, even though it was Mr. Laurence's idea that everyone sign it in the first place. She's never had a detention before. She tugs her sleeve down but it doesn't reach far enough to cover Robbie's picture.

— How's your hand, Emily? Does it hurt a lot?

— Not really. Not as much as it did yesterday.

— Well, that's good. It'll be healed up and your cast will be off before you know it.

Emily nods. She stands in front of his desk, shifting her weight from foot to foot, wondering when he's going to mention the perverted drawing.

— Is everything okay at home, Emily?

Okay at home? What does that mean? It was the same as usual, not perfect, but normal. Normal for them, anyway.

— I guess so.

— You guess so? Mr. Laurence leans toward her.

— You're not sure?

— No. I mean, yes. It's okay. It's fine.

— Well, if there are any problems, if you ever need to talk to anyone besides your parents, just let me know. You can trust me.

Mr. Laurence pauses and looks at her, then at her hand, then back at her.

— How did you fall when you broke it, anyway?

Emily shrugs and pushes at a chair with her toe. There are pencil shavings on the floor.

— Outside. I was running and slipped on the ice and I think I fell on a rock. She looks up and Mr. Laurence smiles at her, but he looks sad at the same time. She doesn't know if he believes her.

— That must have hurt. I bet your parents were really worried.

Emily shrugs again. She doesn't tell Mr. Laurence that they didn't believe her when she said it was broken, and they didn't take her to the hospital until the next day, after she'd been up all night with pain careening through her hand like a chorus of shrieks.

— Well, keep in mind what I said. Now go enjoy what's left of recess.

AFTER SCHOOL, EMILY TRIES HARD not to think about the itch that has replaced most of the pain in her hand. She ignores the tingling under her cast as best she can, counting her steps as she paces across her bedroom to distract herself — she reaches a hundred before the itching subsides. She exhales in relief and looks at the clock; time to get ready for the meeting. Their father has already told Emily and Lenora that they are leaving early tonight, but didn't give them a reason when Emily asked.

— Because we are.

She stares into her closet and cannot decide between her plaid skirt and white blouse, or the blue sweater with the white diamond pattern across the front. She surveys the row of stuffed animals on her bed, even though she knows she is getting too old for dolls.

— What's that, Toaster? Emily leans closer to the grey bear.

— You like the white shirt best?

She pulls it from the closet, slides her arms through the sleeves, then tries to do up the top button. Her fingertips protrude from the cast but when she tries to use them, her knuckles ache and she fumbles and her fingers refuse to do what she tells them to. Her entire hand throbs. Doing her shirt up with one hand is going to take a long time, and she can already hear that her parents are downstairs and almost ready to leave.

— Good idea, Zig Zag. That's why you are lord over all the other animals — you're the smartest. The sweater will be much easier with Plaster Hand.

She pats him on the head, and because no one is watching, kisses him on his plastic-whiskery mouth. Emily wonders if it is wrong to use "lord" like that, since Jesus is the one true lord, but she knows there are regular lords too, small "l" lords who are leaders, but not in a spiritual way. Still, she would never let her dad hear her say something like that. He wouldn't understand. Except for the Bible, her dad's not particularly well-read.

She pulls the sweater overhead easily and tugs on her skirt. Then she looks with dismay at the tangle of tights in her sock drawer. It's too cold to go without; she'll have to get them on somehow. She pinches the sides of the leg and pushes her foot in and pulls up one side, then the other. It's very slow, awkward work and takes a long time just to get the right leg up to her knee.

— Emily! Hurry up! We're leaving in two minutes.

Her father sounds angry and impatient. It's taken far longer than two minutes just to get the tights partway on. She stands up, steps on one side of the tights and hops out of them. She considers asking her mother or Lenora for help, but the idea of them pulling her tights up around her flowered underwear makes her cringe in embarrassment. No way. Everyone will understand if she wears her nicest corduroy pants to the Hall instead — just this once. She gets them done up quickly, snatches up her purse and heads out of her room. At the doorway, she pauses, turns back, and quickly kisses Toaster and Zig Zag goodbye.

At the back door, her parents and sister put on their boots and coats. Emily still doesn't know why they have to leave twenty minutes early. Hardly anyone else will even be there yet, and it will be boring to sit and wait for the meeting to start without anyone to talk to.

— Emily! Get back up there and get a skirt on! What do you think you're doing?

Her father looks as confused as he does angry.

— I did. I mean, I tried. But I couldn't get the tights to work—

— No excuses! Just get properly dressed and hurry up.

Lenora snickers and rolls her eyes. Emily is relieved, and almost surprised, that she is going to the Hall tonight.

— Okay, but— Emily looks to her mother for support. Her mom ignores her, takes one last gulp from her coffee mug, and heads out to the cold car without them.

— Go!

Her father stands with his hands on his hips, expectant, until Emily turns and runs back upstairs.

She slams her bedroom door and tries not to let the burning tears slide out of her eyes. It isn't fair. No one will even help her since she got the cast — her parents said it's her own fault for having a temper tantrum and next time she'll think twice before hitting things. Jesus said to practise self-control, and her father made her memorize a verse from Psalms so she'd learn:

> Let anger alone and leave rage;
> Do not show yourself heated up only to do evil.
> For evildoers themselves will be cut off,
> But those hoping in Jehovah are the ones that
>   will possess the earth.

Emily grabs her longest skirt from her closet and puts that on instead. It's grey wool and itches her bare legs, but she has no other choice. She will just wear her boots into the Hall instead of changing into clean shoes and hope that no one notices that she doesn't have any tights on in the middle of winter.

26

▼

NO ONE SPEAKS DURING THE drive to the Hall. Emily shivers and twists in her seat as the rough wool scratches her legs. When they arrive, there are only a few other cars in the parking lot and they trudge through the gravely snow and inside. Everyone but Emily takes off their wet boots and changes into dry Hall shoes. Emily stomps the snow off as best she can and waits for the rest of them to finish. Her mom looks at her feet and before she can say anything, Emily tells her she forgot her shoes.

— It's no wonder, your father rushing us around for no reason at all. The meeting won't even start for another forty minutes.

The curtains are drawn across the window of the back room and they can't see who is in there. Emily's dad is nowhere to be seen. Is there a special meeting with her dad and the elders? She wonders if he is in trouble, and her stomach drops at the thought. No, she can't imagine her father doing something wrong.

Emily nearly forgets about her aching hand, but then the itching starts again under the edge of the cast. She decides not to ignore it this time, she doesn't care about self-control right now, and takes a pen from her purse. She shoves the end under the edge of the cast and scratches until it feels better. Lenora sits next to her, doodling in the margins of her *Awake!* magazine. Emily strains to see what she's writing but Lenora catches her and scribbles it out before she can read anything. The meeting in the back room goes on for almost twenty more minutes, as the main room fills up with brothers and sisters and kids and bags bursting with Bibles and *Watchtowers*.

Just then she spots Uncle Tyler in the doorway of the cloakroom. He sees her too, smiles and crooks his finger, motioning her over. She hops from her seat and into the aisle, just as her father walks up to their row.

— Where are you going?

— I'm going to see Uncle Tyler!

She scurries past him before he can tell her not to. He doesn't try to pull her back; Emily knows her father doesn't boss her around nearly as much when there are other brothers and sisters around.

In the cloakroom, her uncle hands her a plastic bag. She notices that he has tucked his curls under his shirt collar; he still hasn't gotten it cut.

— Here you go, kiddo. I heard about your busted hand. This should keep you occupied for a while.

He stands back while Emily opens the bag. Inside, there are six brand-new Trixie Belden books. Six! They're all ones she's never read, and not musty used copies either. Real ones, which must have come from the bookstore at the mall in the city. Emily is shocked; she's only ever gotten them one at a time from her mother — her father doesn't like her to read too many worldly books — and the rest from the school library, but they only have a few. Her eyes feel like they're pulsing out beams of sunlight and she can't stop smiling.

— Thank you! Wow, I've never had this many new ones at once before!

She smiles so wide it makes her face hurt. He holds up a hand to high-five her, which she does with her good hand.

— Congratulations on your first cast.

There is a rattle and screech as someone turns on the stage microphone.

— I'll sign it after the meeting, okay? Sounds like they're starting.

— Okay.

Emily rushes up the aisle in her big heavy boots with her bag of books. Her parents look at her when she sits down but they can't ask her any questions because Brother Wilde is at the podium beginning the prayer.

Emily tries to listen but she can't; she's too excited. During the meeting, she nudges the bag open a little with her foot, but it rustles too much and her father shushes her before she can make out all of the titles. She sits and squirms and fidgets and is elbowed by her father. She devises a plan. There is a small flashlight on a ledge in the porch, and she will snatch it on their way back inside when they get home. Then she can read in bed after the late meeting for as long as she wants, tucked under the blankets with her new books. She knows that no matter what strange or scary mess Trixie stumbles into, she will figure it out and fix it and make everything right again by the end.

Halfway through the meeting and after the second song, there is a break. The elder tells everyone to take up their purple copies of *Singing and Accompanying Yourselves with Music in Your Hearts* and turn to page twenty-nine. Emily grins. "Watch How We Walk" is her favourite, the most upbeat song, with a jaunty, bouncing piano score. Unlike the other slow, mournful songs, this one is actually fun to sing. Emily hops to her feet, then tunelessly — but for once with enthusiasm and volume — joins in.

> *Let's watch how we walk, and watch how we*
> > *talk*
> *That thus we may be alert and wise . . .*

As soon as the song is over, Emily smuggles her bag of books into the bathroom stall to look at them. As she waits for a free stall, Sister Bulchinsky waddles in and smiles.

— Hello, Emily. How are you tonight? How's your poor hand?

— Fine, thank you. Better. How are you? Emily knows to be polite; if she is not, her mother will find out.

— Oh, fine, fine. I see your whole family is together at the meeting tonight.

Sister Bulchinsky keeps talking from inside the stall.

— I take it Brother Tyler is over that cold he had last week?

Emily didn't know he had a cold. So much for *alert and wise.*

— I don't know. I guess so.

Sister Bulchinsky rattles open the door and smoothes her red floral dress, and Emily darts into the stall. She no longer tries to be quiet as she rustles open the plastic bag of mystery novels.

There are two she hasn't even heard of: *The Mystery of the Phantom Grasshopper* and *The Mystery of the Midnight Marauder*. She sits down and starts reading immediately, while other sisters and kids enter and leave the bathroom. The toilet in the stall next to her flushes several times before someone knocks on her door and jars Emily from her book. She clears her throat.

— Just a minute, please!

— You all right in there or what?

It's Lenora.

— Almost done. Emily flushes the toilet to muffle the sound of her putting the books back into the plastic bag, then she tries to shove the entire bundle into her purse. They bulge out, and she holds her bag behind her. She unlocks the door and comes out to where Lenora waits, smirking, her hand on her right hip.

— What were you doing in there? Lines of coke?

Emily gasps and swivels her head to make sure they're alone, that no one else heard her say something like that. Talking about drugs is only a few steps away from doing them, and that's why the elders say it's best to avoid talking to worldly teenagers as much as possible.

Lenora just laughs and fixes her hair in the mirror, tugging it down over the shaved patches. It looks almost normal, except for the platinum colour.

— Hurry up, they're about to start again. Something's up too: all the elders were having another secret meeting in the back room during the break. Somebody's in trouble.

Lenora sounds gleeful. Emily straightens her skirt and

they hurry up the aisle as Brother Davies starts the second half of the meeting.

Back at their seats, their father is rigid in his chair and their mother slumps on her right arm, leaning and dozing against the armrest. She jolts awake with an elbow from Lenora, who then giggles and whispers, "That'll teach her for getting mad at us when we fall asleep!" Lenora bites her lip and stares fixedly ahead. Emily tries not to laugh. It's time for the *Watchtower* article talk, which on Thursday nights often goes beyond the meeting's end at 9:30. Emily has forgotten what it's supposed to be about this time.

She pretends to take notes during the talk but actually plays one of her counting games, making a small chart in her notebook: how many blue shirts or dresses, how many white, how many plaid, how many yellow. It passes the time and no one can tell because she is mostly still and staring straight ahead. She tries to play without turning her head at all, which is difficult. Her parents, she assumes, will think her industrious, which is one of her new favourite words.

Emily is distracted from her game as Brother Davies pauses and shuffles his feet and coughs onstage. There are some mumbles from within the rows of the congregation. He isn't supposed to be up next. He grasps both sides of the podium as though holding himself up, and sighs like a deflating balloon. Dark circles ring his eyes and he clears his throat several times, then straightens some papers on the podium. He looks forward and across the congregation, over their heads, and stares at something on the back wall. The curious nudging and neck-craning subsides and the congregation stills as though a breeze has ruffled them, then disappeared. No one whispers or fidgets or moves at all. Even the babies and toddlers are quiet.

— Brothers and sisters . . . His voice is uncharacteristi-
cally low and even, as if he is about to soothe someone
distraught.

Emily has experienced several kinds of silences. Some
are relaxing, like when Lenora has gone out, and Emily
is in the bathtub, still as can be, ears underwater. Then
there are these silences at the Hall, when an elder asks a
question and no one puts their hand up, or when he mentions wrongdoing. Then everyone wonders if it is them,
or who is the unrepentant one, and twists their necks to
see who is red-faced and squirming; the guiltiest will look
the most uncomfortable. This silence is more frightening.
Emily thinks that if she so much as moves, it will be her
that Brother Davies is talking about. And she knows that
everyone else feels the same way.

— It is with great pain and sorrow that I am delivering
this talk tonight. It is always a sad time when a fellow
brother or sister strays from God's ways and follows
Satan. It is a darkness and a blight upon the entire congregation when someone must be removed from our midst.
But it's essential in order to keep our congregation clean
and beyond reproach.

The murmurs surge again, and Emily feels like she's
being pulled below waves by an undertow. The air shifts
and swirls and makes her dizzy as everyone tries to figure
out who is about to be disfellowshipped, and for what.
The air in the Hall feels charged, stretched, as if there are
thousands of tiny rubber bands above them, poised to
snap. Emily is still afraid to move. If she shifts the wrong
way in her seat, even a little bit, everyone will think she
is the guilty one — they will find out about her worldly
books, and she will be removed. Hardly moving her head,
she braves a sidelong glance at Lenora. Her face is blank,

unreadable, and she doesn't fidget or write notes or any-thing. She grips her armrests so tightly that her knuckles strain white against her skin.

— There is always a scriptural reason behind the deci-sion to disfellowship a brother or sister, and this case is no different.

Brother Davies lectures on cleanliness, on being vigi-lant against temptation and bad association, on abstaining from worldly influences, particularly, he drones, "from those of the flesh." The murmurs stop at the word "flesh." Many brothers and sisters now openly turn around and survey the room, stretching out of their seats for a better view of their fellow Witnesses, as though it is a race to identify the unclean one. The meeting is already twenty minutes past its usual length.

Brother Davies goes on to discuss the sanctity of marriage, how Jehovah God created marriage for child-rearing, and that only within that covenant between one man and one woman should sexual activity take place.

Someone must have committed adultery. That was the only other time Emily had ever heard a sermon like this, when Brother Carson was publicly reproved for cheating. Soon after, he divorced his wife, and never came back to the Hall. Sister Carson now takes care of their five chubby kids by herself, and the other sisters make sure that there is someone to help her with them all when she goes out door to door. Emily wonders if she brings all five with her to every house, squirming and squealing and wriggling like piglets.

— The scriptural basis for this disfellowshipping is found in First Corinthians, where the Holy Bible discusses *unnatural acts*.

He cites the chapter and verse, then reads aloud.

— 'Do you not know that unrighteous persons will not inherit God's kingdom? Do not be misled. Neither fornicators, nor idolaters, nor adulterers, nor men kept for unnatural purposes, nor men who lie with men, nor thieves, nor greedy persons, nor drunkards, nor revilers, nor extortioners will inherit God's kingdom.'

— That's right, brothers and sisters. 'Nor men who lie with men.' This most unnatural sin is very serious. Those tempted by homosexual thoughts must fight against them, as hard against Satan as they can.

A murmur ripples through the congregation and seems to stop at Emily's family.

— So for unnatural acts, and conduct unbecoming a Christian, I hereby disfellowship Tyler Golden.

Something huge and heavy pushes against Emily's chest and she cannot breathe. Her entire body stiffens and her throat feels blocked. Colours smear around her and everything blurs into one seething mass.

— Let us now pray for his repentance and his strength to ward off Satan.

Emily clutches her bag of Trixie Belden books to her chest. She can feel the smug eyes of all the other brothers and sisters fixed on their row. She's hot and the room spins. She lets her hair fall over her face as she instinctively bows her head and closes her eyes. She doesn't hear a word of the prayer.

Emily tries to exhale, and the floor drops away, as though she is falling into a gaping canyon. She grips the armrests on her chair and glances at Lenora. She isn't praying. Her eyes are open and she looks straight ahead. Emily can't tell what she's thinking from the look on her face; it's one she's never seen before. Her jaws seem frozen, her mouth slightly open, and she is leaning forward, as though about to say something. Uncle Tyler is across the aisle from them, his head down, his face and neck blood-red and his eyes closed tightly.

The Hall spins around and around and it won't stop and Emily's mouth is flooded with spit and her stomach clenches like there's a giant fist in it and her mouth opens to let it out and before she can do anything about it, she throws up all over the floor. A yellowish pool seeps into the carpet and some has splashed onto her shoes. Her eyes burn and stream and there is a horrible sour taste in her mouth.

Brother Davies ends his prayer with a sombre "In Jesus' name, Amen," but Emily has heard none of it. The stench must be everywhere and her face feels hot and blotchy and people have started to twist around and cough and wrinkle their noses and stare at her.

Ahead of them, Sister Bulchinsky cranes around to look at them. She meets Emily's gaze and shakes her head sadly. Emily narrows her eyes, gives her the meanest look she can muster, and without thinking, bares her teeth. Sister Bulchinsky jolts back, covers her mouth, and turns back to face the front.

Emily feels her mom shake beside her. She is afraid to look. She is afraid to stand as the final song is beginning. She avoids the mess in front of her and moves closer to Lenora, who doesn't pull away. Emily doesn't know where to look or what to do and the last thing she wants to do is sing. Everyone else shuffles to their feet and flips open their songbooks.

Emily shakes her head over and over again and digs her fingernails into her palms. She's still falling, and may never stop.

Her mom blows her nose and doesn't stand. Her dad

puts his arm around her and she pulls away, then jumps up and runs down the aisle and out of the Kingdom Hall. Emily and Lenora stand rigid and frozen but neither of them sings. Emily stares down at the notes and lines but they twist and writhe like snakes.

27

▼

IT WAS FALL. THE COOL air was restless, swirling and darting and filling every corner of the city with its deep, mossy scent of decay. I let it flit across the back of my neck and leave a trail of goosebumps and shivers behind.

I was at the gym that had been converted from a warehouse. I opened the main doors and inside, thick, heavy air rushed to greet me. It was dense with sweat and body heat, echoes of coaches' shouts and tumblers' thuds, and clouds of chalk dust that rose like spectres from the hands of acrobats.

Deciding whether or not to come here was agony. After the initial thrill of finding such a place — of *Circus World* dreams of funambulism — began to wear off, my insecurities rushed in and took over. I paced and debated for days: should I go, should I forget it, should I do it, could I do it, was I stupid, would I fail, was it the right thing to do? Again, I longed for the days when making decisions was simpler, when I was a kid — a precise list of what was allowed and what was forbidden.

Don't be such a chicken.

Would you do it?

If I want something, I do it. I'm not a wimp.

Fine. I'll try it. But don't laugh at me.

So I went. The leaves were falling and I was learning to walk on air. To disappear into memory. Avoid another day of disaster.

That's what I told myself, anyway. What I had actually done, against my better judgement, was sign up for Janice's tightrope walking class.

At my fourth class, I changed out of my black boots and into the soft-soled shoes and took my place by the half-metre practice wire, not nearly as thin as the high and distant real thing. I had yet to progress from there; it was all more difficult than I had expected, and contrary to Janice's optimistic assumptions, I lacked natural balance and grace. After every session, my thighs and calves ached and felt swollen and heavy and didn't cooperate with the most basic of movements. Still, I was addicted to the exotic atmosphere and adrenaline rush of taking one more step on the cord without falling.

As I began my warm-up stretches, bending at the waist over my legs, I realized what I liked most about my tightrope lessons: they kept me from thinking. I focused with a cold intensity on my body — the precise positioning of my feet, toes pointed, and spine straight, eyes looking only straight ahead, one foot in front of the other. No guilt. No memories. No thoughts. Just focus. Nothing else.

— Okay, are you ready for today?

Janice always had a lot of energy and enthusiasm and her blond ponytail always bounced in time to whatever she said.

— Sure.

I turned and put one foot onto the wire.

— Hold on, hold on.

Janice led me back to where I had been standing on the mat.

— We're going to try something else for a while today.

— Okay.

I tried not to let disappointment flood my face. Was I not improving at all? Was I not even good enough to train on the lowest wire?

— Stand straight. And don't move.

I aligned my spine as best I could and stood still. She said nothing, and I was determined not to speak first. Two young girls swung from their knees overhead on the trapeze as other students practised their flips and somersaults and landings. The room hummed with kinetic excitement. I felt conspicuous in my immobility.

— Now close your eyes. Don't open them until I tell you to.

It was harder to keep from thinking when you weren't moving. The sounds of the gymnasium eddied around me and I could no longer tell which direction they came from. It all seemed much louder than usual. Then someone laughed, and though it sounded far away, it was familiar, deep and free but tinged with a hint of malice. I felt like I was falling. My left foot jutted out and my right compensated as my eyes flew open. I looked around, trying to see into every corner of the huge room at once. I touched the bracelet around my left wrist. I didn't see her.

— Again!

I squinted, remembering that I was there with Janice, my instructor.

— What?

— Try to do it again.

She sighed and even her hair seemed to list with disappointment.

— Focus. Work on your balance. The longer you can stand still in one place without swaying or stumbling, the closer you'll be to getting up on the wire.

I looked only at the blue mat, smudged with grey. Pathetic. I couldn't even stand still properly.

— Once you can stay perfectly still for a while, try it on one foot. Do that for the rest of this session, and don't touch the wire.

Janice turned and walked away. I shrugged, shook my limbs out like I had seen others in the gym do, and closed my eyes again.

I felt like I was being punished. Maybe I was.

28

▼

ON THE WAY HOME FROM the meeting, her father drives too fast and her mom stares out the window with her arms wrapped around herself. Lenora turns the pages of the *Awake!* magazine over and over, while Emily picks at the hangnails on her thumbs until they bleed. Lenora doesn't even bother to swat her hands or tell her stop.

— Slow down, Jim.

Her mom peers out the window and Emily follows her gaze. Dark, skeletal trees shiver against the blue-black sky and the stars hide behind the thick, heavy night-clouds.

Her dad doesn't respond, and doesn't slow down. Bits of the road sparkle in the headlights and Emily tries to think this is beautiful, like a street of tiny diamonds, but she can't. It just looks sharp and cold and mean.

Lenora sighs and shifts in her seat and closes the magazine, then her eyes. Emily wonders if she is going to sleep the rest of the way home. How could she possibly relax and rest and dream after this? Doesn't she care that everything is getting smashed up into little pieces and mixed together and no one will ever be able to figure out how to put it back properly again? Doesn't she care about anything anymore? Emily's mouth and throat are hot and dry and all she can taste is sour and her stomach clenches and unclenches desperately, like a heart, but there is nothing left to throw up.

Then Lenora starts to hum — loudly and off-key — the song they sang in the meeting, the happy one, the only one that isn't boring, still with her eyes scrunched closed; over and over again as loud as she can she hums "Watch How We Walk" and no one tells her to stop.

At the same time that the car begins to slide, Emily notices that her bloodied thumbs have dripped all over her skirt in red smeary blotches. There is a bend in the road and the car is going faster and faster and not slowing down at all. Her first thought is that her mom is going to be mad she stained her skirt, and her second is that they're about to be in a car accident. Every pore on her skin prickles, even the ones under her cast, and she can suddenly feel each individual hair on her head and they tingle like they're all alive. Lenora has stopped humming and outside it's black and the headlights streak through the night as they flail all over the road, and her dad isn't driving the car properly at all. Her mom yells, "Jim! Jim! Jim! Stop it!" and he twists the steering wheel one way and then the other and still they slide into the other lane. The back end of the car swerves forward and they are going backwards and sideways and Emily can just make out the tree that her side is heading straight for, closer and closer and she's going to be the one smashed against it, and why doesn't her dad make the car go straight? Then they spin in a circle and Emily grabs the door and they slide more slowly now, until they are facing the right way again. A truck comes toward them and passes and doesn't hit them. They are almost stopped at the side of the road, and her dad pulls into someone else's driveway. They all just sit there, breathing and breathing, and not saying anything.

Their dad clutches the steering wheel and lays his head against his arms and prays. Emily leans forward to make out the words and that's when she realizes he's not praying. He's chanting. He's droning the same phrase over and over again: *never again, never again, never again, never again, never again, never again.*

Emily's throat squeezes shut and so do her eyes, and though she tries not to, she cries a little. She's pretty sure no one noticed, as all four of them now stare out their respective windows and don't dare look at each other.

After a long while like this, her dad starts the car again and they go home, very slowly, and when they get out of the car, Emily's legs don't work very well; they wobble and shake and she falls into the snow next to the car. Lenora pulls her up but says nothing. There isn't anything to say. Emily stands in the snow, staring into the dark sky, watching for something to appear — a sign, stars, the beginning of Armageddon, anything.

Inside, their mom tells them to brush their teeth and go to bed.

— What? Now?

Lenora stands in the middle of the living room and throws her gloves against the back door.

— So we're just going to pretend that the meeting

didn't happen at all? That everything is totally normal? That Dad didn't almost kill us on the way home?

No one responds, and she stomps upstairs and slams the door to her room.

Emily's hands shake and she doesn't know where to go in her own house. After scrubbing and spitting the bile taste from her mouth, she tiptoes back into the living room, picks up a brown velvet-covered pillow from the couch, then puts it back down again. The boots by the back door are jumbled and so she arranges them neatly into two rows of pairs. Her parents are in the kitchen, where her mom slams cupboard doors and bangs her coffee cup hard onto the table. Emily goes upstairs.

The phone rings and rings and no one answers it.

Unchristian conduct. Unnatural acts. Men who lie with men. If her parents start to talk about the meeting or discuss what happened, she wants to be able to hear them, so she drags her blankets and pillow over to her bedroom door and leaves it partway open. She is silent and unmoving, her cast heavy and hard against her chest. Maybe if she is quiet enough, obedient enough, and prays enough, it will make up for everyone else in her family and things will go back to how they used to be.

Please Jehovah, help us to be strong and not sin anymore. Please help Lenora be good so she doesn't get disfellowshipped too, and make Uncle Tyler be repentant for whatever it was that he did.

Her parents start to shout in the kitchen. Part of her wants to get as far away as possible from them when they fight, part of her wants to hear everything they say, and another part wants to leap in between them and kick and scream until they stop.

— So who was it, then? Who opened their big mouth?

Her father doesn't respond.

— Answer me! Was it you?

— It's not that simple, Viv.

— It's very simple! It's the simplest thing I've ever heard — either you ratted out my brother, or you didn't. Which is it?

Emily's heart contracts. Ratted him out for what? She crawls out from under her covers and down the hall to hear them better, then inches down the stairs, along the side where they creak less. So far no one seems to have heard her, so she shuffles along the carpet toward the kitchen, then peeks around the doorway. Her mother's face is bright red, and her arms are rigid at her sides like baseball bats. Her father's head is in his hands on the kitchen table.

— Don't give me that bull! Don't act all sorry now!

Her mom's voice deepens into a near-whisper that Emily finds far more frightening than a shout.

— You sacrificed my brother to get in good with the Kingdom Hall bigwigs. You told them what they wanted to hear for your own greedy reasons. You'll do anything to become a damn elder — even betray your own family!

He raises his head and finally looks at her. Emily ducks back behind the doorway before they see her. Her father sighs deeply.

— That's not true and you know it. It wasn't me. But people know about him, Viv, and maybe this is the best way to get him to come to his senses.

— Come to his senses?! How? By being abandoned by everyone he knows? Being treated like a leper? By thinking that his own sister is ashamed of him? Or that my sanctimonious husband tattled to the elders?

— He needs to have more faith in God, to not be tempted by this wicked system—

— Oh, that's just great! The same JW clichés he hears every Sunday morning and every Thursday night. Lot of good that's done so far.

— Just calm down! Lower your voice!

— Don't tell me what to do.

— I didn't tell them anything, Viv. Someone must have seen him do something.

— What are you talking about?

The chair scrapes and she hears her mother sit down at the table too. They don't say anything for a while. Her father sighs again.

— Someone must have seen him . . . you know . . . with someone he shouldn't have been seen with.

Emily hears footsteps on the stairs and dashes into the bathroom before Lenora can catch her listening in on their parents.

— Where do you think you're going? It's nearly midnight!

Emily flushes the toilet and comes into the kitchen with everyone else.

Lenora wears black leggings and a big black cardigan with safety pins down the front instead of buttons. Her earrings don't match; one is a big silver lizard, and one is a small black hoop. No one says anything to Emily, who stands in the doorway picking her hangnails raw. Lenora pours herself a glass of orange juice, leans against the counter, and downs it one gulp. She belches loudly and grins.

— Excuse yourself, Lenora.

— Yeah, don't be a pig!

— Keep quiet, Emily.

As usual, Lenora smirks.

— Well, excuse me! Yes, it's very important to maintain appearances around here, isn't it?

Emily sits on the floor in a corner and folds her hands in her lap, as best she can with the heavy cast.

Please Jehovah God, make them stop fighting, and make Lenora be good, so no one else gets in trouble—

— Well, isn't it? I mean, we wouldn't anyone to think we weren't the perfect model JW family, now would we? No, no, couldn't have that. Comb your hair, dress all prim, smile politely, knock on doors, sit still at the meetings, tell the elders what they want to hear — that's what it's all about isn't it?

Their mom gets up and starts to wash the few dirty dishes. The window above the sink steams up and the kitchen smells of fake lemons.

I promise I will not complain about going out in service when it's cold, and I will Witness to kids at school, and always listen at the meetings, just please make my family behave—

Lenora slouches against the cupboards, her elbows resting on the counter, her ankles crossed, the empty glass in her right hand.

Their father hasn't moved from his chair at the table.

— That's enough, Lenora.

She ignores him.

— So what were you guys talking about just now, anyway? How Uncle Tyler's a fag?

Emily's father leaps up from the table, toppling over his chair, at the same time that her mom pulls her wet hands from the suds and pulls back her arm. She smacks Lenora across her face. Lenora stumbles against the refrigerator. The juice glass smashes. She covers her nose with both hands but Emily sees the trickles of blood down her sister's chin. Her father stands in the middle of the kitchen, opening and closing his hands.

Lenora runs from the room and upstairs. Her mother stares at the spot where Lenora, moments before, had stood in defiance.

In Jesus' name, Amen.

Emily doesn't know what to do. She walks to the doorway to follow Lenora, then turns back and paces the kitchen five times. Her parents stand still, as though immobilized. Finally, Emily hauls the broom and dustpan from the closet under the stairs and begins to sweep the broken glass from the floor.

— Thank you, Emily. Her father sighs, as though exhausted.

— Give me that. Her mom snatches the broom from her.

— You're making it worse.

Upstairs, Lenora opens and slams shut drawers in her room. Emily wants to see if she's okay, if her nose has stopped bleeding, but she's scared to do or say the wrong thing. She's scared to move. The three of them stand, rigid and immobile, staring at the floor or the wall, but not at each other.

Lenora's footsteps crash down the stairs and snap them out of their paralysis. Emily backs out of the kitchen and into the living room, where she straightens the cushions on the sofa and then stands in front of the television, unsure if she should turn it on or not. As her parents start to yell again, demanding where Lenora is going, Emily pulls the On knob and cranks the volume on a late-night newscast. People far away sob and wring their hands. A massive earthquake has destroyed a town. A little boy, wearing just a diaper, cries alone on a dirt road, amid smashed houses and crushed cars.

The Last Days.

Lenora stomps to the back door. She pulls on her big black boots and furiously laces them up. She wears a leather jacket Emily has never seen before; it's black and the sleeves are too long, and there's a big red letter A with a circle around it painted on the back. Emily doesn't know where she got it; their parents would never buy that for her.

As she bolts from the house, Lenora grabs one of their father's huge old camping backpacks from a cluttered corner of the back porch. Emily wonders how long she's had it waiting there, and what she packed in it. It doesn't even look half full. Lenora tugs it onto her back and runs down the driveway toward the road. No one tries to stop her. She's a black blur zigzagging across the white snow. Emily is about to close the door behind her and right the boots Lenora has toppled, but she doesn't. Without even thinking, she grabs her coat and boots and follows her.

29

▼

THE MOON IS BRIGHT AND round and white like a plate and the stars are back out, pricking the sky above her. Emily prays as she trails her sister: *Please Jehovah, don't let me lose Lenora, I have to be vigilant and watch over her, please give me the strength to keep up with her, I have to, please God, please, and forgive all my sins, please, I promise to be better, please.*

Her lungs burn as she stumbles quickly through the snow along the cold, quiet road. *Please God, please,* she chants, eyes half shut, panting, *please, please, please,* until it is a mantra. She nearly forgets to say *in Jesus' name, Amen.*

There are few cars on the road this late, but when she hears one coming she ducks behind a tree or crouches in the iced-over ditch until it passes. Her furious parents will come after them soon, if they haven't already. If they get caught, they must be together. She has to protect Lenora, though she isn't sure from what. All she knows is that ever since the meeting tonight, since Brother Wilde's horrible announcement, her entire body has been tense and cramped with pain. She feels like if she can keep Lenora in sight, everything will be okay, and when they get back home, their parents will explain that it was all just a big mistake, a misunderstanding, that nothing is wrong with Uncle Tyler, that he is not disfellowshipped after all and can still be in their family.

Please God, please, make it all be a misunderstanding. I promise I'll never complain or disobey again. Please.

Lenora is still striding a couple hundred feet ahead of her. Emily knows that if she stops moving, if she loses sight of her, things will become even worse. The wind gusts and the snow lifts from the ground around her in spirals. Emily shivers and tries not to be scared. Other than the crunching of her feet in the snow, the night is quiet and she focuses on the rhythm of step, *please*, step, *please*, step, *please*, but then a dog barks and it sounds big and close, and he's going to chase her and knock her down with his big paws and tear her throat open with his razor teeth, and her heart lurches and she doesn't know what to do. Her skin flushes hot even though she is cold and she shudders, stippled with goosebumps, especially across the back of her neck. The dog barks again, he must be nearly on top of her now, and though she knows she shouldn't, she runs. She runs faster than she ever has, and her lungs burn hotter and still she mutters *please please please please,* knowing that a huge, snarling German shepherd is snapping his drool-filled jaws at her boots, and will tear her apart like the wolves in the book of Jeremiah.

When the cramps in her sides are so sharp she can

hardly move, she slows and looks behind her. Nothing. The bark is distant and faint. She is close to town now. Lenora is still ahead of her but much closer, so she jumps behind a hedge as her sister slows almost to a standstill and digs into her coat pocket.

She stops at a phone booth and makes a call. Emily sneaks closer, hiding behind a parked car, but is too far away to hear. Lenora hangs up quickly, leaves the booth, and turns down a side street. Emily waits at the end of the block so as not to get too close, and peers around the corner. Lenora is sitting on a bench near Emily's school, the backpack leaning against her feet. There is a street-light over her like a spotlight in a play, as though her sister is the star. Emily stays crouched behind a pickup truck, watching, waiting, knowing that as long as she is there, nothing can happen to Lenora.

Please please please please. Please God, Jehovah, don't let anything else bad happen.

Lenora touches her nose gingerly and cringes. Emily touches the bridge of her nose too, and makes the same face.

Turn the other cheek.

Lenora didn't even cry when she got hit.

She must be waiting for whoever she called from the payphone. Emily knows it is a worldly person, and her stomach twists again.

Please God, I hope you're listening, I'm sorry for everything. I'm sorry that Lenora said that stuff about Uncle Tyler and I'm sorry—

Emily wipes her runny nose and drags her coat sleeve across her wet, blurred eyes.

Please God, I'm sorry, I ruined everything. It should be me that gets in trouble, not everybody else. Please, someday, please forgive me.

A long brown car pulls up to the bench and idles. A tall boy in a black bomber jacket gets out, loud music seeps into the night, and he waves to the driver, who squeals his tires and jolts away. It's Theo. He sits down next to Lenora and she leans against him. She rests her head on his shoulder. Emily gnaws on the inside of her cheek.

Please Jehovah God, please make them be good, please help them do what's right so they aren't killed at Armageddon—

Lenora leans up toward his face, puts one hand on the back of his neck, and kisses him. They kiss for what seems like an hour. Emily feels her stomach flip over a few times, but she can't look away. She shivers on the hard, icy ground, her hands shoved deep in her pockets.

Please make them stop, I promise I'll be good for the rest of my life, if you just make them stop—

And finally they do. Theo helps Lenora from the bench and they walk down the street. Emily doesn't know what to do. Anyone could see them, anyone from the Hall could drive by and call their parents, or their parents themselves could be here at any time, and just like that, her sister could be called before a Judicial Committee. They would probably bring their father in too, and the elders, and Lenora would be forced to confess every last detail to them. They could even disfellowship her. Emily is pretty sure what she's doing is *fornication* and there aren't many things worse than that.

Emily follows them in the dark for a few more blocks to a park. More kissing, this time for even longer. Emily, who didn't think to grab her mittens, is blowing on her frigid hands, half hiding behind a slide.

Despite the cold, Theo unzips Lenora's coat and walks her backwards until she's leaning against a tree. He pushes himself against her and Lenora wraps her arms around his waist. His hands are inside her jacket.

Emily starts, then stops. Should she pretend she just found them and yell? Her sister would be furious, both at being interrupted and at getting caught, and would be ruthless. But she can't let her keep going, she can't let her get in trouble.

Please please please, I don't know what to do, I really don't—

And then they seem to stop on their own. Lenora pushes him away a little, and Emily can't hear what they're saying. They stand there and talk for a while. Theo frowns and leans toward her, then he steps back a few paces, about to walk away, then turns and comes back. It looks like he's asking her a question. Lenora shrugs, then looks down and rubs her forehead. Theo just stands in front of her, hands on his hips, waiting for her to say or do something, and neither of them seems to know what.

After a long impasse, Lenora looks up at Theo and shakes her head and says something, then scrunches her eyes shut. Theo stumbles back and nearly trips, then rights himself. He shouts but the words swirl in the cold wind that rushes across the park, as though dragging their argument far away so that no one has to hear it. Then they're both yelling at once and the only words that Emily can make out is Lenora's choked, "It's all your fault!"

Then Theo really does stomp off, walking at first, then breaking into a jog across the far end of the park, through the arc of one of the streetlights and into the dark. As Emily watches him disappear, a car rounds the corner toward the park entrance, too quickly for her to hide, and the driver brakes hard and leans on the horn. It's as though a hole's been torn through the night.

— Emily Morrow! her mother shouts.

— Get in the car — now!

Emily jumps from behind the slide. She doesn't look back. They are caught. She walks slowly through the snow to the car and gets in the back seat, as her mother yells, seemingly unconcerned that lights in nearby houses have begun to blink on.

— Are you crazy?! Walking into town by yourself at midnight — anything could have happened to you!

Emily looks down.

Please please please please God, let Lenora be okay.

— Where's your sister?

Emily looks at her father and then into the park, where she now sees no one at all.

— Emily! I asked you a question: Do you know where your sister is?

She shakes her head and doesn't look at either of her parents. She doesn't even bother to ask Jehovah for forgiveness this time. Her dad puts the car in park, gets out, and strides through the park, calling Lenora's name. He comes back alone. Her mother is silent and squints through the window as they drive home. Emily doesn't even bother to wipe her dripping nose. She is suddenly more exhausted than she has ever been before.

30

▼

TEN IS A PERFECT NUMBER. Divisible, easily fractured into equal shards. Ten is a milestone, commemorated with tin or aluminium. Tin, the metal that resists corrosion, that which preserves. Aluminium, lightweight, a good conductor. My sister — always silvery and fluttering out of sight.

Anxiety rattled my vision and constricted my throat; I would see Lenora on the streets, out of the corner of my eye, but when I caught up to her, panting and flustered, she would turn into a scowling stranger. The worst part was that I knew I was being irrational, but I didn't try to stop. I let myself slip into the world where reality and memory overlapped and shimmered like the metallic glint of the hottest summer afternoon.

The day that threw off my routine entirely was the windiest I'd ever seen in the city. Snarls of air tore the branches from trees and tossed them onto sidewalks. Pedestrians bent forward, shielding their faces with their forearms. Window casings howled like vengeful, too-near wolves. Doors rattled but when I opened them, no one was there.

First, I cleaned my apartment. The hall closet was full of every chemical disinfectant and cleanser available — bottles for windows, for bathtubs, for floors, for dust, for dishes, something to kill every household germ, imagined or otherwise. The air in my apartment burned my eyes, and always smelled synthetic. This time, unfortunately, sterilizing my place didn't make me feel any better.

Next I decided to make lunch. I wasn't hungry, but couldn't remember the last time I had eaten. I'd defrosted some chicken the night before and knew never to leave it uncooked for long. I slid the pan into the oven and closed the door. Then I dragged a chair into the hallway beneath the smoke detector and removed its batteries.

While my chicken quarter cooked, I opened the small blinds to let in some light. I stood on my toes and peered outside. Twigs were scattered in the snow and a woman hunched forward as her useless umbrella bent upward. Her hat flew off and she turned to chase it. A car swerved to miss her and its horn sounded distant.

My place lacked light; shadows would hover and parry, as though amorphous shapes constantly darted around me. It set me on edge. Often I'd see something hiding in a dim corner, but when I jerked my head, everything would be still.

I straightened the magazines on the coffee table and the books on the shelves, and suddenly smelled smoke.

Grey curled from the oven and swirled upward like a mist. I snatched the potholders. The chicken was charred, almost entirely black, and I set it on top of the stove to cool. I opened the two small windows to air the place out. Cold whipped in and rustled the pages of the magazines. I shivered and wrapped my arms around myself, but it didn't help.

The chicken cooled and I scraped away the blackened layer and inspected it.

Perfect.

After I ate, I decided to go out and buy some groceries, since I had no milk or bananas and my last bit of bread was fringed with green fur. The temperature had plummeted when the wind began, and the slush that had melted was frozen into a varnish of ice, thick over the sidewalks. The sun glared down at me from the sky, and up at me from ground. It hurt my forehead. My scarf whipped around me and my eyes streamed. I squinted my way to the grocery store, counting, purely out of habit, the three hundred footsteps per city block.

I bought more than I had intended, not just milk and bread but cans of beans and a big bag of rice, some new kind of energy bars with ginseng and coated in chocolate, and a dozen eggs. The bags were heavy and it was lunch hour for other people and so the streets were crowded. I had two bags in one hand and one in the other, and every hundred steps I switched so my arms wouldn't get too sore. I was halfway home when I swung the heaviest bag from my right hand to my left and hit a woman in a fur coat in the leg.

— Watch where you're going! She glared at me through what looked to be expensive sunglasses.

— Sorry.

I tried to balance my groceries and ease the burning in my arms. Then a vicious gust of wind shoved me, and my heel slid on a patch of ice. My legs slid and buckled and I fell. My tailbone hit the sidewalk first. It felt like being stabbed in the spine, and the white hot pain jolted up to my neck. I couldn't move. My groceries were scattered on the sidewalk, the eggs were broken, and I couldn't help it, I just gave up. I sat on the icy concrete amid oozing yolks and grains of rice, unable and unwilling to bother moving, while busy people huffed and surged past me as though I'd deliberately blocked their way.

— You all right?

A tall guy in a black leather jacket loomed over me, blocking the sun and covering me in shadow. He extended a gloved hand. I looked at the groceries strewn around me. It looked as though there had been an earthquake that had affected only me. I cried harder and still couldn't get up. He withdrew his hand, squatted down, and put my fruit and vegetables and cans and boxes back into the bags. He tried, unsuccessfully, to pull me up.

— I suggest you leave the eggs behind.

He smiled and pushed his dark glasses up onto his head. That face.

Is it him? Is it?

Yes. Don't let him get away.

— Are you okay?

He cocked his head and glanced around nervously, then looked at me again.

We stared at each other on the sidewalk. I didn't know if he recognized me. The last time he saw me, I was only ten years old. Instinctively, I closed my eyes and fingered my bracelet, then ran my cold hand over my forearm. *53235.*

Deuteronomy 32:35 —

Vengeance is mine, and retribution.
At the appointed time their foot will move
unsteadily,
For the day of their disaster is near . . .

— Sorry, did you say something?
He leaned in closer and I opened my eyes.
I shook. I raised one of my arms and it felt like it was attached to a concrete block. Slowly, I pointed at him.
— I know who you are.
He took a step back from me.
— I don't think so.
— Don't lie to me!
He shook his head and handed me back my shopping bags. I hadn't meant to be loud, but I must have been, since he was walking away and other people stared or went wide around me.
At the curb he hailed a taxi.
— Wait!
I shouted, dropped my bags again, and waved my arms. I'd found him and lost him again all in the same five minutes. Finally, I could move again, but it was too late.
A single piece of red paper fluttered to the icy pavement as he slammed the door and zoomed away. I ran to the curb and snatched the flyer before it blew into the eddies of the cold afternoon.

31

▼

LENORA DOESN'T COME HOME THAT night, and Emily, overtired, sleeps in fragments, waking up at every sound, listening for the door to creak open and her sister to sneak back into her bedroom, but instead she hears only her parents' low murmurs and the occasional clink of a spoon against a coffee mug. In the morning she dresses for school as quickly as she can with her cast still on, and asks her parents the question she already knows the answer to. Both her mom and dad still wear the same clothes as last night.

— Is she back yet?

They shake their heads and her mom tries to smile but it's only with her mouth and it isn't very convincing.

— I'm sure she's just at her friend's house and will come

home after school tonight and try to pretend nothing happened. Don't worry.

Emily nods. It's possible, she supposes, that Lenora is at Marla's. She might have called her from a payphone after Theo ran out of the park and asked her to pick her up in town. Maybe Marla's mom was at work and so they sat up all night talking about what a jerk Theo is and how bad an idea it was to get a worldly skinhead boyfriend in the first place, and she would come home soon and everything would get back to normal. Or maybe she had caught up with Theo and they had made up after their argument, kissing and groping some more in the cold, steely air. Maybe she would skip school with him today. She can't get in much more trouble than she is already.

— What is it, Emily? Her dad looks at her without blinking.

— Is there something you're not telling us? Did you see where she went last night?

When she doesn't respond right away, her mom jumps in.

— Did you? Did you see her at all? If you did, you have to tell us. She's in big trouble right now, and I don't think you want to be part of that.

Her mom's lips have dark burgundy stains on them. Emily can't remember the last time she saw her mom wear lipstick, even to the Hall.

Emily decides to tell them part of the truth. Enough to make them leave her alone, but not enough to get Lenora in any more trouble.

— I followed her into town. Toward the park. Then I lost her.

— Was she with anyone? Maybe Marla? Anybody?

Emily chews the insides of her cheek and sighs.

— Not when I last saw her.

That part, at least, is technically true.

— Maybe she went to Marla's after that?

— Maybe.

Her mom turns on the tap and steam smudges the window.

— I'll drive you to school, Emily.

Her dad hands over her lunch and wordlessly they go out to the car.

WHEN THEY GET TO EMILY'S school, they're early. He puts the car in park and shuts off the ignition. They sit there, staring straight ahead, until Emily begins to tap her fingers on the glass and count how many cars drive past. When she picks up her school bag and reaches for the door handle, her father speaks.

— Wait. I have a question for you before you go in. What, for you, is the most important thing about being a Jehovah's Witness?

He still just stares straight ahead. Emily sits back again and puts her bag on the floor. Why is he asking her this? What's the point right now? Don't they have more important things to worry about? She knows the right answer, the response he is looking for, and tells him.

— Um, serving God?

He surprises her by shaking his head.

— I mean for you personally. Not what you're supposed to say. Is there anything in particular that is more important to you than anything else?

It must be a trick question. They never ask this at the Hall.

— I don't know.

They sit and sit and he says nothing and it starts to get cold in the car. More and more kids arrive and Emily blows on her fingers to warm them and keeps looking over at the school doors. She doesn't look at her father and he doesn't look at her.

— For me, it's the Resurrection.

Emily finally looks over toward him. He is staring, as if seeing them for the first time, at his half-missing finger stumps. She looks away.

— That's the most crucial part for me. It keeps me going. That we can look forward to one day seeing the dead come back to life.

Emily nods. She rubs her eyes, then pulls out a couple more of her lower eyelashes. She puts her hands back into her mitts and tries to distract herself by imagining what the dead people will look like when they're alive again. Will they look like they did at the moment they died? What if they were beheaded, like John the Baptist? Or got shot to death in a bank robbery? Would they still have bullets in their chests? Or would they be resurrected as the person they were before? How would God decide what moment of their life to choose to bring them back from?

— Are you listening, Emily?

She nods again.

— Yeah. I was just thinking about the Resurrection.

— Good. Me too.

The bell rings and Emily lifts her bag up again. Will her dad, who hardly ever says anything, keep talking and make her late for school? It's not fair. Everyone is doing everything wrong. She feels hot and cold at the same time.

— There's one person in particular I want to see when Jehovah brings him back to life.

Emily knows she is supposed to ask who, but can't say

anything. She knows he must be talking about his dead brother. The little brother he murdered. May have murdered. By accident.

He turns toward her and smiles but it makes him look the saddest she's ever seen anyone look instead.

— I'm talking about my younger brother.

Emily sucks in her breath and doesn't want to let it back out.

— I used to have a little brother. But there was a terrible accident.

Emily whispers her response, staring at her ragged nails and scabby cuticles.

— The same accident when your fingers got cut off?

— Yes. It was a terrible car crash.

Emily nods.

He starts the car again.

— His name was Christopher. I'm waiting to apologize to him.

He sighs and slumps his head against the steering wheel. She doesn't ask him what he's sorry for.

— It was all my fault, the accident was all my fault.

Emily gets out of the car and runs into the school and doesn't look back.

32

▼

AFTER SCHOOL, EMILY'S DAD PICKS her up and she can tell by his face that Lenora did not come out the front doors of the high school at 3:30. They drive back there and sit out front for forty-five minutes as dozens of teenagers thrust open the doors and lurch out. None of them is Lenora.

At home, her dad makes them spaghetti and when it's ready, the sky is completely dark and Lenora still isn't home. It begins to snow, the kind of tiny, icy flakes that look like they could cut you. Her mom walks from room to room peering out the windows into the night.

— I called Marla's and her mother said she isn't there, but she doesn't know about last night. She was at work.

— Okay. You should eat something, Vivian. I'm sure she'll be home any minute now.

Their father says a long prayer before they eat, and Emily starts when the wall creaks. It's not Lenora opening the door. Wind rattles the sharp branches as though tapping out a message, and Emily listens to it instead of her father's prayer.

— In Jesus' name, Amen. Their father sighs loudly and they begin to eat, without Lenora.

Her mom bangs her fork on her plate, over and over, harder than she needs to.

— Vivian, is that really necessary?

— Yes, it is. She mumbles back through her coffee cup and thumps it hard onto the tablecloth. A dark, purplish splash stains the white and Emily holds her breath, unable to reach across and cover it. Her mother, after chewing another forkful of pasta, sets her mug over it. Emily exhales and briefly closes her eyes.

— Are you okay, Emily? Her father watches her, his head slightly tilted.

— Yes. She quickly slurps some noodles.

— Do you have homework still to do tonight?

— A little bit. The pasta feels stuck somewhere between her throat and her stomach, as though her stomach is shut tight and won't let anything in. She moves her food around on her plate and hopes that drinking a whole glass of water will help. It doesn't look like any of them are eating very much. The room seems empty but at the same time thick with Lenora's absence.

Emily and her mom wash and dry the dishes, and she is careful not to leave any streaks or wet spots on the plates or silverware or glasses.

She does her math homework at the table, her father

goes upstairs with the new *Watchtower* issue under his arm, and her mom continues to pace through the house. She leaves the television on mute but doesn't watch any particular program, just strides around, picking up dishes or books and setting them down again a few feet away and constantly looking out the windows. Nine passes, then 10:00, and no one tells Emily to go to bed. Her mother goes upstairs and leaves Emily pretending to read in the kitchen. She can't quite make out what her parents say, but she can hear her mother's voice getting louder. The bedroom door slams and her mom stomps back downstairs.

— You don't give a damn about anyone but yourself! she yells into the otherwise silent house.

— You'd rather risk your own daughter's life than have the elders think you're anything less than the ideal Witness.

Her mother stands in the doorway of the kitchen, her head cocked up toward their bedroom, but Emily's father does not respond.

— Well, I'm calling the cops.

As soon as her mother mentions the police, Emily's father comes downstairs.

— You are not to call the police. Do you understand? His face gets red and he leans toward her mom.

— They won't listen anyway. She's probably just at some other friend's house. She was angry at both of us last night, and is just trying to scare us.

— I'm not just going to sit here and do nothing while our daughter is missing! Just because you're too embarrassed to admit we have problems—

— Keep your voice down. You're hysterical.

— I am not hysterical!

Lenora has never stayed away overnight before, not

without permission, and never at a worldly person's house. There are a few other teenagers at the Kingdom Hall, but Lenora isn't close friends with them. She once said they were bland and without an original thought of their own, which is when their father assigned her a long Bible reading about pride. She isn't mean to the other kids her age in the Truth, but she doesn't hang around with them.

— She might have been abducted!

Her mother paces the kitchen, shredding a tissue she pulled from her pocket. When she notices the white bits all over the floor, she sweeps frantically, empties it into the trash, and throws the dustpan at Emily's father.

He dodges it and picks it up — very slowly, while staring at his wife — and puts it away in the closet.

— Calm down, Vivian. Perhaps a prayer to Jehovah for a little more self-control is in order—

— Yeah, you know, sometimes I pray that Jehovah will help me fall asleep more easily at night and protect me from demons, and I think it's working—

— Shut up, Emily. Her mother runs her hands through her coarse hair.

— And go to bed.

— I highly doubt Lenora's been abducted. She's probably just with some worldly friends and will come home in the middle of the night.

— What does 'abducted' mean?

Her mother grabs her shoulders and turns Emily toward the door.

— It means go to bed now, Emily!

Upstairs in her room, she pulls an old dictionary out from under her bed. *To carry away by force, to kidnap.* Emily pictures a tall man dressed in black with Lenora — kicking, punching, screaming — flung over his shoulder. He carries her off in the sharp whorls of snow, and they disappear into the dark beyond the streetlights.

33

▼

AT THE GYM, I CHANGED out of my black boots and
into the soft-soled shoes. I was still on the half-metre
practice wire and it was more difficult to master than I
had expected. My quads and calves always ached and felt
heavier the next day, just from an hour or two of these
tense, halting steps. One foot in front of the other. Exhale.
Exhale.

— Concentrate, Morrow! Focus! the indomitably
perky Janice yelled over at me.

— You're relying too much on the mat! Pretend it's
not there, pretend it's a pit of vipers. Remember, Philippe
Petit didn't even have a net!

Janice's idol was the self-taught French master — he
was infamous, he even upstaged Nixon in the newspapers

when he strolled between the twin towers in New York City. A feat, no question, but I wasn't trying to impress anyone. I just wanted to be alone. I ignored her, and started again. Janice, hands on her hips as usual, watched from nearby.

She had said I was a fast learner, dedicated, and calm. In each lesson, I'd get a few steps further along the wire than the last time. It was addictive. A pattern emerged, a cycle of emotion and release, and I was emboldened not just by the thrill of it all, but also by knowing what to expect. My psychological routine would still usually begin with fear and self-consciousness, followed by a debate about whether or not to abandon the tightrope altogether, but then I would force myself to go anyway. Once I got there, I trained harder than anyone else in the gym, and temporarily overcame my fear of failure.

— Let's call it a day, Morrow.

I was sitting on the mat, rubbing my foot.

— Why? We're not out of time yet.

— Because you're not concentrating, and it's wasting our time. And because it's Saturday night. Go have some fun.

She was right, I was preoccupied, and I did have plans, but I'd been trying to take my mind off that by coming to my tightrope lesson. I nodded as she tidied up the studio and turned off lights.

It's all your fault I couldn't focus.

Too bad. Are you ready for tonight?

I don't know.

Don't worry. I'll tell you what to do.

When I got home, I sprayed disinfectant on the counters and wiped them down, then began to wash the small linoleum area in my kitchen again. I had done the same less than twenty-four hours ago, but bacteria could sneak in at any time. The harsh chemical smell obliterated all other thought, and I lulled myself into the rhythm of scrubbing the floor. Right, left, up, down, killing any and all germs that may lurk: no less than two hundred strokes across the floor. My hands were red and the cracks were split open again, but the apartment was spotless. Gradually, the turbulence buffeting my stomach slowed its wings.

After a shower, I dusted my face with white powder, painted my eyelids with cold, black liquid, and smoothed on two coats of red lipstick. It took only ten minutes to tease and spray up my hair; I had gotten better at it. Next, I pulled on the old black and white striped tights, then slid into the short black skirt. Next came the black lace bra, slightly too big, followed by the satin camisole, red lace-trimmed blouse, and black cardigan. I folded the cuffs of the sleeves up and looked at my chafed hands. Disgusting. I rolled them back down and let them cover my knuckles. Finally, I laced up the boots and tentatively glanced into the mirror.

Relics and masquerade. I was a spectre.

I took another dusty box from beneath my bed and pulled out a small, folded piece of paper. I slid it into my pocket, and ran my fingertips over its brittle edges. I pulled my hand out as though burned.

The note was for me. I was terrified to unfold it, but I had no choice.

I turned off the lamps in my apartment, and I closed the blinds. With an engraved silver Zippo, I lit a series of ten candles and arranged them in a semi-circle on the floor of my small, damp living room. Careful not to trip over them and burn down the house, I took out the necessary items from the box.

One tiny flame for each year that had passed.

I'm creating a ceremony. Just for us.

My hands shook as I laid out the ratty old Misfits t-shirt — frayed, stained, and chewed through with holes — between me and the flickering arc of candles.

Next I stood up and walked over to the freezer. I took out the small package of Belmont Milds. Then I sat back down and lit a cigarette from the flame of the tenth candle. I inhaled, coughed, and inhaled again. The smoke filled my lungs and my head felt hot and prickly. My nostrils burned when I exhaled. I tried hard not to think about the ash and tar coating my throat and lungs as I flicked the ashes into the lumpy black and red clay candle holder that served as an ashtray.

After I smoked the entire cigarette, I flushed the butt down the toilet and washed my hands three times, then returned the pack to the freezer for next time. I wished there was a way to cleanse myself on the inside too.

I slid the CD into my portable stereo and skipped to the right track. The low, mournful song began — the same one I used to hear behind her bedroom door.

I barred all other thoughts and concentrated only on the baritone vocals — silence and danger — until my breathing slowed and my hands stopped shaking.

Careful to avoid contact with the candles, I took from my pocket the dirty piece of folded paper. By then, the creases had started to tear. I placed it in my lap and closed my eyes.

I'm trying to make things right. I'll do what you tell me to.
Good.
Please don't be mad at me anymore.

It was time to unfold the paper. I waited until the song finished, then put it on "repeat." My hands started to tremble again. It had been almost ten years since I'd looked at it.

My stomach heaved when I saw the familiar handwriting. My lungs shrank to impossible specks. I gasped and wheezed as though being strangled, the page blurred, and I fought for air.

I want whoever finds this to know the truth. The real truth, not the hypocrisy that calls itself the Truth. Then give it to my sister, Emily. She isn't too young to know what happened to me.

I grabbed the nearest candle and held the flame against the scabs on my arm for as long as I could stand it. I read her words as small hairs burned away and the air smelled bitter. I dug my teeth into my lips to keep from crying out. Her note was two and a half pages long. My arm erupted in blisters and a corner of the note started to burn. I quickly put it out with my fingers and pulled the candle away from my flesh.

I want her to keep this letter, this chronicle, and remember everything. Ems, maybe things will turn out better for you. I don't know. Just don't get trapped in the lies that other people tell themselves, and tell you.

I pressed her t-shirt against my face and there was still a faint scent of vanilla.

I won't, Lenora. I'm sorry.

I finished rereading the letter, put it and the t-shirt back into the box beneath my bed, and blew out the candles. Their smoke eddied in the air, sharp and sweet.

Outside, snow fell in a thick, white shroud, smothering the city.

How do I look?

Undo two more buttons.

But—

Do it.

34

▼

EMILY CAN HARDLY MOVE in her own house. The
rooms overflow with elders, Ministerial Servants, their
wives, and other brothers and sisters from the Hall. They
perch on the living room sofa, cluster around the kitchen
table, huddle in groups of three or four in corners, while
another van load pulls into the driveway. It's as crowded
as a party, but the atmosphere — the reason everyone is
here — is the opposite.

Someone has taped the service map to the wall and
they're organizing who will take each area for the search,
like they do on Sundays before going out door to door.
Emily weaves through the fray, wondering where her
parents are. No one looks at her, just at each other, and
then they shake their heads when they think no one is

watching. Emily feels something on her shoulder and she jumps. Sister Bulchinsky pulls her hand back and looks away. On the far side of the living room, flanked by two sentinel-like elders' wives, sits her mom with her hands over her face, crying.

These must be the Last Days. Emily can feel the panic in the room as it erupts into goosebumps on her arms and scalp. She shivers. She is afraid to move, lest her tiny action trigger further catastrophe, so she stands rigid in the middle of the room as adults drift past her. Everyone's murmurs meld together into the sound of wind keening at the windows. She holds her breath and the room blurs. She tries to conjure up Lenora's face, Lenora's laugh; she needs Lenora's strength today more than ever, but her mind is fogged.

Then Emily falls to the carpet, into a black hole, and everyone surges into the space she left behind. Someone picks her up and sets her on the couch and gives her a glass of water. Still, she won't open her eyes. Not until she can will everything to return to normal.

Please Jehovah God, make Lenora come home. Please don't let her get in too much trouble. Please forgive Lenora for running away.

Lenora has been missing for three days.

The congregation, a tidal wave of search-and-rescue, has taken over their home. Emily knows she cannot just chew her hangnails and eavesdrop anymore; she has been swept up into this tsunami and must save her sister. She is the only one.

Please Jehovah, let me be the one to find Lenora and bring her back home. It has to be me. I know that you understand this. Please God, this is very important.

The phone rings while her mother sobs amid the elders' hushed tones and surreptitious glances. Emily's father answers, tells whomever it is that no, there is no news, and he must keep the line clear.

Emily has to get out. She wishes she'd thought of it earlier, before their house had so quickly filled with all these brothers and sisters. She knows what to do.

Thank you Jehovah God, and forgive all my sins. And Lenora's too, especially Lenora's. She doesn't mean it, I promise. In Jesus' name, Amen.

It's weird to have everyone in their house — in the kitchen, the bathroom, sipping from their mugs, looking at their things. Someone is bound to find something else wrong with their family.

With the group's attention on her parents, Emily darts upstairs, grabs a handful of change from her piggy bank, and slips out the back door.

She walks quickly down the road, almost running, shoulders hunched, hoping that no passing carload of fellow Jehovah's Witnesses recognizes her. She clutches a tiny piece of folded paper in her pocket.

It takes Emily about fifteen minutes to reach the pay-phone outside of the truck stop on the highway, the same one she'd watched Lenora use the other night. She wishes she'd had time to find her mittens before she left.

Please God, Jehovah, please don't let them notice I'm gone. You know I'm just getting Lenora to come home. Please don't let them worry any more. Please make this work.

She takes a deep breath and unfolds the paper, chanting, *Please let me find my sister. Please let me find my sister. If I can make Lenora come home, I promise I will always pay attention during every single meeting, even the assemblies. I won't fidget*

anymore or daydream during sermons. Please just let me find my
sister. And make her not be mad at me. In Jesus' name, Amen.

Emily's hand no longer aches beneath her cast, and it's due to come off in a week. Still, it takes her a little longer to do things with her hands, and her awkwardness frustrates her. She rallies what shreds of patience she has left and unfolds the page torn from the H section of the phone book, picks up the phone, drops in her coins, and dials the number for Lenora's secret, worldly boyfriend.

The phone rings four times.

— Hello?

— May I please speak to Theo?

— You got the wrong Hansen. Try P. Hansen in the phonebook.

Emily thanks him and digs in her pocket, hoping she's brought enough change. She hadn't planned for wrong numbers, but there are three Hansens on the same street. She dials P. Hansen's number and again asks for Theo.

— Yeah. That's me. Who the hell's this?

— This is Emily Morrow. She pauses, cringing.

— So?

— I'm Lenora's sister.

— Like I said, so what?

There is laughter in the background, shrill like a banshee. Emily doesn't know if it is the television or a real person, but it is definitely not her sister. Lenora's laugh is deep and full and sophisticated.

— Well . . .

— Spit it out, kid. What do you want?

Emily rushes, spits it all out as fast as she can, before he laughs at her or hangs up or both.

— I'm trying to find Lenora. Is she there? I'm not at

home, I'm calling from a payphone, and I promise I won't tell, she won't get in trouble, I just need to know if she's there, and I need to talk to her for a second. I'll be really quick. It's important. It's an emergency.

Theo laughs, but he doesn't hang up. Not immediately.

— Listen, kid. Your sister and me aren't going out anymore. I don't know where the hell she is, and I don't give a damn. So you and your freak family can fuck off and leave me alone.

The dial tone hums indifferently in her ear.

Emily stares at the numbers on the telephone for a long time. Her hands are numb and she drags her coat sleeve across her nose.

— I'm not crying, I'm not crying, I'm not crying.

This wasn't what was supposed to happen. This is what being punched in the stomach must feel like; this is what people must mean when they say, *I got the wind knocked out of me*. Emily lets the receiver dangle in the phone booth and puts her hands on her knees and leans over, breathing like someone who has been running for hours.

A few cars zip past the truck stop, and Emily starts to breathe normally again, though she feels like she has just woken up and doesn't know where she is. The incessant recording tells her to *please hang up and try your call again*. Emily shakes her head, hangs up the phone, and stuffs the page from the directory back into her pocket and, having no other great plan to find her sister, starts toward home.

When she gets back, another couple of elders — Brother Maxwell and Brother Bouchard — are just coming up to the back porch, so she stashes her coat there and enters the house with them, as though she is letting them in. Her absence appears to have gone unnoticed.

She pushes through all the men in the living room, past Brother Wilde pointing at the map with his pen, past the brothers pulling on their coats and getting ready to leave. She heads into the kitchen, where a clump of elders' wives cluck and sigh and shrug.

— Well, you know what I heard, don't you?

Sister Bulchinsky purses her lips, narrows her eyes, and glances sideways at the sister standing closest to her.

— She was running with a worldly crowd, those freaky kids with the spiky hair and safety pins.

— Bad associations spoil useful habits. Amen.

Someone nudges Sister Bulchinsky and they stop talking and look at Emily, their eyes glassy, their heads tilted in pity.

Stupid gossips, Emily thinks. They don't even care about Lenora, not really; they're only here so they don't miss anything. Emily glares at each of them in turn. Sister Bulchinsky puts an arm around her and coos softly.

— There, there, let's pray together and ask Jehovah—

Emily pulls away as though burned.

— Don't touch me!

Her voice bounces off the fridge and stove and back toward her and it's far louder than she meant it to be. She tries to walk away, but the kitchen is thick with grasping women and sniffling toddlers and she is surrounded; they all move as one, and she cannot escape the throng. They all stare at her.

— Get out of my house! I hate you, I hate all of you!

Like pillars of salt, they fall silent and unmoving, and Emily hears an echo of herself, someone unfamiliar and horrible.

— Get out get out get out!

Emily stops in the middle of the kitchen, looks down at the green and yellow linoleum, closes her eyes, and tries to pray silently to Jehovah. She wants to ask to be forgiven for hating her fellow sisters; hatred is a sin. But this time, praying doesn't work. She cannot force the words out. She pretends to pray, but it doesn't calm her down or make her believe that everything will be okay.

— Oh, you poor lamb. Sister Bulchinsky clucks and sing-songs.

— Everything will turn out fine in the end. Are you hungry? I left a tuna casserole in the fridge. Do you want some?

Emily fights back the urge to scream or, better yet, throw all the dishes and cutlery — including the knives — at their heads. She doesn't need their pity. They don't understand Lenora, her beautiful and complicated sister, no one does. Except maybe Emily. At least, a little bit.

— I hate tuna. She glowers over her shoulder and leaves the kitchen.

In the living room, her dad has his arm around her mom, something Emily has rarely seen. The others organize who is driving where to look for Lenora. Some are going as far as King Street in the city, where all the record stores are. It doesn't seem as though anyone heard her outburst in the kitchen, or if they have, they don't say.

— Excuse me, Brother Wilde. Emily taps him on the elbow and he starts, as though he hadn't noticed her before. He looks at her, then at her parents, then back down to Emily.

— Yes?

— Which car will I be going in?

— What do you mean, Emily?

— Who am I going with to find Lenora?

His arm flops down to his side and he looks back toward her parents.

— You're going to stay here, Emily. Her mom looks up at her from the couch.

— But why? I have to go! I'll find her! Emily squeezes her eyes tight, trying not to shout. She had truly believed that Lenora was just at Theo's, and that he would tell her the truth, that they would be co-conspirators, together, for Lenora.

She has to make up for that mistake.

Her mom takes her hand and pulls her into the bathroom. She puts the seat and lid down on the toilet and sits. She pulls Emily onto her lap, and even though she is too old for that, Emily slumps against her.

— We're going to stay here in case Lenora, or someone with information, phones. We need to maintain a home base, okay? It's the most crucial job of all.

Emily doesn't believe her but knows enough not to fight. She is tired of being told to stay home, to keep out of the way, to be quiet. She knows her sister best, so surely she should be the one to find her. But does anyone ask her to help? No. And so she must find Lenora herself. That will show them.

Twenty minutes later the house is empty except for the two of them. The cushions are dented and askew, mugs sit half empty on the coffee table, there's a pool of slush by the back door, and someone has dropped a black woollen scarf on the floor. When her mom goes into the bathroom and shuts the door, Emily knows exactly what she must do.

She slips silently to the back door again, pulls on her boots, and gets her coat and hat from the porch, as well as the emergency flashlight they keep out there. This time she remembers her mittens. She puts them on as she runs across the back field toward the woods.

The snow slows her down — it's slippery and she falls once, bashing her knee against a rock, but scrambles up quickly, ignoring the pain. She knows her mom might see her from the kitchen, so she runs full speed and hopes she doesn't look out the window. Once in the trees, she knows no one can see her.

Emily has no plan. She thought she'd find Lenora because that's how it should be — she deserves to be the one to find her. Now she has no idea how to do that. She decided on the woods out back because that's where Lenora goes on long walks. And besides, no one else thought to look out there. She doesn't know which path through the trees to follow first. The wind hisses through her coat, and so she decides to start walking in the same direction as the wind.

Emily pulls her hood over her toque to shield her eyes from the late afternoon sun glaring off the snow, and thrusts her hands deep into her pockets. She walks for half an hour, finds nothing indicating that Lenora was recently there, finds nothing at all, but isn't ready to give up. She yawns and slaps at her cheeks.

— Keep going, keep going, keep going. She must stay alert, she must find a clue, just like Trixie Belden, who would never give up just because it's cold out. Then again, Trixie always had Honey and Jim to help her, but today, in the woods, Emily has no one. She walks faster. The sun is behind the trees now, between layers of blue and yellow and purple — the colours of a bruise. There's less than an hour left before it will be completely dark.

The snow crunches where it had melted and frozen

over again. Trees glint in the remaining light and she squints. Her only plan is to look for footprints. Her eyes scan the snow for Lenora's Doc Marten imprints or anything indicating that someone has been trudging through there recently. Maybe Lenora found an abandoned cabin, once used by hunters, and she's warm and dry, hiding out with her friends. Maybe Theo lied about breaking up, to throw her off. Even though Lenora's not supposed to have a worldly boyfriend — or any boyfriend, for that matter — Emily doesn't want to believe that they've broken up.

— Concentrate, concentrate. She mumbles aloud as the leafless branches continue to shake around her, as though they're trying to tell her something, as though they know something she doesn't, and far past the trees, on some farm on the other side of the woods, a dog howls. Emily wraps her arms around herself and pulls her thick wool toque down over her ears.

Please Jehovah, let me find Lenora's footprints. Emily trudges along, counting her own steps as she prays. *Let me find her footprints before it gets too dark. Please.*

35

▼

DJ MORG AT THE CAVERN. New Wave & Punk. Every Monday night. Dress code enforced.

There was no lineup when I arrived. I checked the address on the flyer that Theo had dropped on the street. This was the place. My feet throbbed and my empty stomach gurgled in fear. I had never been to a place like that, or to any night club, and I was so nervous, I hadn't eaten all day, afraid I might throw up. What if they didn't let me in? What exactly did the dress code consist of? What was I supposed to do when I found Theo? He'd been so scared of me when we collided on the street. Maybe, because of all the makeup, he wouldn't recognize me. I deserved another chance.

The bouncer was impassive, his face, a boulder. He

glanced at my identification and waved me in. I exhaled in relief and tossed my license back in my purse, not bothering to shove it in my wallet. I had been terrified that I may not pass the dress code. Inside, the lights were dark, with occasional flashes of blue or green or red. The music was loud and the bass rattled the floor. I didn't recognize the song, and it was far too early for anyone to dance. There weren't many people there yet, just a few ageing punks with mohawks playing pool, a group of girls in black eyeliner reading Tarot cards by candlelight in the corner, and a dozen or so others in black leather, crinolines, and army fatigues clustered around the bar.

I felt conspicuous as I weaved between a handful of small tables along the sides. I hoped no one could tell what a fraud I was. Could they kick me out? What was I doing there?

I locked myself in a bathroom stall for as long as I could stand it. The graffiti was the same as anywhere: who loves who, who's an asshole, favourite bands, and pseudo-philosophical quotations. Despite my obsessive and pathological need for solitude, I wished I had a friend with me, someone who would encourage me to talk to Theo, and reassure me when I panicked.

I'm scared. What do I do when I find him?

You're always scared. I already told you what to do.

Pick up where you left off.

That's right. You owe me.

The person next to me flushed the toilet. My cheeks burned. I hadn't heard anyone else come in. I waited until she left before I came out, and washed my hands and smoothed my hair at the mirror. Then a girl with spiked pink hair and a pierced lip lumbered in. Her fishnets were torn and she had a bottle of beer in each hand.

Black Label. She didn't acknowledge me. A drink seemed a good enough way to kill more time until Theo showed up. I headed for the bar.

It was the first beer I'd ever bought for myself. Despite all the drinks I served at work, I never stayed afterwards for a pint with Kameela and Grant and the other staff. They thought I was a freak, and I didn't want to unintentionally do anything else to reaffirm their opinion.

It didn't taste as bad as I had expected, and I sipped it slowly, getting used to it, alone at a small bistro table on the edge of the dance floor. I had a good view of the entrance area and the bar, and watched more and more black-clad new wavers and punks arrive. I was relieved that I wasn't the only person to show up alone; apparently it was the kind of place where it was cool to be solitary. People gradually straggled onto the dance floor, kicking their legs to guitar chords and slamming into each other. I didn't know all of the songs, but I recognized a few from Lenora's tapes or the radio, which was better than I expected.

I craned my neck to survey the growing crowd around the bar. No sign of Theo. I didn't want it to look so obvious that I was waiting for someone, but no one appeared to watch me anyway. They either chatted to one another in the booths along the sides of the club or stared at the floor while dancing. I went to the bar for another beer.

— Thanks. I nodded to the bartender and dropped my change into the tip jar. Both his arms were covered in multi-coloured tattoos. Then I felt a hand on my shoulder.

— Black Label, huh?

I looked behind me. My stomach turned inside out. The crowd cheered as the opening bass line from Alien Sex Fiend's "I Walk the Line" boomed. Theo laughed.

If he recognized me from last week on the sidewalk, he didn't let on. I took a huge swig from my beer and nearly choked.

— Easy there!

— Uh . . . yeah. Black Label. I stared at him. He lifted his own bottle of Black Label.

— Cheers.

— Cheers. My heart beat so hard I thought my ribcage would shatter. I was grateful for the loud music.

Theo held out his hand. He wore a plain black t-shirt, black jeans, and eight-hole boots like mine.

— I'm Zack.

Zack? Isn't this Theo?

Yes. He's lying.

Instinctively, I shook his hand, still staring at him in disbelief. His hand was rough and dry.

— And do you have a name?

— Uh, yeah. Sure.

He watched me.

— So what is it?

I took a deep breath and exhaled.

— My name is Lenora.

36

▼

EMILY TAKES OFF HER MITTS and blows on her hands again to warm them, then struggles into the left one, tugging it over her cast. The light is now bright orange and dark purple and blazes through the trees as though chasing her, and the icy branches rattle dully in the wind. Her skin prickles and she shivers and trudges farther into the woods.

If Lenora really is out here, Emily hopes she's warm enough; there's no smell of wood smoke in the air, and the ground is so cold it crunches when she walks. She hopes she found somewhere warm and dry to sleep, and has enough food. After three days, she must be hungry. Emily should have brought something for her to eat, even just a peanut butter sandwich. Why didn't she think of that? Why can't she do anything properly? She could have made a sandwich, even with her broken hand. Then again, maybe Lenora is just hiding out at some friend's house like everyone keeps saying, listening to music and laughing at them all for trying so hard to find her.

— You'd better not be!

It feels good to say it aloud. Maybe Lenora doesn't know how worried everyone is, or how much trouble she's going to be in when she gets home. It's better that Emily gets to her first, to warn her, to advise her on the best time to come back. Like tonight, while everyone else is out of the house. Lenora should say she was out walking in the bush and fell, hit her head hard on a rock and got amnesia, and that's why she couldn't remember how to get home. Emily's familiar face would snap Lenora out of it, and they'd come home together like nothing had ever happened. Lenora will be impressed that Emily thought of that. Everyone will be so grateful to Emily for bringing her back, they won't even be mad at Lenora anymore. Emily will be a hero.

The wind whistles like a living thing and pushes at her back, coaxing her to keep looking. It's almost dark, and Emily is glad she remembered the flashlight. The exhilaration of having escaped the house has worn off, and she fights off the fear that seeps through her coat and into her skin and chills her blood. She must be brave. Trixie Belden was never scared away from solving a mystery, and Lenora isn't afraid of anything. Emily starts to sing to make herself feel stronger.

She runs through all of "Frosty the Snowman," as loud as she can while scanning the ground for footprints or other clues. It's one of the few songs they're allowed to sing at school in December, since it's not actually about Christmas, just winter. Some people at the Hall won't sing it though, because they say it's close enough to a Christmas carol, and worldly people think that it is, which makes it bad enough. Emily's parents don't think there's anything wrong with it though, and they even watched the cartoon *Frosty the Snowman* on television this year.

Next she sings her favourite Hall song:

> *Let's watch how we walk, and watch how we*
> *   talk*
> *That thus we may be alert and wise,*
> *Buying out the opportune time,*
> *Since this world in Satan lies.*
> *Yes, watch how we walk and watch how we*
> *   talk*
> *That thus we may be alert and wise.*

Alert and wise. That is what Emily is trying to be, so that she might be the one to find Lenora. She doesn't even get to the second verse before she sees something in the arc of the flashlight ahead of her. It's red and looks like a glove — one of Lenora's.

— Lenora! Emily sounds more panicked than she means to, and she tries to sound more calm, so she doesn't chase her away.

— Lenora! It's just me!

If her sister is nearby, she doesn't answer back. Emily runs, sliding a little, toward the glove. A little farther ahead rests a huge rock at the edge of a ravine.

Emily rounds the boulder and shines the light over it. She stops so suddenly that she skids and nearly falls. It's her. It's Lenora. It's her sister, just sitting there, lounging in the snow against the rock. She found her. She grins and calls her name again.

She has never been so relieved in her life.

— Hurry up, you have to come home, they're gone and we can sneak in, only Mom's there now. It's your perfect chance!

Lenora says nothing, only stares straight ahead. There is something in her right hand.

— Seriously, come on! We're going to tell them you had amnesia, but you're okay now. Let's go!

Lenora is playing a trick on her, refusing to answer. She's mad at Emily for finding her, and giving her the silent treatment. Emily will not be ignored.

— The entire congregation is out looking for you. They might even call the police soon, so you have to come with me!

Nothing.

— It's not funny! We have to get home right now!

— Stop it! She stomps her foot on the hard ground and steps closer to her sister.

— Cut it out!

Lenora doesn't move. She doesn't answer. Her profile looks different, somehow wrong. The wind rattles the envelope crumpled under Lenora's hand and Emily snatches it from her. Then she looks down and on Lenora's left, under a thin dusting of snow, is a rifle.

— Lenora!

Emily pulls her scarf away from her throat and screams and pushes her sister. Lenora's body is rigid and slides sideways. Emily's hands shake and the flashlight jerks over the scene, lighting up fragments that won't stay still, like living shards of a nightmare.

Red all over the rock. Red in the glaring snow. Red ice clumped in her hair.

The back of her head clean gone.

Emily vomits. She falls to the snow beneath her and vomits again. She loses count of how many times. She can't breathe. She can't hear. She sees only streaks of light around her as the flashlight rolls down the hill. She kneels in the snow, heaving. The wind shakes the trees and the branches crack and rattle, driving ice and snow into her face as she looks up into the dark. The world is spinning and sharp like broken glass and Emily cannot see anything else above her.

The wind carries her screams high into the empty sky and leaves them there.

37

▼

I FINISHED THE SECOND BEER and felt detached but no more relaxed. My fingernails dug hard into my forearms, and I winced when I gouged one of my blisters through the bandage. I felt like I was going to explode.

Thankfully, there was no lineup at the women's washroom, and I locked myself in a stall again. My chest heaved even as I sat on the toilet, so I waited a few minutes until my breathing slowed down, then I opened my purse and took out my penknife. I pushed up my left sleeve. There was a bit of room left. I hadn't been etching as much since I'd started the tightrope training with Janice, but I needed it tonight. Things felt overwhelming and out of control, and I was scared of what I was about to do with Theo.

I drew a half-dozen Xs on the inside of my forearm,

and felt better. One of them went a little deeper than I meant to, and blood dripped onto the floor. I tore off a wad of toilet paper and held it on my arm for a while. I felt much more poised.

I reapplied my dark red lipstick, fought back a grin, and left the washroom. This was it.

In a matter of hours, I would lose my virginity.

I had another beer and swayed with the others on the dance floor. I felt lighter, airy, somehow separate from myself. Despite some sort of unspoken code in the club, I was smiling. I felt free, finally, and transformed. I was Lenora. I danced and drank and danced and danced and drank until the music and the lights and the crater inside were nothing but one big far-off blur.

The strobe lights pulsed and the fog machine hissed and everything eddied into afterimages and blurs. When the lights came up, he kissed me. The floor seemed uneven and I stumbled, and he put his arm across my shoulders to steady me as we left the club.

We went to a dingy all-night coffee shop, where we sobered slightly, but not so much to prevent us from holding hands across the stained table. We ate stale butter tarts and drank black coffee and talked about music. His hands were dry and lightly calloused. After the dark haze of the Cavern, the coffee shop was too bright and I squinted.

I excused myself to go to the washroom, and nearly tripped over a chair. I reddened and hoped that Theo didn't see. I stared at my teased hair and red stained lips in the mirror.

I think it's working.

Good.

But I don't get it. Why do you want me to sleep with him?

Because you're me now.

Yes.

Someone flushed the toilet and left the stall. I jumped. I hadn't noticed that anyone else was in there. It was one of the waitresses and she stood next to me, watching my reflection.

— Don't worry, honey, I won't bite.

Her hair was blond with dark roots, and frizzed out from her head in a big perm. She reapplied her pink frosty lipstick and smiled. I held on to the edge of the sink and tried to look sober. I couldn't tell if I was still swaying or not. My ears rang from dancing too close to the speakers.

— You better have a decaf and sleep it off. Don't worry, it will all seem better in the morning.

Her heels clicked across the floor and she was gone.

38

▼

EMILY, HER CAST OFF AND fingers working again, pulls on her black wool dress and sits on the edge of her bed. The house has never been quieter. She feels like she can't wake up. She pinches her arm, but it isn't enough. She claws at the inside of her elbow. There is some blood, and that feels better. All of her lower eyelashes are gone. Red rings her eyes. Even though she is too old for stuffed animals, she grabs Zig Zag and clutches him tight to her chest and doesn't let go. Her dad stands in her doorway, looking down at the blue carpet.

— It's time to go.

She can't get up from the bed. Her mind tells her limbs to move but they refuse. Her father walks over to her and gently pulls Zig Zag from her arms. He sits down next to her, puts his arm around her, and says nothing. They sit like that for a while.

— I know, Em, I know. It's hard. It's . . . I don't know. His voice breaks.

— Is this the Great Tribulation?

He doesn't answer this but hugs her to him, hard.

— Is it?

He smiles sadly.

— Kind of.

— Then why is it only happening to us?

He stands up and pulls her off the bed.

— I don't know, Em. I don't know.

In the car, Emily sits in the back, and at first, no one says anything.

— Why isn't the funeral at the Hall?

Her father sighs and her mom turns and looks out the window, her jaw tight.

— It's complicated, Emily. We can talk about that another time.

Her mother makes an unmistakeable sound as she takes a drink from her travel mug. She snorts.

— Oh, just tell her the truth! She's not stupid, Jim.

— Vivian—

— Don't 'Vivian' me!

Her mother turns toward the back seat, one arm across the headrest, and faces Emily.

— Viv, don't.

— It's because your sister committed suicide, Emily. She killed herself. The elders won't allow a funeral in the perfect, holy Kingdom Hall if it's a suicide. We're not allowed to bring Lenora there. It might send the wrong message to all the true and faithful sheep—

— Enough!

— She wanted to know. That's the truth. No suicides allowed! Pretend it doesn't exist! Pretend everything is perfect and righteous.

Why wouldn't they let Lenora be there? Was she disfellowshipped? Can you do that after someone's died? Worse, was she demonized? How would anyone know? Emily doesn't ask her parents if the brothers and sisters from the Hall will be there. The rest of the drive is silent.

There are a few other cars in the parking lot when they arrive, but none that Emily recognizes. Inside, the people who work there whisper and shake her father's hand and lead them down the hallway. There is a big room with flowers and rows of chairs, kind of like the Kingdom Hall. No one else is there yet.

At the front of the room is a big wooden casket. Emily can't see her from the doorway, but she knows her sister lies inside of it. Emily's whole body tenses. Her mom holds her hand and they stand there, in the doorway.

Emily hasn't seen her sister since she found her. She can't remember the last thing she said to her before that day in the woods. She can't remember anything except Lenora's red mitten on the ground, and the red splatters across the snow, and she tries hard not to see that every time she closes her eyes, but it doesn't work.

Her mom is crying, and Emily can't stop shaking, her teeth rattle like marbles, but she doesn't cry. She's scared that if she cries, something unspeakably terrible, somehow even worse than this, will happen. She doesn't even want to move.

More people begin to arrive, and there are relatives she hasn't seen in months or years who hug her and say "You poor thing" or "What a shame" or "Don't you look like a grown-up these days" or else nothing at all, just leaving wet teary patches on the shoulders of Emily's dress. She picks at her arm, letting it bleed into her sleeve.

She wonders how they fixed up Lenora's head.

Lots of Lenora's friends from school come, and some of the teachers, but not Theo. She sees Lenora's friend Marla, wearing black lipstick like the last time Emily saw her. Some of the relatives nudge each other and whisper.

— Hey there, girl. How you holding up? She punches Emily lightly on the arm. Emily doesn't know what to say, she has no idea how she is holding up, but she smiles gratefully at Marla.

— I brought a poem to read. One of Lenora's favourites. That okay? Marla isn't really asking anyone in particular, and both of Emily's parents answer.

— Of course—

— Sure, yes, absolutely—

Emily didn't know that Lenora read poetry. What else about her sister doesn't she know? She wonders if she will ever find out. The envelope she found still sits hidden under her mattress, but she doesn't want to know what it says. Not yet.

More and more teenagers arrive, and some cry, many hug, but no one else besides her family is from the Kingdom Hall. Emily wants to ask if at least the elders will come, but she knows the answer.

Emily and her mom and her dad are allowed to go into the room with Lenora before everyone else. The funeral director closes the door behind them. It's too hot and Emily puts her hand on her chest and clears her throat. The flowers smell thick and sweet and disgusting. Though she can't remember the last time she ate, her stomach hurts. She closes her eyes.

— Are you okay? Her mother brushes her hair from

her forehead. They stand near, but not too near the casket. They don't look at each other, and they don't look at Lenora.

Then her parents go over to Lenora first, together. They hold hands, which Emily never sees them do, and they cry. Emily stands to the left of them and a few steps behind, and she can see Lenora from there. She is motionless, her expression blank, and Emily shivers. She looks clean and plastic, like a doll. Worse, she's dressed like she's going to the Kingdom Hall.

— I'm so sorry—

Her mom slumps against her dad, who sways and stumbles. Emily can't look at them any longer. It feels wrong. She sits down at the back of the room, puts her hands over her ears and closes her eyes, and wishes for a way to not smell the thick, syrupy reek of the flowers. She feels like she's drowning. After a while, they come back and sit next to her, then motion Emily closer to the casket.

The dead are conscious of nothing at all. She has heard that statement a hundred times at the Hall, yet still she knows that Lenora can hear her. She's not really gone. She's probably, somehow, faking all this too.

Emily walks over to her. She steels herself, holds on to the edge of the coffin, and leans in. She whispers, speaking quickly, as though she doesn't have much time.

— It's okay, Lenora. Don't worry, it's just me. No one else can hear us right now. I have your letter safe and sound, hidden in a secret place. No one will find it. I got it before anyone else . . . Emily's throat tenses up but she continues.

— I didn't know what you wanted, but I brought you some stuff. Things I think you'd want. Mom and Dad don't know.

Emily opens her Hall purse and pulls out a few of

281

the mixed tapes that Lenora's friends had made her and puts them next to her right hand. She slides her Walkman under the pillow.

— I didn't want them to put you in that boring outfit, but Dad insisted. I said, 'She hasn't worn that in ages, she hates that outfit,' but he did it anyway. Mom said, 'What does it matter' and just let him. I wouldn't have though; I would have put you in your favourite striped tights and big boots and black skirt and one of those weird band t-shirts. I'm sorry I couldn't do that. I'm sorry I didn't try harder.

Emily cries for real now, but still whispers.

— I'm sorry I didn't come and look for you sooner, and I'm sorry I didn't make you stay home instead of going out with stupid Theo. But I'll make it up to you. I promise. I'll do everything you wanted to do, and it'll be like you were never really gone.

Emily takes a pair of Lenora's tiny nail scissors from her purse. She turns to look behind her. Her parents' heads are bent close together and they aren't looking at her. She reaches toward Lenora and very quickly clips off a chunk of her hair. Her hands shake and she shoves the lock and the scissors back into her bag.

She doesn't know if there's a name for what she's just done, but she knows it's a sin.

Emily has a hard time paying attention during the funeral. She has to sit at the front with her family, but she keeps turning to see who is there. Most of the kids are unfamiliar to her. Finally, a tired-looking Uncle Tyler comes in and sits by himself near the back. She starts to wave, then stops, remembering that she isn't supposed to acknowledge him anymore. It's too late though; he's seen her and nods, with a sad smile on his face. Emily looks away.

After the funeral director speaks, other people go up

and talk about Lenora. Everyone says she looks so beautiful. Everyone is a liar. Lenora doesn't even look like herself. It's kind of like being at the Hall, with the microphone and podium and the quiet, but with hardly any Jehovah's Witnesses. Marla reads a poem called "Poppies in July" and Emily's parents squirm uncomfortably. Emily can hear people crying, but doesn't know who they are. Lenora's English teacher gets up and talks about how creative she was and what a good student with a great sense of humour. Lastly, Uncle Tyler goes to the podium. Her parents tense up. Emily doesn't know where to look.

— Lenora is my niece. His hands shake and he looks like he hasn't slept in a few days. Emily doesn't know why, but she's scared of what he's going to say.

— I loved her very much. She had a lot of energy, a lot of passion and intense emotions. Things are never easy for teenagers, but doubly so for religious kids. Sometimes, they have to conform to expectations that are unrealistic. Sometimes, this is impossible. There is a murmur throughout the room. Her father looks down, but her mom looks straight at Uncle Tyler. He pauses for a long time, then looks down too.

— I'm going to miss her a lot— He starts to cry hard now, and everyone near Emily looks at their shoes or out the window. When he tries to speak again, it sounds like he is choking.

The funeral director takes his elbow and walks him back to his seat.

After that, their father prays, his voice wobbling the whole time. His prayer says the usual things about forgiveness and sin, guidance and wisdom, but this time he mentions the Resurrection a few times, and Emily can tell he is trying hard not to cry in front of everyone.

At the cemetery, they walk — as though in slow motion — toward the freshly dug grave. Emily is dizzy. A big hole in the ground. They are going to put her sister in there. She knows this, she knows what death is, but this doesn't make any sense. Lenora, hidden away in a big hole. It doesn't seem like she's faking anymore.

Emily is paralyzed. She cannot walk over to the pit where they're going to put her sister. Her mother takes her hand and murmurs something but she pulls away and shoves her. Her mom doesn't even get mad. They let her stand there, back by the road, away from everyone.

They lower the casket and start to put the dirt over it. Lenora's friends cry. Uncle Tyler cries. Her parents cry. Everyone but Emily cries. The funeral director says something else and Emily can't hear. After he stops, her father says another prayer, and when everyone lifts their heads back up, people start to leave. They go back to their cars, dust off the windows, and drive away.

They just leave.

Her parents wait in the hearse and leave Emily there by herself for a while. She can move again, and slowly she walks over to the grave. It starts to snow, big heavy flakes. The air is thick and white and it's hard to see. She kneels beside the mound. Snow lands on her eyelids and melts and runs down her hot face.

— I promise I promise I promise I promise I promise I promise I promise . . .

She chants until all the dirt is layered over in white. She doesn't even know what she is vowing, but Lenora will. Lenora will know.

She will be Lenora when she grows up.

Emily doesn't care that her knees are all wet. She doesn't feel the cold. She doesn't feel anything. She lies on top of the grave on her back. The elders would think this was wrong, maybe even pagan, but she doesn't care.

She stretches out her arms and legs and makes a snow angel.

39

▼

HIS APARTMENT WAS A MESS, the air was too warm, and it smelled of stale smoke. I tripped over a guitar case and gouged my shin on an amplifier when we came in. He took me by the hand and led me to the edge of his unmade bed, where we kissed some more. Theo's lips were soft and insistent, and it felt good, but I was distracted by thoughts of whether or not I was doing everything properly, and if I should be doing it at all. That, and the place was filthy. I tried to ignore the dirty dishes that littered the small table, stove, and counter.

— Do you want some water?

I nodded and he filled a glass for me. After checking that nothing was visibly floating in it, I gulped it until it was empty.

Don't think about the germs, don't think about the germs.

I was careful not to say it aloud.

We rolled around on his bed and I let him undo the rest of the buttons on my shirt. My kilt soon followed and joined the shirt on the floor. I wasn't sure what to do next.

What should I do?

Undo his pants.

I did as she instructed and he moaned. He undid my bra and licked my nipples. I sighed and arched my back. No wonder Lenora liked this.

A tiny twinge of guilt singed me but I ignored it. *Neither fornicators, nor adulterers, shall enter into the Kingdom of God.*

I closed my eyes and concentrated on Theo's tongue teasing my stomach instead. He swirled and nibbled and I moaned out loud. Then he stopped and stood up.

— I'm going to put on some music. Any requests?

Joy Division. 'Atmosphere.' He'll know why.

— Joy Division. 'Atmosphere.'

— Sure. Good pick.

He put on the CD, lit a couple of candles, and returned to the bed. We made out for a while longer, then he stopped and sat up.

— I'm going to get a condom, okay?

This was it. The moment I'd both anticipated and feared. I hoped I would do everything right, I hoped I wouldn't panic, I hoped it wouldn't hurt.

Tell him no.

What?

No condom.

But I might get pregnant!

You want to be me, don't you?

I didn't know what to do. That wasn't fair. My heart was pounding and the beer sloshed in my stomach and the room spun and tilted and I almost threw up. I grabbed the sheets in my fist and focused on a faraway light across the city until the room stopped moving.

It wasn't fair. While Theo rummaged through a nearby dresser drawer, my eyes welled. She had no right to ask me to do that. Was this her vengeful way of getting back at me? To make me have the baby she didn't? I had no idea what good that would do.

No. I don't want to.

Then you're a fraud.

I don't care. I don't even think it's really him.

Don't be stupid. Of course it is. You're just too scared.

She was right; I was scared. I was scared it was going to hurt a lot, I was scared that he would think I was a loser, and I was scared — still — of Lenora being mad at me.

And I was scared of getting pregnant.

Theo finished rolling the condom on and I didn't stop him. The candle nearest the bed flickered and went out. I closed my eyes.

It did hurt, but not that badly; it was more like a strange pinch. He moaned and I clenched my teeth.

— You're not Theo, are you?

— Huh? Droplets of his sweat fell from his shaven head onto my chest and face.

— Theo. My sister said you were him.

— You can call me whatever you want. He kind of laughed.

I counted ten more thrusts, then he made a gurgling, growl-like sound. He tossed the condom into a nearby garbage bag, and fell asleep with his arm across my chest. I lay like that, afraid to move, for a long time.

It was too dark to check his wallet, but I didn't need to. She had tricked me. It wasn't him. She just wanted me to end up like her. I was so naïve and gullible. I thought I was doing her a favour, I thought that I could make up for everything, and most of all, I thought that she would forgive me, even miss me. I was wrong. It was my first time being drunk, but it seemed to offer a strange clarity. I knew I wanted to stay there and figure out, if I wasn't going to be Lenora, who I really was.

I DIDN'T KNOW WHERE I WAS when I woke up. I felt sick. The room smelled different from mine, damp and musty, like a laundry hamper. The streetcars' clang sounded nearer than usual, and I could hear music above me — a horribly repetitive thumping that hurt my already throbbing head. I squinted through the sunlight and saw an old poster of The Cure, one corner curled in, obscuring "Boys" in the title, leaving just "Don't Cry."

Lenora had had the same one hung on the back of her bedroom door.

I was sore. But I knew that would go away, and that the next time would be better. If there was a next time.

Fragments of the night before began to seep back, bits in a kaleidoscope falling into a pattern. Whether or not it was the right configuration mattered less to me than creating some sort — any sort — of cohesion to the evening.

I was in Theo's apartment. Zack's. Zack wasn't Theo. At least, I didn't believe he was. But I was sure that I wasn't a virgin anymore.

He was already awake, sitting on the end of the futon with his back to me. I ducked my head under the covers and quickly scanned the sheets: no blood. I didn't want him to know he'd been the first.

I wanted a shower, I wanted to leave, I wanted my

own clothes. I wanted him to kiss me. But I wanted, more than anything else at that moment, to not throw up. His grey t-shirt was still lying next to the bed and I pulled it on. A nearby clock radio said it was nine in the morning. I vaguely remembered that he'd said something about having to work sometime later that day, but I didn't know when. Or where. I really needed to use the bathroom.

— Good morning. My first words as a non-virgin, and they were so anti-climactic. What did people usually say?

He didn't respond. Nor did he turn around. He ran is hand over his shaven head and ignored me.

I found my underwear in the folds of the sheets, pulled them on, and scrambled out of his bed. My head seemed to spin one way and my eyes another. On my way to the bathroom, I tripped over my own purse. The contents spilled, but I didn't stop, I'd clean it up when I came out. I stumbled into the bathroom and closed the door. I didn't dare sit down on the toilet seat. There were nine dark curly hairs on the edge of the bathtub, and seven more in the sink. My stomach heaved again. I started to sweat and my heart sped up, as though it were bouncing down a steep hill. Flashes of bright white and red surged behind my eyelids.

— Oh no, please no, please God no, no no no . . . It was so easy to slip back into that old prayer habit.

Breathe, I could hear Janice coaching me, *just breathe*. I inhaled and exhaled slowly twelve times. My pulse slowed, my stomach calmed. I was safe. I had to be. After so many years, I wasn't going to let myself throw up again. Ever. I splashed my face with cold water and dried it off with what appeared to be the cleanest towel.

When I came out, my purse was on the bed, and the wallet and lipstick and keys were no longer on the floor.

He sat on the edge of the mattress, still naked, this time facing me. He had his head down, and he fiddled with something in his hand. I stood there in front of him, stupidly, not knowing what to say. Maybe he wasn't a morning person. Maybe he wanted me to leave. Maybe he even had a girlfriend. Maybe he was onto me. I took one more deep breath and decided to get out and go home as quickly as possible.

He lifted his head up. His huge brown eyes stared at me, unsmiling. I rubbed my temples and tried to grin. How did people behave after they had sex for the first time? I had no idea, no basis for comparison. I stood there and waved a goofy little wave.

He didn't wave back. He stared at me. A dare, a challenge. I wavered, I looked away, I swayed. Someone slammed a door in the hallway. I jolted.

He had my driver's license in his hand. He stared hard at me. I couldn't tell if the look on his face was of fear or disgust. Or both.

— You told me your name was Lenora.

My stomach muscles constricted. An acrid, sweet odour that only I could smell, then a sour nausea.

— You told me your name was Zack.

— It is. He tossed his own license at me. It landed next to my feet, facing up at me. Nowhere did it say Theo Hansen.

— Give me that! I lunged at him. He held my identification above my head. I stumbled and scraped my knee on the corner of his futon frame.

— Lenora's not even your middle name.

I clawed his chest and pulled at his arm but he held it out of reach.

— That's mine! I intended to sound commanding,

but it came out cloying and desperate. Then he abruptly threw my license onto the floor next to his.

— Who are you?

— No one. Nothing. None of your business.

— I don't get it. What kind of game are you playing? I know we moved pretty fast, but I like you. I mean, well, I'd like to get to know you better. But you lied about who are and then had sex with me. That's kind of weird.

He looked at me, waiting.

— Are you hiding from someone? Do you have a boyfriend? Jesus Christ, you're not married, are you?

— No. Of course not.

I scrambled into my clothes and grabbed my coat.

He pulled on his plaid boxer shorts and leaned against the window ledge, smoking a Camel Light. I opened his door to leave.

— I'm sorry. It's hard to explain.

— I'm a pretty good listener.

He took a step toward me, then stopped.

— It's impossible to explain.

— Well, if you change your mind and want to hang out and talk, call me. I left my number in your purse. But no bullshit.

I walked out, pulling the door closed behind me, and ran down the three flights of stairs to the icy street. Instinctively, I reached for the bracelet around my left wrist, then stopped and grabbed the handrail, trying to catch my breath. Light as it was, made of braided hair, I had worn it every day for a decade, and I had never lost it. I checked my purse — not there. My stomach lurched. I pushed open the door to the street, desperate for air. And I recognized nothing in the neighbourhood.

My head still throbbed with pain and the light was too

bright. It had started to snow again, whirling and surging around me. I scoured my pockets and found nothing. I was disoriented, as though my frantic race down the staircase had catapulted me back in time. I looked down, trying to steady myself. White glares smeared with red. I closed my eyes but it was too late.

My mouth filled immediately with bile. I had no time to stop it. Cramps wracked my entire body, and I contorted rigidly, my arms clenched at my sides. I fell to my knees and vomited three times on the sidewalk.

Tears streamed down my face. The snow was just like it was back home, and it stung my face like a thousand tiny daggers.

A full decade, to the day, since I had last thrown up. I had no idea what would happen next.

40

▼

THOUGH ALWAYS A STRAIGHT-A student, Emily can hardly concentrate anymore. Her appetite has vanished and lunches go straight into the garbage can. Whenever she sees a police car on the street, she shakes uncontrollably and has to close her eyes as though blinded by red and blue swirling lights. The sound of sirens, the scent of vanilla — these are the details that immobilize her. Nightmares and panic attacks shred what little sleep she gets, and she often wakes up panting, sweating, and disoriented. On the edge of her bed, she forces herself to open her eyes, and reality surges back. She clenches her blankets in agony, unable to get back to sleep, and eventually, unwilling.

Most days, Emily is a zombie, drowsy and distant, as though on the other side of a pane of frosted glass.

Everything had changed overnight; the world is nothing now but threat and peril, and she doesn't know how to make it otherwise.

She still goes to the meetings at the Hall with her father, and sometimes her mom comes too, though unwillingly. Emily can concentrate no better at the Hall than she can in the classroom. Her mom shifts angrily in her chair, then blatantly sighs when she disagrees with something, such as *men are the head of the household*. Everyone can tell what she's thinking; it's uncomfortable, even embarrassing, to sit by her.

Emily is convinced that their house is full of black holes. There is no other explanation. Her mother disappears into hers and does not re-emerge from her bed for days. Her back is always the last thing Emily sees as her mother supports her thin body with her hands on either side of the door frame, her head slumped forward and dark hair askew. She heaves a sigh, then closes the door behind her. No one knocks or opens it until she stumbles out on her own.

Except for the Bible and *Watchtower* magazines, her father appears to be afraid to touch things. When he reaches toward his hat or a fork, his hands shake and he pulls away and tries again. The den, lined with bound volumes of the magazines and other Watchtower Society books, is a safer place for him, so he spends most of his time there, and at the Hall.

Certain parts of the house have become off limits. No one sits in or even puts a jacket or bag on Lenora's chair. Whether intentional or not, they walk widely around it. Dust has begun to layer it, and one morning, Emily stands over it, as close as she can without touching it, and blows it off.

Her bedroom door is kept closed. When Emily walks past it, she feels the air sucked from her lungs. She stops and stares and listens for her. Emily convinces herself that it was all a bad dream, and that Lenora is just away, and will eventually be back. If no one else is watching, Emily will stay as quiet as she can and hold her breath, then put her ear to the door. Maybe she has secretly returned and is living in her room, unbeknownst to anyone. Emily wouldn't tell on her; she could sneak in food and water and notes. She is sure that all of this is possible.

One morning, Emily faints right there in front of her door. When she comes to, her dad is kneeling beside her, crying.

— It's okay, Dad. I'm all right. I think I just blacked out, that's all.

She sits up and he crushes her in his arms, his rough cheek wet against her neck. Then he abruptly pulls her to her feet and walks away.

WHEN EMILY NEARS THE AGE Lenora was when she was baptized, her father starts to pressure her to do the same. He says it is for her protection, to ensure her everlasting life, but Emily doesn't believe him anymore. She is determined to avoid taking such a drastic step, one that is impossible to undo.

— You wouldn't want to miss the Resurrection, would you? He doesn't have to mention Lenora.

— I don't think I'm ready yet.

— You're getting close. Let's go over some of the questions.

Her father closes the *Watchtower* issue he had open on

the kitchen table and folds his hands together, perfectly centred on top of the cover.

— What is the significance of the year 1914?

Emily hesitates. She knows the answer, but she also knows that Lenora wished that she hadn't gotten baptized so young.

— Is that when Jesus Christ returned to Earth?

— Yes, but what else?

Emily bites her lips and scrunches up her face as though searching hard for the correct answer.

— What did 1914 mark the beginning of?

— I forget. Emily looks down at the table and traces the grain of the wood with a ragged thumbnail. Her father sighs loudly.

— It was the start of the Last Days. Remember? Let's try another question, an easy one.

— Okay.

— What is signified by the Wild Beast in the Book of Revelation?

— Satan the Devil?

— No, Emily. Concentrate. The Wild Beast. You know this.

A full five minutes pass and neither of them speak, until her father clears his throat and tells her the answer.

— It's the United Nations. You should have gotten that one. You need to read fewer worldly books and more of the Bible and *The Watchtower.* We'll try again in a couple weeks.

When they do, Emily misconstrues several prophecies, and bungles the chronology of several simple Old Testament stories. Her father appears to give up on the idea for a while, telling her that she is too immature and unprepared for baptism. She overhears him explaining to an elder on the phone that it is their shared trauma that has arrested her religious development.

AT THE BEGINNING OF EACH school year, Emily's parents write a note to her teacher excusing her from any activities or assignments that focus on Christmas, Halloween, Thanksgiving, Easter, or birthdays, as well the national anthem and Lord's Prayer. All Emily has to do is hand the teacher the note. Usually, they've taught other Jehovah's Witnesses before, so they just nod, fold the note back up, and put it in a drawer.

But after eighth grade, Emily is on her own, like the other Witness teenagers. It is up to her to explain to her grade nine homeroom teacher why she cannot stand for the anthem. Emily is now old enough to Witness to teachers herself.

Jehovah's Witnesses are to be No *part of this world,* which means . . .

Other kids obsess over their first-day-of-high-school outfits, and Emily worries a little bit over what to wear too, but mostly she dreads trying to explain their religion to a new teacher. She practises what to say, and hopes she can get there early, before any other students arrive.

Well, it means . . . that we have to keep apart from politics . . . stay neutral about government . . .

Every rehearsed explanation sounds awkward and ridiculous, so she asks her mom what to say.

— Just tell them it's against your religion. She doesn't look up from the television and just waves her away. Emily wishes she could remember what her parents used to write in her notes in public school. Maybe she could just forge a note. What had Lenora said to her teachers? Her explanation was probably concise and confident; she would never have been this afraid.

Emily barely sleeps the night before her first day of high school and the insides of her cheeks are raw from biting them and grinding her teeth.

She wakes up disoriented and nauseated, but doesn't call out to her parents for comfort. They barely speak to her or to one another at this point anyway. Emily knows they still care about her, at least she thinks they do, but they are too preoccupied with their own guilt. It's as though they've crawled into the damp caverns of grief, lain down, and forgotten about Emily.

She can't shake off her unease as she waits until it's time to go to the monstrous high school. She switches on the light and picks at her gums until they bleed, then scratches her sister's initials into the margins of the *Watchtower* article lying open nearby.

The secondary school's hallways are wide and dim and loud with teenagers. The older kids lounge in clumps along the lockers and jeer at the nervous ninth graders. Emily keeps her head down and ignores taunts of "Minor niner" and "Loser." She finds her locker and fusses with the lock but eventually gets it open, puts her jacket away, and finds her homeroom. She pauses in the doorway. The classroom is almost full and there are very few familiar faces. In the front corner of the room, there's a girl in a tight denim dress and bright pink shiny lipstick, her blond hair crimped to a nearly impossible volume. If it wasn't for her same thick, round glasses, Emily would never would have recognized Agnes the Pentecostal. She stretches up in her seat and waves. She looks like an exotic bird taking flight. Emily smiles back. A few boys from her old school sit together near the back, all elbows and pimples and rattling chairs. The room smells like a combination of sweat, wet wool, and cheap perfume.

The teacher is young, probably new, with her long dark hair clipped back, and she wears a black skirt and white blouse. She fidgets with a small gold cross around her neck, and Emily knows she won't like her rehearsed speech about abstaining from the national anthem and the Lord's Prayer. Emily stands in the doorway for a moment, unsure what to do. Then she closes her eyes briefly and remembers when Lenora pulled Tammy Bales off her in the ditch, and when she would change out of a mini skirt and into corduroy pants on the way home from school, and when she would do her hair before going to the Kingdom Hall, and tell Emily her secrets. Then she has a flash of the last time she saw her. Her stomach constricts briefly, and another student elbows her out of the doorway.

Emily knows what to do.

As the rest of the students file in and slump down into seats, she walks over to a desk near Agnes and sits down. Agnes smiles and Emily grins back. She doesn't even look at the teacher and doesn't hear the woman's name when she introduces herself. Emily grips the side of her desk, steeling herself.

When "O Canada" crackles through the public address system, her heart thuds like a huge bird against the cage of her ribs — the entire class must be able to hear it over the music. Then she stands up. She doesn't leave the room. She just stands up like everybody else. Her head feels light, she's dizzy and feels more conspicuous than if she'd been standing outside the room in the hallway like every year before. She twists around to look at what her classmates are doing, how they're standing, if they're looking up or down or straight ahead, if they're singing along. Emily doesn't even know the words to the national anthem. She stands next to her desk, shuffling from foot to foot and wills it to be over quickly.

When she sits back down with the rest of her class, she feels a rush of adrenaline. She can't stop grinning. She knows that there's no way she can get away with it; the town is just too small and sooner or later, she'll be found out. She's going to get in big trouble, not just with her parents, but with the elders too. But for once, she doesn't care. For the rest of that day, she holds her head high, sailing from class to class, sitting where she wants, talking to whomever she chooses, as she imagines Lenora had. At 3:30 the bell rings and she smiles, amused that her first act of rebellion has been one of conformity.

That night, she sleeps better than she has in a long time.

41

▼

THE BACK ROOM AT THE HALL smells like damp
carpet and old books. Emily breathes carefully through
her mouth, then slumps into a chair and yawns. She's so
tired she feels disconnected from her body, as though she
is watching everything happen just a short distance away.
She has been summoned to an "informal meeting" with
Brother Wilde and Brother Davies. As if there is any such
thing. Once the elders decide you're a wayward sheep,
there's no reversing it. Emily's hands tremble slightly,
but she is determined not to let them see. She must be
in trouble for something, though she doesn't know what.

— Thanks for coming in on a Saturday to talk with us,
Sister Emily.

Emily says nothing, just grips the armrests and stares

at a torn bit of beige-flecked wallpaper just behind, and slightly above, Brother Davies' head. Brother Davies looks at Brother Wilde before he continues.

— We have some concerns about you and your family. We are worried, Sister Morrow, about you and your mother's absence from so many meetings lately. She was supposed to be with you today to talk to us.

They look at Emily expectantly, waiting for her to tell them why her mom hasn't come with her, as though she'd tell them what they want to hear, simply because they've asked. But Emily won't tell them anything. Besides, what can she say? That her mother just isn't interested anymore? That most of what the elders say makes her angry? Emily doesn't look up from the hangnail she picks at. For a few moments, she concentrates on breathing: inhale, exhale, not through her nose, focus, don't tell them anything they want to hear. Don't tell them anything.

Emily shrugs. Brother Wilde takes a turn.

— Is your mom ill? Is there anything we can do to help?

Emily doesn't remember how she got there. Surely her father drove her to the Kingdom Hall, but she doesn't know where he is now, or why she is trapped in this stuffy room with a pair of elders.

Emily yawns again and shakes her head.

— Has your mom been keeping up with the readings at home? Are you still having your weekly Family Study?

She wonders how many Witness families actually have Family Study. There is no set time for it; you just fit it in whenever it's convenient, on a night when there isn't already a meeting. But they have to go to the Hall three times a week, and that's not including the hours spent in door-to-door service. Emily and her parents rarely have Family Study, all of them around the table reading and discussing the latest *Watchtower*, like they're acting out a miniature meeting.

Emily squints as though trying hard to remember. Her dark hair is in her eyes and that is somehow making it very hard to concentrate. She is acutely conscious of hundreds of hairs shrouding her periphery. She wills herself to focus by biting the inside of her lower lip.

— I don't know. Sometimes.

Brother Wilde and Brother Davies look at each other.

— You don't know?

— That's right. I don't know. I have no idea if she's doing the readings or not.

— I see. Brother Wilde adjusts his blue striped tie.

— We're disappointed she isn't with you today. We thought that some words of encouragement might help her, might strengthen her faith.

— Oh. Emily snickers and tries to disguise it with a cough. Brother Davies raises an eyebrow and looks at her. His face suddenly fascinates her.

— How do you do that?

— Do what?

— Lift up just one of your eyebrows. It looks really cool.

Brother Davies frowns.

— Emily, we know that your family has been through a lot. This is the time to turn to Jehovah God for support, to praise him, not to turn your back.

Emily grips the armrests so hard her knuckles glare white and throb. *Been through a lot.* What do they know? The only suffering the elders know is what they read in the Bible. They haven't had their favourite uncle or only sister ripped away from them. Emily sits up straighter and looks at them. They look at each other. They shift in their chairs and loosen their collars. Maybe Emily will be disassociated from the congregation. She's not baptized, so they can't disfellowship her, and though she has never heard of anyone so young being disassociated, she doesn't put it past them.

Perhaps they want to eradicate Emily's entire family.

Just as Jesus said in the book of Matthew, *there will be great tribulation such as has not occurred since the world's beginning until now, no, nor will occur again.*

Maybe the elders are trying to create their very own, uniquely local version of the Great Tribulation. They took away Lenora and her uncle Tyler. They're trying to make her crack. They're playing God.

— Are you okay, Emily? Brother Davies' upper lip is wet and glistening with sweat.

— Is this a Judicial Committee? What did I do?

Lenora was called before a Judicial Committee, shortly before Emily found her. In her long note, she described the leering, beady eyes of the four elders, how they kept her in this very same room for hours, asking her detailed, personal questions about Theo and what they did together.

She was smart though, and even though you're not allowed to make any record of a Judicial Committee hearing, she wrote everything down.

There were questions about her *gross misconduct*, her *grievous sins*, her *fornication*. Questions about what she wore, where they met, who touched who first, and where, how many times, dates, places. At first she resisted but they wore her down, they kept her there all day, and it was dark when she left. They wouldn't even let her take a break to go to the bathroom. Finally, she gave up denying anything. She couldn't hide it anymore. Nor did she want to.

I told them what they wanted to hear, and more. I told them

everything. I just didn't care anymore. What did I have to lose?
When they asked me what underwear I was wearing the first time
with Theo, I didn't just tell them 'black lace' — I showed them.
I made them look.

They didn't even try to stop me. Eventually they said, 'Lower
your skirt, Sister Morrow' in that same condescending voice
they all have. But not until each of them took a good look.

In order to disfellowship Lenora, they were supposed
to have an eyewitness to her sins. They didn't. But they
knew it was only a matter of time, so they started the pro-
cess to subdue her. It was a game with them. They didn't
try to help her, to counsel her, or to forgive her mistake.
They didn't offer her the chance to repent.

They told me I'd be disfellowshipped as soon as it was
obvious that I was pregnant. That then everybody would be a
witness to my 'sin.'

Emily sits there, in the room she's been in hundreds of
times but that she will never look at the same again. The
room where the elders draw the curtains when someone
is in trouble. The room they kept Lenora in, relentlessly,
and probably Uncle Tyler too, and now her.

— Of course not, Emily. You're not in any trouble.

Emily says nothing, but wishes she'd brought a notebook and pen with her. Just in case.

They said, 'You'll be alone. Just you and your worldly bas-
tard child. No one will help you. And that is what you deserve.'

Emily would have helped. Even if it had meant sneaking
around, she would have helped her sister. She wouldn't
have abandoned her. She would have babysat for Lenora,
and helped her cook and clean and change diapers. She
would have played with her little niece or nephew.

At least, now she thinks she would have helped. But

maybe at ten or eleven years old she would have been too afraid to defy her parents and the elders. Maybe she would have been just like all the other faithful sheep in the congregation, shunning her own sister when the elders decreed it. She would like to think that she would have done the right thing, but she isn't sure. Fear is what made her do nothing to prevent Lenora from getting into trouble in the first place, so maybe she would have just renounced her along with everybody else. Because it was easier.

She wonders about her parents, if they would have cut off their own grandchild after Lenora was disfellowshipped, or if they would have visited, brought presents, looked after him or her.

They wouldn't let me take notes during the hearing, but I wrote everything down when I got home. Keep the transcript safe. There's a false bottom in my top drawer.

Both Brother Wilde and Brother Davies are staring at her when she looks up. They probably think she was praying, and Emily doesn't tell them otherwise. She's too tired to be afraid of them and too angry to care, and that makes her feel free. She doesn't know if she has any faith in God left, but she definitely has none in the elders. She knows they have already made up their minds about her; she's beyond redemption, just like her uncle, just like her sister.

They don't want her anymore.

That's why they'd been so hard on Lenora. They didn't want her back either. Their star pupil, then their biggest disappointment. They treated her more harshly than anyone else who had done what she'd done because they resented her. Such a bright, eager young Witness, learning difficult concepts easily, never being ashamed of the Truth, or intimidated by being different. She was fearless, yes, and bold, but they had failed to harness that. They couldn't control her, and when she rebelled, it was with the same intensity and passion she'd formerly applied to the Bible.

And that was unforgivable.

Emily starts as Brother Davies clears his throat.

— Did you hear me, Sister Morrow?

— No. I wasn't listening. She is careful to allow no expression to betray her face.

— I said that, no, of course this isn't a Judicial Committee meeting. What makes you ask such a thing? We're just trying to help your family.

They wanted to know how long each time was, what we did beforehand, what we talked about afterwards. What he said when he climaxed. If I had an orgasm. 'You bet,' I said, grinning, and looking each of them in their hypocritical eyes. 'I sure did. A lot.' I didn't care anymore. They may have caught me, but I won't give them the satisfaction of punishing me. I'm not going to let them win.

Emily looks up and leans forward. Her voice is low and even.

— Help us? Like you helped Lenora?

The room goes silent, then seems overwhelmed by sound. The fluorescent lights hum, a fly buzzes against them, a lawn mower rumbles outside. Everything is too loud. Emily covers her ears.

Brother Davies and Brother Wilde look at each other again.

— We know that your family is still grieving. It is a natural response to loss, but it's been a long time now. It's been long enough.

— It has? I didn't know there was a time limit.

— Playing with fire is dangerous, Emily. Don't forget

that. You're older now, and we don't want you to follow the same treacherous path. Keep your faith in Jehovah, and try to focus on what's right. What happened to your sister, tragic as it is, should also be a lesson. Don't forsake God for anger and self-pity during these times, Emily.

A lesson. She's learning all right, but not what they want to teach her. What Emily understands is that it's more important to maintain the appearance of faith and virtue than to actually have any.

And she has proof. A detailed account of what happened. And no one knows she has it.

She stops listening to the elders. She wonders how Lenora felt at the very end. Scared, probably. Trapped, like there was no other option for her. Maybe if Theo hadn't broken up with her, she would have just run away to be with him instead. Maybe she would have had the baby. But she'd run out of choices, and refused to let the elders control her. So once again, she made up her own rules. Emily fingers the soft bit of braided hair around her wrist.

— You don't think God will resurrect Lenora, do you?

Her eyes dart back and forth between their scowling faces.

— Do you, Emily?

The elders' usual response to a difficult question: another question. She tosses her hair and takes four deep breaths, pushes her hair away from her blue eyes, and stares back at Brother Wilde and Brother Davies. They shift some more in their chairs. She stands up.

— Yes, I do. If there is such a thing.

The two elders suck in their breath at the same time and both lean back, then slightly forward toward her. They begin to talk at once, quickly, and she cannot understand either of them. Then they both stop and each motions for the other to speak first. Emily takes this opportunity to interrupt.

— I know what really happened.

Again Brother Wilde and Brother Davies exchange glances.

— What do you mean, Emily?

She feels her eyes narrow.

— I know what you did, and I have proof.

Emily waves Lenora's letter at them.

— I know everything.

They don't respond.

If the District Overseer finds out how they handled Lenora's situation, they could lose their positions as elders. Maybe she should contact him, and let him read it. No. She shakes her head. Inevitably, everyone would find out, and Lenora would hate that. Worse, the overseer would probably stand up for the elders, and claim they did everything right. They might not even get in trouble.

— What happened to her is your fault. You made her feel trapped, like she had no choice. She didn't know what else to do. You did this to her. I know, and Jehovah God knows.

— What do you have there, Emily?

— The truth.

— Did your sister write that?

— It's mine.

— You'd best pass that over to us. I'm sure it only brings back painful memories for you. Brother Wilde hoists himself from his chair, his hand outstretched, and takes a step toward her.

— No.

Emily shoves a chair between her and Brother Wilde.

— Hand it over, Emily.

Brother Wilde stands in front of the door, while Brother Davies twists in his seat and looks toward the back door, as though contemplating whether or not he should block that one too.

— Never.

She doesn't wait for them to dismiss her. She jumps up and runs out the back door and down the hall toward the exit. They yell after her, and the floor shakes with the weight of their heavy footfalls behind her. She is in the cloak room now and will soon be outside, where it's almost dark.

— Stop right there, young lady! Brother Davies, the heavier of the two, is behind Brother Wilde and calls after her.

She keeps running, but Brother Wilde is close and reaches out to grab her. He gets her sleeve and grips it tightly. Brother Davies lumbers toward them, almost caught up. Emily's eyes dart left then right and she knows that if Brother Davies reaches them, she will be outnumbered, and they will have her. And Lenora's letter.

Emily shrugs out of her jacket and sprints outside.

— Hey!

She doesn't hear them running down the sidewalk behind her, but she doesn't want to turn around to check and risk slowing down. She runs and runs and then hears a car start in the Kingdom Hall parking lot. She tucks the envelope down the waistband of her jeans and pulls her shirt over it, then cuts into the next backyard she passes, jumping over kids' toys and bikes and pushing through thin, sharp hedges.

She runs and climbs fences and runs and falls and runs and ignores the burning in her chest. She zigzags through side streets, cuts through more yards, and hides behind parked cars whenever anyone drives past her. By the time she reaches the outskirts of town, the sky has darkened and the wind has died down and Emily slows to a walk. She walks and walks and she doesn't know where she's going, but she doesn't care. A light rain begins to mist her thin arms and she shivers. She is far from her house, where the elders are probably drinking instant coffee in the living room with her parents, waiting for her. Her father is most likely apologizing, her mother, sipping sloppily from her travel mug and refusing to either speak or leave the room so they can talk about her. As Emily imagines the scene, she forgets to hide from the passing cars and there is a crunch of gravel behind her. She spins around and is about to run across the lawn of the nearest house, when she hears her name.

— Hey, you need a lift?

Emily stops, turns, then shields her eyes from the glare of the headlights. It's not the elders. She puts her head down and rests, her hands on her knees, and decides right then that she can't go back home. Not that night, anyway. She wraps her arms around herself, then checks that the envelope is still safe in her pants. It is. The driver is waiting, his window still rolled down, a hesitant half-smile balanced on his lips.

— Yes. Emily nods up and down, up and down, too many times.

— I do. Thank you. Yes.

She looks up into the purple sky above her head and smiles. For a moment, everything is silent and perfect and for once, she is not afraid.

She opens the passenger door and slides in next to her uncle Tyler.

— Let's go.

42

▼

FOR A FULL DECADE, I was terrified of throwing up.

They say Joan Baez had the same problem, that she'd do anything to keep from triggering it. I could relate to that. A checklist of what to avoid, memorized and learned the hard way: boats, roller coasters, drunkenness.

I was convinced that if I ever vomited again, it would mean the loss of control, everything would change, my world would dissolve and another, scarier one would take its place. Again. It would mean the loss of everything I knew.

And so I spent years concentrating on breathing deeply, placing one foot in front of the other, exhaling. After all that, I had risked it. I had gotten drunk, puked on the sidewalk, and made it, intact, back to my apartment.

Nothing calamitous had happened. My stomach was still sore and heaving when I collapsed onto my couch, but I had stopped vomiting. I drank as many glasses of water as I could, and started to feel better.

It was then that I realized I was sick of being afraid. I decided that that day was to be a day of lasts and of firsts. It would be the last day I would be scared of my own reactions, the last time I would allow the familiar burning surge of fear in my stomach. It started with the early morning hours of first-time sex, and would end with, for the first time, making it to the other side.

Don't you want to know why I'm doing this?

I waited. Nothing.

This is your last chance. Don't try to change my mind. It's something I have to do.

Still, silence. Never had she made me wait; she had pounced on our dialogues like a hungry, feral cat. She'd had no one else.

Then just like that, it was over. For the first time in ten years, there was no response. She really was gone.

She made the ultimate sacrifice — her life, for truth. An escape from hypocrisy. A vengeful refusal to surrender. For a decade, that's what I'd clung to.

But maybe it was meaningless. Maybe hers was another senseless, preventable suicide. A statistic. Maybe her strength was in fact her weakness. Maybe neither of us had really understood what we were up against.

And maybe it didn't matter anymore.

THE ROPE LADDER SWAYED AS I climbed. One hand, one foot, one hand, one foot. Don't look down. When I reached the top, I felt as though I was swaying, but there was no wind up there, and couldn't have been. I steeled myself.

What I would have told her was, I wasn't doing this for her; I was doing it for both of us.

— This is it. Almost there. Don't think about it. Just keep going.

I pulled myself up and stood, my toes curled around the edge. My eyes closed, I held out my arms, palms up, a supplicant. I breathed in, then out, in, out, and felt nothing. Perfect. Then I opened my eyes. People say to never look down, just straight ahead, keep only your goal in mind, nothing else.

I looked down.

Blurred shapes moved in what looked to be synchronized, darting waltzes below. A loud buzz surged through me and I gritted my teeth and closed my eyes for a moment, then opened them wide.

— Here's to us, Lenora.

And then I stepped from the platform.

▼

THANK YOU TO THE IMPOSTORS — my sporadic writing group — whose support and feedback helped to get this project out of the shadows. I am especially grateful to the inimitable Julia Tausch for her friendship, enthusiasm, encouragement and editorial insights throughout several drafts of this book. Thanks for keeping the faith.

With gratitude, I acknowledge the support of the Ontario Arts Council, whose Writers' Reserve and Works in Progress grants bought me some much-needed time to write.

Thanks to misFit editor Michael Holmes for taking on this novel, and to all the talented, dedicated folks at ECW Press.

**Get the
eBook free!***

*proof of purchase
required

At ECW Press, we want you to enjoy this book in whatever format
you like, whenever you like. Leave your print book at home and take
the eBook to go! Purchase the print edition and receive the eBook
free. Just send an email to ebook@ecwpress.com and include:

• the book title
• the name of the store where you purchased it
• your receipt number
• your preference of file type: PDF or ePub?

A real person will respond to your email with your eBook attached.
And thanks for supporting an independently owned Canadian pub-
lisher with your purchase!

CPSIA information can be obtained at www.ICGtesting.com
Printed in the USA
LVOW06s2325021214

416801LV00002B/3/P